Alan Titchmarsh

The Last Lighthouse Keeper

POCKET
BOOKS

LONDON · NEW YORK · SYDNEY · TORONTO

First published in Great Britian by Simon & Schuster UK Ltd, 1999
First published by Pocket Books, 2000
This edition published by Pocket Books, 2004
An imprint of Simon & Schuster UK Ltd
A CBS COMPANY

7 9 10 8

Simon & Schuster UK Ltd
Africa House
64–78 Kingsway
London WC2B 6AH

www.simonsays.co.uk

Simon & Schuster Australia
Sydney

A CIP catalogue for this book is available
from the British Library.

ISBN-13: 978-0-7434-7845-8

Typeset in Goudy by SX Composing DTP, Rayleigh, Essex
Printed and bound in Great Britain by
Cox & Wyman Ltd, Reading, Berkshire.

Praise for Alan Titchmarsh

'Splendid . . . I laughed out loud'
Rosamunde Pilcher

'Absolutely charming . . . made me understand a
lot more about men'
Jilly Cooper

'A steamy novel of love among the gro-bags'
Observer

'A fine debut . . . great fun, but also sensitive and
sensible with a tuneful storyline. Titchmarsh fans
will lap up *Mr MacGregor*'
Independent

'I admit it, I like *Mr MacGregor*. It's as satisfying
as a freshly-mown lawn'
Daily Mirror

'Humorous, light-hearted and unpretentious.
Titchmarsh's book is strengthened by authenticity.
Ideal for romantic gardeners'
Mail on Sunday

Acknowledgements

I am very grateful to the many folk who have helped me with background information for *The Last Lighthouse Keeper*. Breda Wall of Trinity House arranged for me to visit the Lizard light in Cornwall, and Eddie Matthews the Lizard's principal lighthouse keeper (who was almost the real Last Lighthouse Keeper and remains custodian of the Lizard light) showed me around his domain and provided masses of useful information about a keeper's life. Both were subsequently patience personified on the telephone when I remembered questions that I had forgotten to ask.

Rob Stokes of the Association of Dunkirk Little Ships was helpful in providing details of this club of indomitable enthusiasts, and David Bintley of the Birmingham Royal Ballet patiently advised on dancing injuries and their likely consequences in spite of a manic rehearsal schedule.

Nigel Rickman of Bucklers Hard Boat-builders has answered all manner of boating questions during the course of repairing my own vessel, without once becoming irritated.

I am also grateful to two unnamed members of the Metropolitan Police Force, who were happy to answer questions on the elasticity of police procedure, and the Kent policeman who furnished me, at my request, with the caution! Surrey Police were helpful in other ways. Any irregularities in police procedure at St Petroc police station are down to me!

Several books have been a rich source of inspiration, particularly Christopher Nicholson's *Rock Lighthouses of Great Britain*, Craig Weatherhill's *Cornish Place Names and Language*, Peter Collyer's *Rain Later, Good* and Frank Cowper's *Sailing Tours*.

As ever I'm tremendously grateful to Clare Ledingham and Peta Nightingale, my editors, who know just when to encourage and when to admonish, and to Hazel Orme, my copy editor, who always does more than that.

Luigi Bonomi continues to be unflagging in his encouragement.

The chapter titles throughout the book are names of English lighthouses or lightships under the jurisdiction of Trinity House, every one of them now automated. It is up to the reader to decide why I considered each one appropriate for a particular chapter. Start Point is obvious; St Anthony and

Varne might take a little more working out.

This is not a book about lighthouses, just a story about one fictitious lighthouse and its keeper. You will not find Prince Albert Rock on any map, but you may be able to find the part of Cornwall that it occupies in my mind. If the story leaves you with a feeling of admiration for the work of the men of Trinity House I will be well pleased. It is no more than they deserve. Along with a lot of others who go down to the sea in ships, I am sad they have gone.

A.T.

For Bill and Sue
with thanks

The Corporation of Trinity House
TRINITAS IN UNITATE

There are 72 lighthouses and 11 light vessel stations
under the jurisdiction of The Corporation of Trinity
House.
Every one of them is now automated.

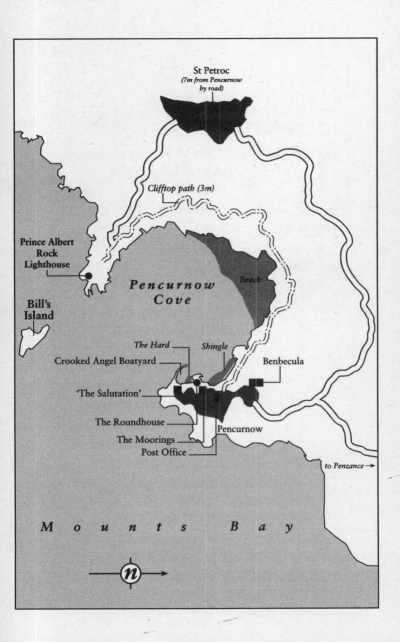

Prologue

"Viking, North Utsira, South Utsira." The varnished oars slipped silently out of the sea. "Dogger, Fisher, German Bight." Salt water dribbled off them, disturbing the glassy ripples. "Sole, Lundy, Fastnet." The oars dipped in again, propelling the little wooden boat towards the shore with practised ease. "Channel Light Vessel Automatic." One oar tumbled clumsily from its metal rowlock, a seagull shrieked in mockery and the oarsman cursed.

The litany of sea areas he recited to himself as he rowed was more familiar to him than the multiplication tables he had learnt at school, but Channel Light Vessel Automatic? It was the thin end of the wedge. A wedge that had now been driven home.

Still, it was too late to grumble about all that. Too late to cherish comfortable dreams of the distant future. The future was here. He suspected that what

1

really rattled him was the prospect of his failure to make those long-held dreams come true.

The bows of the clinker-built skiff met the pebbles of the shore with a sliding crunch. The rower shipped the oars and heaved the boat a yard or two further up the shingle bank. He looked up at the sky – as blue as a heron's egg, with just the occasional wisp of cloud. A perfect April day. A perfect day to begin a different life.

Chapter 1: Start Point

Will Elliott pulled off the thick, grey, hand-knitted fisherman's sweater that had kept out the chill April air on his half-hour passage across an unusually calm Pencurnow Cove. He tied its sleeves around his waist, checked that the skiff was well clear of the tide line and began the climb up the shingle bank.

It was a strange feeling. For the first time in his life there was no grid to his day, no timetable that would tell him where to be and when, just a clear sky and a clean slate. He felt half elated, half terrified at the prospect, glancing back at the lighthouse on the other side of the bay to make sure it was still there, even though it need no longer concern him.

As he crunched up the shore, his welly-booted feet sinking deep into the shingle and slowing his progress, he made a mental checklist of the positive aspects of his future. First, he would stay in Cornwall – for the time being at least: coping with a new set of people and a new place all at once held no appeal. And, anyway, he loved this outpost at the toe of Britain, where the sea and the rugged coastline appealed to his solitary nature. He might have spent just a sixth of his life here, but he felt Cornish now, not Oxonian.

He had to find a boat. If the dream was to become reality he'd better get it soon. Put that sort of thing off and you might just slide into indolence. That scared him more than anything. And he didn't want to live in a house – certainly not one without a view of the sea, and those with sea views in this part of the world were beyond his means.

The logistics of his plans swam around in his head, as did his concerns as to whether or not he had thought this thing through properly. The boat he would buy would probably need attention before he set off: with the amount of money he had to spend he was unlikely to find a vessel in the first flush of youth. While he repaired it in readiness for the Grand Voyage he would have to find some way of earning a living. With any luck he'd be able to sell his little boats – but for how much? He'd started making his scale models of local boats – the clinker-built rowing boats they called Cornish cobles – during his first winter at the lighthouse. Ernie had told him he'd need something to occupy himself on dull, uneventful shifts and Will had found that his steady hand, keen eye and irritating perfectionism had suited him well to a hobby he had previously regarded as the province of sad old men whose idea of excitement would be watching the bacon slicer in the Penzance Co-op.

He would never make a fortune with his models. But, then, he only wanted enough for food and drink, and a book or two. The days of high ambition were long gone, with another life in another place with another person. Now he had to be positive. There were a few thousand pounds in the building society, and the small legacy left to him by his Aunt Alice the previous November should see him all right for the big boat at least. Lucky, and unusually well timed. Thirty thousand would hopefully get him something without too many holes in it. But it was all so iffy.

He reached the top of the bank and struck out for the lane that led to the village. He stopped abruptly. There was no need to rush. His mouth twitched. He turned round, squeezed his hands into the pockets of his jeans and looked back across the bay once more, at the squat white finger pointing upwards into the blue. Prince Albert Rock Lighthouse had been his home, and his refuge, for the last six years. Now he needed to find another. Sadness and irritation, anger, fear, excitement and anticipation vied within him for the upper hand.

He'd had enough warning about the demise of

manned lighthouses. He'd come to terms with the fact that his chosen way of life – or the life that had been chosen for him – would come to an end. He was resigned to it, even if he still resented its inevitability. How could a machine replace a man? How could electronics and automation be a substitute for observation and intuition? But there was no point in being obsessed by it. The lighthouse had served him well. If he was honest, it was time he struck out on his own now.

Trinity House had been pleasant enough about his redundancy. The principal lighthouse keeper, Ernie Hallybone, had officially retired a month earlier but would stay on as custodian of the newly automated light, showing visitors around in summer. Will and the other assistant lighthouse keeper, Ted Whistler, could stay in the blockhouse until they found alternative accommodation.

Ted had left already. Couldn't wait to get out, he said. He'd packed his stuff the previous morning, muttering under his breath as he thrust the few possessions he had accrued over the years into an ill-assorted collection of cardboard boxes and carrier-bags. He moved straight into rooms in the Salutation, the rough-and-ready hostelry on the quayside. Ernie remarked that at least he'd be nearer to his daily pint (or three) that way. Ted grunted.

Will cast his keen, practised eye over the short stretch of coastline he now knew so well. Prince

Albert Rock Lighthouse sat on its rugged granite promontory a mile to the west of where he stood, and beyond it the hazy blue-grey hump-backed whale that was Bill's Island surfaced from the glinting Atlantic – which today was the colour of blue-black ink, though he'd seen it in every shade from deepest purple to evil brown and menacing battleship grey.

In front of him Pencurnow Cove arched gracefully round to the right, its pepper-coloured sand fresh washed by the retreating spring tide, and beyond it, over the cliffs and crags, the spire of the church at St Petroc came and went in the morning haze. Herring gulls shrieked and wheeled over the bay and the beach, which at this time in the morning and so early in the year, was mercifully quiet and free of tourists. Only the matchstick figure of a local woman in a headscarf was visible in the middle distance, throwing a stick into the waves for a yellow Labrador that clearly had the courage of Hercules and the brain of a pea.

He listened, as the waves lapped on the sand, which curved round towards the short headland nearest the village. This small knob of tussocky ground sheltered the shingle bank on to which he'd pulled *The Gull*, the clinker-built, copper-riveted skiff it had taken him two years to complete. He looked at it and smiled, pleased with his handiwork. The varnish on the pitch-pine timbers glowed in the sun. But it wasn't big enough for what he had in mind.

Above him crouched the village of Pencurnow, and at the end of the promontory to his left, an arc of granite sheltered the three fishing boats that still endeavoured to bring home lobsters, bass and whatever else they could catch.

It was, admittedly, a small world. But it suited him. Correction, *had* suited him. He squinted as the keen rays of the morning sun bounced off the sea, then turned and walked up the lane towards the Post Office.

The bell pinged brightly as he pushed open the battered bottle-green door of Pencurnow Post Office and General Stores. He walked towards the un-manned counter, but before he reached it a strangulated voice from the back room instructed, "Hang on, I'm on my way. I'm just getting these damn papers out." A series of grunts and the popping of plastic webbing came to Will from the rear of the tiny shop, which was piled high with a thousand things that might be useful to somebody, if not to him.

On either side of the metal-grilled post-office cubicle, festooned with exhortations to buy Premium Bonds and Post Early for Christmas (and April, indeed, was early) stood perilously lopsided pyramids of tinned peas and butter beans. A tower of red plastic trays containing the day's supply of fresh bread leaned Pisa-like towards him, backed by shelves stuffed with cigarettes and corn plasters, matches and Mintoes, and an array of cleaning substances that would have impressed the most zealous daily help. The stone floor presented itself as a maze of cartons, pop bottles, garden tools and galvanized buckets. Gold-painted fire guards enveloped coppery companion sets, and the smell that reached his nostrils was compounded of cardboard and paraffin, soap powder and mothballs.

Tucked here and there Will noticed such irresistible temptations as pink shampoo in a poodle-shaped bottle, an implement for taking dents out of car doors (handy in Cornish villages with narrow lanes), and bottles of Mrs Pengelly's Home-made Piccalilli – a villainous-looking yellow decoction that would probably take the skin off the roof of your mouth before you had a chance to swallow it.

Above the bare Formica counter, magazines hung from a washing line, *Practical Boat Owner* alongside *The People's Friend*, *The Lady* sandwiched uncomfortably between *Farmer's Weekly* and *Cosmopolitan*. *Loaded* and *FHM* were under the counter for a local youth who aspired to the fleshpots of Newquay.

Beneath this literary fringe, appeared the Amazonic figure of Primrose Hankey, her face only half visible above the pile of daily papers, which hit the counter with a thud. She greeted her customer with a warm, toothy grin and boomed, "Morning, Mr Elliott. Come to look at your picture?"

Will looked suitably embarrassed and asked, "What have they said?"

Primrose took a copy of *The Cornishman* from the top of the papers and read out the headline: "'Farewell To Britain's Last Lighthouse Keeper.' Nice photo of you – and Mr Hallybone. Ted Whistler don't look too pleased. But, then, when do he?" She tutted disapprovingly and handed Will the paper.

He took in the front page and its banner headline, the black-and-white picture of the six keepers in their uniforms – his shift of three and the other shift – and of the Elder Brethren of Trinity House who had come down to Cornwall for the momentous occasion. Evan Williams and his team stood to the left of the picture, Ernie Hallybone, Will and Ted Whistler to the right. They made an uneven trio, Ernie short and stocky with white hair and a face seemingly carved from English oak, Ted tall and gaunt with hooded eyes, and Will at the end of the row, not quite six feet, square jaw, high cheekbones and black curly hair under the peaked cap. He looked good in uniform. He felt better out of it.

The sextet of lighthouse keepers stood in a semi-circle, hands clasped neatly in front of them, surrounding the Master of Trinity House – the Duke of Edinburgh.

"What was he like?" enquired Primrose, anxious for gossip to recount for the rest of the week to her avid customers. Not for nothing was Primrose known as 'the human telescope'. Her shop had a panoramic view of the village and none of her windows boasted net curtains. Little passed her by, and there was even less on which she was unable to offer information, thanks to a multitude of sources.

"He was very nice," offered Will.

"But what did he say?" Her beady eyes were bright.

"Oh, he thanked us all and told us we'd done a valuable job very well and that he hoped we'd all remember our days at Trinity House with pleasure."

"Is that all?"

"Well, just about, yes." Will felt a bit of a failure. Nothing there with which Primrose could impress her customers. "Mr Elliott said the Duke of Edinburgh was very nice." Hardly spicy. "I did notice a bit of shaving foam behind his ear, though."

"Really?" Primrose's eyes lit up and she leaned forward on to her counter. "So he wet-shaves, then?"

"Must do." Will tried to conceal a grin, and held up the paper in front of his face as camouflage, knowing that Primrose would now be a happy woman and could speculate for weeks on whether the Queen's husband used Gillette or Old Spice shaving foam.

"Well I never." Will lifted his eyes over the top of the *Cornishman* and noticed that Primrose's had already glazed over, and that she was playing with the single grey-brown plait that hung over her right shoulder. She chuckled to herself and made chomping noises with her mouth. She tossed the plait behind her with a jerk as Will said, "Hey-ho," and fished out some change.

"I see Spike made it, then!" remarked Primrose.

"Sorry?"

"Into the photo."

Will unfolded the paper again and looked at the picture. There, at the feet of the Master of Trinity House and curling his tail around the highly polished brogues, was Spike, the lighthouse cat, in his own black uniform with a white bib, clearly aware of the gravity of the occasion.

"Cheeky blighter," laughed Will. "Now I know why he was looking so pleased with himself this morning." Spike had turned up on Prince Albert Rock two years ago and had latched himself firmly on to Will. "I only hope he takes to his new home just as well."

Primrose scented another potential snippet of gossip. "Oh? You've found somewhere, then?"

"No, not yet."

"Not much for sale in the village at the moment. Or will you be moving away?" The tentacles were out.

"No. I plan to stay – hopefully – but I don't want a house."

Will was momentarily undecided as to whether or not he should reveal his plans to the human telescope, but decided there was little harm in telling her. It might even result in him finding a boat, although like as not he'd have to move into grotty rooms until something suitable turned up.

"You don't want a house?" Primrose broke in on his thoughts.

"No."

"Well, what, then?" She looked at him quizzically, wondering if he planned to become a cave-dwelling hermit.

"I want a boat."

"A boat?"

"Yes."

Without looking upwards, Primrose reached above her head and yanked at one of the magazines that formed the proscenium arch around her ample frame. She slapped it on the counter in front of him. "There you are. Two pounds sixty."

Will looked down at the glossy cover of *Boats and Planes For Sale*.

He looked at Primrose, and she looked right back, smiling. He fished into his pocket and found three one-pound coins. "Suppose I'll have to start somewhere."

Primrose punched at the buttons on her cash register. It made a few grinding noises then spat out a drawer from which she extracted his change. She

13

pressed the coins into his hand and asked her next question. "What sort of boat do you want?"

"Oh, an old sailing boat."

"Just to live on?"

Will was trapped. Either he became evasive, or he would have to admit to Primrose that the real reason he wanted a boat was to sail around Britain single-handed. Every time he thought about it he felt self-conscious and a bit embarrassed. If he told the postmistress this, the entire village would soon know, and he'd never escape the repeated enquiries: "How's the boat doing?" "When are you going?" and "Haven't you got it sorted out yet?"

He tried not to be rude and fudged his answer. "Oh, I just want to be near the sea, and I can't afford a house with a sea view." Which was quite true.

"You could try the Crooked Angel."

Will looked at her incredulously. "What?"

The small boatyard, adjacent to the cobbled hard where the fishing fleet was pulled up during its off-duty hours, was not an obvious place to start looking. Its proprietor, Len Gryler, was not highly regarded within the community: he had a shady past and a shadier collection of boats at his disposal – the Arthur Daley of the waves.

"You're not serious!" said Will scornfully.

"Oh, I know he's a bit of a rogue, but even rogues have a decent boat every now and then."

"In Gryler's case I wouldn't bet on it," muttered

Will, running his hand through his unruly hair.

"Well, I know for a fact he got a new one in a couple of days ago. Told me it came from some old sailor who was devoted to it."

"Oh, I see. One careful lady owner – probably an ex-Wren – only ever pottered around the bay on a Sunday. Kept in a heated boathouse since new?"

"You're teasing me!" Primrose admonished him. "I'm only trying to help. I know Len Gryler isn't the most reliable type . . ."

Will raised his eyebrows.

" . . . but you never know. It might be just what you want." She went back to her newspapers.

"Well, I might have a look on the way down."

"You've nothing to lose, have you?"

"Only thirty thousand quid," he said, under his breath.

She looked up. "Pardon?"

"I said, I'll try an early bid."

Primrose eyed him suspiciously. She'd always thought he was such a nice, quiet young man, but she had now detected an element of spirit she hadn't noticed before. She looked at him sideways. He wasn't going off the rails, was he? Funny lot, lighthouse keepers. Loners most of them. Men with secrets.

She snapped out of her reverie. "If you're going down there, can you give these to young Applebee?" She fished *Loaded* and *FHM* from under the counter, slid them quickly into a brown paper bag snatched from a nail on the shelf behind her and handed them to Will. "I've put them in a bag to save any embarrassment."

Christopher Applebee was Gryler's general dogsbody at the Crooked Angel, and clearly yearned for more excitement than he could find in Pencurnow.

Will slipped the bag between the folds of the *Cornishman*, realizing that he would now have to visit the boatyard whether he liked it or not. He made for the door.

"Oh, and don't forget to look in on the Round-house," said Primrose, through a mouthful of crisps.

"Mmm?"

"The old capstan house. It's being done up. Some artist is renting it."

"What for?"

"As a gallery. It'll make a change from all that junk the old woman from St Petroc has been selling in there for the last couple of years. I hope it's a success, for the sake of the village. The Roundhouse has never been the same since they retired it from hauling the fishing boats up the hard, but it's a lovely building. I've always thought of it as the heart of the village. It's time someone brought it back to life."

"Yes." But Will was miles away, his mind on the boatyard. He hardly looked round as he tossed a vague " 'Bye" in Primrose's direction. Nor did he notice, in the early-morning light, the shadowy figure through the window of the old capstan house as he walked past it towards the boatyard. But she noticed him.

Chapter 2: Longships

The sign attached to the high granite breakwater certainly had romantic appeal. Its royal blue paint was flaking, but the words 'Crooked Angel Boatyard' were still visible in ornate, once-gilded script, coupled with the additional information, 'Berths and Servicing'. A crudely painted, lopsided figurehead of a seraph, plundered from the wreck of some ancient schooner, was bolted to the wall above the sign, and another piece of wood tacked beneath it proclaimed 'Boats for Sail'.

Will was unsure whether this betrayed an aptitude for puns or ineptitude in orthography. He sighed, took a deep breath, and went through the solid blue gates fastened back against the walls into the boatyard.

It was a modest marina, but then it probably had a lot to be modest about, he reflected, as he looked at the motley collection of vessels that creaked and groaned alongside the half-dozen wooden pontoons.

But in spite of its general air of decay the place was not unappealing. Funny, he thought, that what in a town or city would be looked upon as ramshackle and down-at-heel was regarded on the coast as charmingly rustic. Add water, stand well back and you had allure rather than atrophy. The Crooked Angel Boatyard was undoubtedly picturesque in a tumbledown way, from the robust wooden piles that penetrated deep into the Cornish mud, to the limpets and lime-green seaweed that festooned them.

Even the boats – mostly old and worn – had an air of contentment about them. About a dozen and a half were scattered across the still, dark grey water, straining gently at their mooring warps as the effects of the tide disturbed the water. They came in all shapes and sizes, from small, brightly painted fishing smacks filled with tangled skeins of line and tethered while their owners took breakfast in the Salutation, to larger 'Tupperware' boats of uncertain age. Nothing here to inspire a millionaire intent on finding a gin palace, thought Will.

There were boats with tattered canvas cockpit covers, and boats with punctured white plastic fenders and the occasional car tyre slung over the side to protect once-pristine paintwork from the ancient cobbled jetty. Masts towered above him, their frayed burgees lifting gently in the breeze, with the occasional ting-ting of a halyard as it rattled against hollow alloy.

The boatyard was barely a couple of miles from the lighthouse, as the fish swims, but Will could not recall ever having set foot in it. Most of the locals disapproved of Gryler, and Will had never needed to come here. It was not a public marina, more a nautical builders' yard.

Several small motorboats of relatively recent vintage bobbed alongside larger ones of greater antiquity and ugliness, and one or two of the ancient wooden vessels clearly owed something of their ancestry to Noah. Their names were as varied as their condition. Will walked down one of the pontoons, past *Racy Lady* and *Pinch of Thyme*, *Ultra Vires* and *Sokai* – perhaps the owner had Japanese associations. Beneath his feet, the water made glooping noises as the floating pontoon rose and fell gently, anchored by robust yet rusty fixings to the tall piles that towered eight feet above him on the falling tide.

"Can I help you?"

Will turned at the sound of a youthful voice. Its tone was neither solicitous nor aggressive. Before him stood a tall, scrawny youth of nineteen or twenty, a lopsided mop of sandy hair falling over his eyes. He wore a paint-spattered sweatshirt that had once been navy blue, and a pair of jeans with more holes than a colander, though less symmetry in their layout. There were two rings in his left ear. He looked like a latter-day pirate.

"Oh. You're one of the lighthouse keepers, aren't you?"

"Yes."

"I'm Chris Applebee. I work here."

"In that case I've got something for you." Will pulled out the bag with the magazines from the folds of the *Cornishman* and handed them to the lad. "Primrose sent them."

"Oh, thanks." The youth looked up at Will with a grin. "I bet she's read 'em both!"

"More than likely."

"We've never seen you here before, have we?" asked Christopher Applebee, tucking his magazines under his arm.

"No. I've not got around to it until now."

"Plenty of time now, eh?"

"Yes." Will was unsure whether he detected a note of mockery in the lad's voice, but chose to ignore it anyway. "I hear you've a new boat in for sale."

"Yeah, that's right. But you'd better see the boss, not me. I'll go and fetch him." He turned and walked down the pontoon towards a peeling, blue-painted shed on the jetty.

"Where is it?" Will called after him.

He didn't look back. "Pontoon number three."

Will looked up at the white numbers painted on the piles at the end of each pontoon. He was standing on number one. Number three was in the central part of the small pool, so he retraced his steps and walked back towards the main jetty. He turned left past the shed which he could now see was in the terminal stages of collapse. In this part of the world that probably meant it would last another twenty years.

As he passed the door, a short, round, oily man bounced out of it. "Mornin'," he growled, and offered a fat, greasy hand. "Len Gryler." The oily fist gripped Will's.

Len Gryler looked as if he was of Italian ancestry. He was balding, but the hair that remained on his spherical head was black as pitch and joined to the dusky stubble on his chin with long sideburns. He wore a dark blue one-piece overall, a stranger to the laundry, and carried in his left hand a monkey wrench. "So you're after a boat?" He wiggled the wrench.

"Well, yes. I hear you've got one for sale, but I'm only in the early stages of looking. Nothing's certain yet." Will was anxious to cover himself.

"Oh, don't you worry. You'll love this little beauty." Len Gryler slid effortlessly into his sales patter. He was a born trader. Here was a man who could not only sell ice-cream to Eskimos but a deep freeze to keep it in. He put his hand gently in the middle of Will's back and propelled him in the direction of pontoon number three.

A couple of small day-boats were bobbing at the end nearest the jetty on which they stood, and on the pontoon's starboard side, at the far end, lay an old, green-painted Cornish yawl, perhaps fifty-feet long, with the name *Florence Nightingale* carved into her gunwales. She had a squat wooden cabin amidships, behind the varnished wooden mast, and was littered with an assortment of nautical paraphernalia from an old brass binnacle to lobster pots in the process of repair, voluminous coils of old rope and assorted pieces of timber.

Will took to her immediately. "Very nice."

"No, not that one. That's Aitch's boat. This one."

Gryler pulled Will by the arm so that he faced the port side of the pontoon. There he beheld an altogether different vessel.

It was an ageing motor yacht, rather shorter than the sailing boat, with a row of portholes running from six feet abaft the bows to somewhere amidships. She was clearly a pre-war vessel, with wooden wheel-house and aft cabin, once-varnished rails and two wooden masts, from which hung rotting ropes. She had once been someone's pride and joy, but those days were long gone.

"Ah," said Will. "She's a motor launch. I wanted a sailing boat. Stick and rag man, I'm afraid." He offered Gryler an apologetic look, but before he could make his escape, the man blocked his path.

"She's got two masts," he countered, defensively.

"OK, so they're not what you might call powerful sails but look at the workmanship. Pitch pine on oak. Built in nineteen thirty-one by Staniland and Company in Yorkshire. On the River Ouse. Wonderful lines. Piece of history."

"But the engines—"

"Work of art. Twin diesels, Perkins M30s, recently reconditioned. And I'm going to have a look at them meself." He waggled his monkey wrench again as if to emphasize his skills. Realizing he had more work to do on this particular customer, he moved into second gear. "I dunno. These sailors. Make such a fuss about motorboats, rave on about the joys of 'proper' sailing then spend three-quarters of their time battling against the tide on a windless day with a piddling little engine that just about stops them going backwards. You'll be able to move in this one whether there's wind or not."

Will tried to interrupt, but Gryler was in full flow. And although the villagers considered him a rogue, he sounded as though he knew his boats. "A gentleman's yacht, without a doubt. Length overall thirty-six feet, beam nine foot six, draught two foot six – get you well up any estuary, that will."

"But what about her sea-keeping qualities?"

"What do you want her for? Crossing the Atlantic? All right, so I wouldn't recommend her to Sir Francis Chichester, but for estuaries and inshore waters she'll be fine. Built to last. Very sea-kindly." He slapped at her bulwarks and dried white paint fluttered off like a flock of miniature doves.

Again Will tried to protest.

"I'll tell you what, just look her over. I won't hassle you. I'll go and put the kettle on. The cabin door's open so hop aboard and see what you think. Needs a bit of work, I know, but for someone with time on their hands . . ." He paused to let the point sink home. "She'll repay any work that's put into her. Great live-aboard. For one." He looked up with a twinkle in his eye. "Or two. She's a little cracker, even if she has got a man's name."

Will looked at the bows of the old motor yacht and saw the engraved board fastened to the gunwales: *Boy Jack*, it said.

How can you call *Boy Jack* she? thought Will. He looked at her, or him, frowning, and opened his mouth to decline the offer, but Gryler was already at the end of the pontoon, heading kettlewards.

"Oh, well," he muttered to himself, and stepped up on to the deck. It was the first step in his en-snarement.

The mooring warps chafing against the fairleads caused the boat to let out a sound that was not so much a creak or a groan, more a sigh. "Yes," said Will, half aloud, "I'm not surprised you're sighing. Look at the state of you."

The deck was littered with herring-gull droppings. One of the culprits shrieked from the masthead and took off angrily. Will rubbed his hand along the timber, and remnants of varnish came away in crisp, translucent flakes. But the timber itself seemed sound.

He looked at the decks. Plenty of green algae, especially on the shaded areas. He glanced about to see that the coast was clear, took out his penknife and sank it into the planked decking in a particularly damp spot. Surprisingly it was hard and unyielding.

He leaned over the side to look at the hull. The seams between the planks were cracked. There would be plenty of recaulking needed if she were not to leak like a sieve. He hopped off again to see how the hull lay in the water. Quite evenly. A second surprise.

Will scolded himself for bothering to go through all these checks. He wanted a sailing boat. A Cornish yawl like the one in the next berth would do him nicely. He did not want a pre-war motor yacht. He made scale models of Cornish cobles, not motor boats.

Yet he climbed aboard once more and walked around the deck, past the old anchor winch at the bows and the iron jack-staff atop the stem. Well-balanced lines. He walked astern. She had plenty of deck space and the stanchions seemed well anchored to the topsides. He turned and pushed open the cabin door. It wouldn't budge. Gryler had said it was open. He put his shoulder to it and it yielded with a crack followed by a loud creak as the old brass hinges reluctantly turned on their spindles.

He stepped down into the wheelhouse, where the smell of mildewed carpet and cloth hit him. A thick layer of dust had settled on every surface, except where it had been recently disturbed, clearly in bringing the vessel to its final resting place. Black mould speckled timber and fabric alike. A small galley with a filthy porcelain sink was built into the starboard side. It was unclear whether the metal fixtures and fittings, from taps to knobs, portholes and the cabin-door lock were of brass or base metal, so dark and dull were their surfaces.

He tugged at a curtain to let in more light, and a swatch of rotten brown cloth came off in his hand. He pulled it away until the morning light beamed in diagonally, highlighting the dust motes that hung in the air. Will sneezed, and blew his nose.

The wheel was of the traditional type – wooden spoked and varnished. There were aged instruments on the fascia and a tarnished bell hanging from the bulkhead. Will resisted ringing it in case it summoned the boatyard owner.

Instead he searched for the entry to the engine room. Under assorted lumps of rotting carpet, he discovered a metal ring, and found that the hatch came up quite easily. He removed it and stood it to one side before lowering himself into the bowels of *Boy Jack*.

He had no torch, but the hatchway was large enough to let in sufficient daylight for him to be able to inspect the two Perkins engines. They were not in the first flush of youth, yet were excessively oily, rather than rusty. Will dredged up from the back of his brain the information he'd digested on a marine diesel-engine course a couple of years ago and married it to his knowledge of the generators at the lighthouse. He was relieved that the engines were not petrol-driven: diesel was far safer, and low-horse-power engines like these, could go on for a long time – if you looked after them.

He spotted a loose wire here, a leaking pipe there, but not the seized-up piles of rusty metal he had expected. He put his hand down into the bilges. About an inch of water. He licked his finger. It was fresh water, not salt. That boded well. Then, again, he chastised himself for going through all this rigmarole, even if she was a boat with character. He heaved himself up from the engine room, and replaced the hatch.

Three steps led down into the aft cabin where he discovered a double berth with a damp, stinking mattress that sported a number of unidentifiable stains, and a wooden-doored cubicle that contained a small marble basin, an antique-looking hip bath, and an old lavatory – a Blake's head of the sort with two hand pumps, one to pump in salt water, the other to let it out. He pumped at the latter and was rewarded with a loud gurgle and a vile stench. He turned on his heel and moved through the wheelhouse to the fore-cabin, lit by several port-holes and a deck hatch.

He fought with the catch and finally succeeded in pushing it upwards and outwards. Light streamed in and he gulped at the fresh air.

The forward cabin was longer than he'd expected, and quite narrow, with one curving berth to port and another to starboard. Lockers filled the space between the hull and the inboard side of each berth and he opened them to take a look at the state of the boat's planking. Some of the caulking was coming away and he could see faint signs of moisture. The timbers were clearly not the originals: the boat had been restored and the hull replanked within, he guessed, the last twenty years. The pitch pine was in good condition, and many of the original mahogany stringers had been replaced with new.

The locker beneath the berth on the starboard side was empty, except for a few 1960s newspapers, old beer cans and some rusty spanners. He opened the locker on the port side to make a similar inspection and found a pile of sacking. He tugged at it and it fell out with a hefty thump. He picked it up and a hessian-wrapped lump dropped on his toe. "Bloody hell!"

He looked down, and saw a clumsily tied parcel, held together with fishing twine. He took out his penknife again and carried the parcel into the wheelhouse. As he cut away the twine and pulled off the rough hessian wrapped around it, the brass plate became clearly visible, as did the legend upon it. It bore a name and a date, and marked the point at which Will Elliott knew that there was no escape from the clutches of *Boy Jack*.

The plaque read simply: 'Dunkirk 1940'.

Chapter 3: Needles

It took exactly eleven days for the surveyor's report to confirm that *Boy Jack*, in spite of her appearance, was seaworthy. Gryler was asking £25,000 for her but Will managed to knock him down to £23,000, to include three months' free berthing at the Crooked Angel – time enough, he hoped, to do the boat up. With any luck the spare £7,000 would be enough to fund repairs sufficient to make her seaworthy. He'd be on his way by midsummer.

With an armful of cardboard boxes, courtesy of Primrose Hankey, he walked up the rough gravel path from the lane that led to Prince Albert Rock, conscious that this was a journey that from now on he would make as a visitor.

The wind had swung round to the north-east and had more bite than of late. Leaden grey clouds ballooned up from landward and the sea looked restless, breaking heavily on the rocks below the clean white tower. It had lost the blueness of mid-April and seemed to hark back to winter in its chill grey tones.

Will walked around the side of the building and pushed open the door into the engine room.

"You all right, then?" It was Ernie Hallybone, broom in hand, sweeping the floor by the old foghorn compressors.

"Fine. Just got some boxes for my stuff. Should be out by lunchtime."

Ernie smiled thoughtfully and carried on with his sweeping. They'd had all their conversations about the rights and wrongs of automation. "Loony," Ernie called it. "You can't get instinct and experience from a computer."

Automation had been on the cards since the sixties and had begun in earnest in the eighties. Few keepers regretted the conversion of rock stations such as Longships and Wolf Rock, Bishop Rock and Eddystone – Ernie had been stuck on Wolf Rock once for three and a half months, thanks to the weather. He'd regaled Will with stories of storms that shook the tower, waves that passed right over the lantern, and boats standing off in violent seas to relieve the keepers of their watch, then having to go away again, the sea too rough to transfer the men.

Will had arrived too late for such a posting: today

the rock stations were visited only by helicopter when maintenance was needed. At the time he had longed for such isolation. The suddenness of the tragedy had left him oblivious to anything but his grief. The healing process was slow. Even now it was far from over, and there was still a huge part of him that he dare not explore too deeply. But he had learned to live with that. In time it might change, perhaps not. Whatever the future held, the Cornish coast and the kindliness of his principal lighthouse keeper had done much to ease him back into life.

When he had arrived Ernie had found him difficult to communicate with, but had been wise enough to give him time to come to terms with his future. As a rule, lighthouse keepers were a patient breed, and Will knew that the service had something of the Foreign Legion about it. It was a way of life suited to a few, usually those who needed an escape. Every man joined the service for a different reason. Those who stayed had in common only a unique brand of self-containment, their patience and, often, a love of nature. Few other vocations could satisfy such men, except the monastic life, and that precluded certain activities that many lighthouse keepers would have been reluctant to forgo.

Will climbed the brass-railed stone staircase to his room, opened the door and dumped the boxes on the floor. His packing was almost complete. There were just a few more odds and ends to wrap and box before he could load the whole lot into the back of Ernie's van and transfer them to his new floating home.

He looked out of the small window towards the sea, crashing on to the rocks, its crests blown back by a brisk offshore wind. He knew that stretch of water in every mood and yet really hardly knew it at all. It was totally unpredictable; every day was different.

The half-dozen completed models of Cornish cobles had already been packed. He put the remainder of his wood, his knives and twine, the paint, varnish and assorted bits and pieces together in a box, pushed bubble wrap carefully around it, sealed the box with sticky tape and wrote in neat script on the lid: 'Boat Bits'. To a man, lighthouse keepers were tidy. They had to be, to avoid falling over things in confined spaces, and irritating each other.

As with every other lighthouse in Britain, six men had been assigned to Prince Albert Rock, divided into two sets of three, each three working one month on, one month off, a twenty-eight-day tour. Ernie Hallybone was the principal lighthouse keeper, Ted Whistler and Will Elliott his assistants. The other team, led by Evan Williams, had left the service at the end of their last tour a month ago.

During their month on duty the keepers would live in the lighthouse; some – Will, Ted and Ernie – lived there all the time, others moved inland to their homes during their month off.

The eight hours on and sixteen hours off had been

a routine that helped Will rebuild his life. Each watch was different. From 4 a.m. till noon you could see the sun rise over the cliffs, hear the dawn chorus of land and sea birds and feel justifiably virtuous. From noon until 8 p.m. you could take things steadily and in summer enjoy a watch entirely in daylight. From 8 p.m. till 4 a.m. you were up and about while the rest of the world slept. For many it was the unfavoured watch, but for Will it was the ultimate escape, a time to look out to sea and watch the sun go down. Never had he experienced the fabled "green flash" that Ernie boasted of seeing on the horizon twice in his life – when the sun sets over a flat, calm sea and the weather conditions are just right – but he had seen and enjoyed, times without number, the moon glistening on the Western Approaches.

He would miss it. He would miss the ships passing in the night. They were often lit more brightly by the moon than the sun and even when there was no moon, they were clearly visible under the stars in darkness illuminated only by the light from the lantern, one flash every three seconds.

He emptied the chest of drawers, five sweaters and ten shirts, three pairs of jeans, underwear and socks, and packed them into another box, before clearing his bookshelves. A small pile of CDs – Rameau and Philip Glass, Pat Metheney and George Shearing – were tucked alongside the books: the five volumes of

Frank Cowper's *Sailing Tours*, Joshua Slocum's *Sailing Alone Around the World* and Libby Purves's *One Summer's Grace*. He was relieved that, unlike her, he would not be battling around Britain accompanied by fractious children.

He filled another box with back numbers of *Classic Boat* and the exercise books he had used as diaries since his first day at the lighthouse six years ago. He flipped open the one dated "Apr – May '94" and read a paragraph. "Noon. Better today, I think. Still hard not to think of E all the time, even when trying hard to concentrate on something else. Thought of what she said about the colour of the geraniums down the steps at Oriel. Saw a skiff rounding the headland and remembered that day on the Cherwell in the rowing boat."

He felt a pang in the pit of his stomach, and flipped the pages. "4 p.m. Sea vile. Almost black. Terns trying to stay airborne. Painted wall behind generator. Wish Trinity House knew what it was like using this shitty-coloured paint. Ted being equally shitty to all and sundry. Must be his time of the month. 6.30 p.m. Watched fishing boat PZ 291 picking up lobster pots around Bill's Island. Two men getting a soaking. Seemed to catch quite a few."

Will smiled, closed the book, and stacked it with the rest.

That was almost it, bar the sweeping up. Oh, and the certificate. He walked over to the windowsill and picked up the framed citation that had been presented to him the day before:

This is to Certify that
William Elliott
entered the Service of the
Corporation of Trinity House of
Deptford Strond on
19th April 1993 and left
the service on 7th April 1999

This Certificate is issued as a mark
of the Elder Brethren's appreciation
of many years of faithful service
rendered.

Trinity House   Patrick Rowe
Tower Hill   Deputy Master
London EC3

Not that many years, thought Will, but maybe enough. He slipped the frame on top of the diaries and closed the box.

He had left the most difficult job until last.

"Come on, then. We've got to go."

The cat was asleep at the bottom of the iron-framed bed, curled up on the neatly folded blankets. Or, rather, he was pretending to be asleep, having watched carefully the previous preparations through one half-open eye.

Will walked over to him and prodded him with a finger. "Are you coming or staying behind?" He eased his hand under the animal who remained relaxed until he caught a glimpse of the cat basket, at which point he became rigid and totally uncooperative. It would have been easier for a camel to have passed through the eye of a needle than for Spike to have entered the kingdom of the cat basket. He travelled to his new home on Will's knee, both eyes tight shut.

"Are you sure you want to be moving out now?" Ernie Hallybone was driving towards St Petroc, through which they had to pass to get to Pencurnow Cove.

"Yes. The longer I leave it the harder it will be. I've got to get on."

"I can't believe it's all happening, really. It's been so long coming I suppose I should be ready for it, but I still can't take it in."

"Nor me."

"Forty-three years. It's a lifetime, isn't it? A bloody lifetime."

"At least you'll still be living here. I'm being kicked out into the big wide world."

Ernie looked across at him. "It's a bugger, isn't it?"

"Yes."

They passed through St Petroc and turned west towards Pencurnow village.

"Are you taking all this lot with you?"

"Can I leave a few boxes with you until later?"

"Course you can. May's got plenty of storage space in the spare room. What about the state of the boat?"

"Oh, I can cope with that. I've got rid of all the old carpet and curtains and scrubbed it out. It's clean . . . ish. Bit spartan, though."

"And cold."

"I've got plenty of sweaters, and a good sleeping-bag. It's been recommended by an Antarctic explorer."

"Scott?"

"No. Someone who survived."

Ernie was trying to make light of the occasion. He'd grown fond of the lad who'd worked with him for the last six years. He'd miss him. He had more rapport with him than he'd ever had with the dour Ted Whistler. Will had regularly been invited into Ernie's flat at the lighthouse for supper, cooked by his wife May, who had a smallholding in the village. He always ate well at Ernie and May's – fresh eggs and ham and home-grown vegetables. May was the sort of figure Will had always imagined as a farmer's wife – amply proportioned with grey hair dragged back into a bun – one wisp always managing to escape, and rosy cheeks. She had a high-pitched, sing-song voice, almost always wore a brown overall coat and wellies, and looked, Will thought, like Beatrix Potter.

Ernie's face was as weatherbeaten as that of a deep-sea fisherman. He seemed always to be smiling, and he and May, a childless couple, rarely had a cross word. It was, Ernie claimed, because they had always let each other have their own space. Ernie loved nature and bird-watching, May loved her livestock, and the one complemented the other. They were married, said May, "for better, for worse, but not for lunch".

"You'll keep comin' to see us?" asked Ernie with concern.

"Course I will. What's started you worrying that I won't? I'm only round the corner."

"Ten miles. A long way round 'ere, ten miles."

"Yes, but only by road. It's closer across the water and the cliff path. You've got too used to your van." Will turned to look at Ernie, whose eyes had glazed over. His jaw was set firm and he looked straight ahead.

Will hesitated. "There's something I want to ask you."

"Mmm?" Ernie's response was distant.

"The boat. The rowing boat – *The Gull*."

"What of it?"

"I want you to have her."

Ernie began to protest, but Will cut him off: "I'll have a bigger boat, and the *Gull* will be too heavy either to mount on davits or to tow behind. Anyway I want you to have her. No arguments, that's it."

"OK," Ernie said quietly. "Thanks."

"You all right?" Will had not seen him like this before. He'd always been relaxed and sanguine about anything life threw at him. But right now Will detected a note of apprehension in the older man's voice.

"Fine. It's just been a long time, that's all." He brightened unconvincingly. "I'm fine."

Ernie had worked on almost half of Trinity House's seventy-two lighthouses, ending up back on home territory in Cornwall. The only time Will ever saw his feathers ruffled was when Ted Whistler droned on about the inevitability of automation. "We're not coastguards," Ted would moan. "We don't have to look out for anything, just clean things up, that's all." When this happened Ernie would give him chapter and verse on the benefits of manned lighthouses, on how many potential disasters had been averted because of a lighthouse keeper's observations and instincts, and how many lives had been saved because of man rather than machine.

"Look, it might be ten miles by road, but it's only a couple of miles by sea," Will repeated reassuringly. "You can row over when it's calm. And when it isn't I'll get on my bike, when I've got one."

"Course you will. Don't mind me. Just bein' daft."

"Old bugger!" Will mocked him, and nudged his arm.

"Aye, daft old bugger." He laughed and jerked a thumb in the direction of the slumbering Spike. "He don't seem to mind, then?"

"You wouldn't have said that if you'd seen him half an hour ago."

"How are you going to stop 'im comin' back?"

"No idea. He'll do what he wants to do, I suppose – always has."

The cat began to purr.

"May says you 'ave to butter their paws. It makes the smell of their new place stick to them and then they don't try to go back home."

"I can't afford butter. Does it work with marge?"

"Now who's a daft bugger?"

Ernie laughed again. Their journey to the Crooked Angel boatyard continued in silence, except for the hum of the engine and the purring of the cat.

Chapter 4: Portland Bill

Their first night together passed uneventfully. The gentle swaying rocked both man and cat to sleep at around midnight, and Will awoke to the sound of scratching and seagulls at seven in the morning.

One thing he had not done was buy food, so there was no margarine to put on the cat's paws. But he couldn't leave Spike cooped up while he walked up the hill to Primrose's: the boat had an ample sufficiency of aromas already, without adding one of a feline nature. What's more, the ship's timbers were beginning to suffer the effects of Spike's claws.

Will struggled out of the sleeping-bag, stretched, pulled on a fisherman's sweater and a pair of shorts, then opened the door and let the cat out.

Spike crept gingerly over the threshold into the bright morning, his whiskers twitching and his tail held vertically aloft. He looked, thought Will, like a little boy who had just been introduced to a fairground. Eyes wide, he padded around the boat, familiarizing himself with his new territory. Then he hopped off and went down the pontoon in the direction of the jetty.

Will considered calling him back, but resisted, thinking that he might wake his boating neighbours. Instead, he watched through the window of the wheelhouse as Spike plodded towards the jetty. Gryler would not be in his office yet. He had told Will he generally started work at around eight. The cat reached the jetty and looked to left and right before disappearing behind a pile of old wooden crates. For fully five minutes he was lost from view and Will was getting ready to go in search of his lost shipmate when Spike emerged from behind the crates with the remains of a fish.

Will's thoughts turned to his own breakfast. Then he gazed at the bare interior of the boat, and wondered yet again if he had done the right thing. But he'd had no option. The boat had spoken to him that day a couple of weeks ago and he'd felt responsible for it somehow. What he had to do now was make it more reliably seaworthy and more comfortably habitable.

He sat back on the hard wooden bunk, acutely aware that his daily timetable had gone. What he did now, and when he did it, was up to him. It was tempting just to stay in bed and brood or, at least, it would be when he'd found a mattress. He could put off the voyage for a year or two if he wanted. It was a hare-brained scheme anyway. Why was he preparing to do it? How long would it take? Cornwall alone had 417 miles of coastline, counting all the twiddly bits. The distance round England, Scotland and Wales amounted, geographically, to 6,872 miles, though the voyage would be nearer 2,000 miles in reality. And what would he find at the end of it? Would he be back where he'd started in more ways than one? He wanted to voyage alone, but part of him wished he didn't have to. If things had gone according to plan . . . But they had not.

He took stock of himself. It was no use thinking like this. He had to be positive, practical. For three years he had promised himself this voyage. It was now or never. He had a year to do it – he could probably eke out his present funds over twelve months but no longer. Then he would have to find another job. He would probably have to go back to making clocks. Unless something else turned up. There. Sorted.

He pulled on a pair of deck shoes then sneaked off the boat. He walked down the pontoon, across the jetty, let himself out through the blue gate and went up the hill in search of provisions.

Primrose could not disguise her surprise at his appearance. She said nothing, but her eyes spoke volumes. It amused Will to think of the gossip she'd be passing on today: "Mr Elliott, the lighthouse keeper, has really let himself go. Used to be so neat and tidy. You wouldn't know him now. Such a pity."

He walked back down the hill towards the boat, loaded with four carrier-bags. The threatening clouds of the day before had blown away, and the sky was clear. There was a faint nip in the air. He looked across at the lighthouse and thought of Ernie, hoping he'd soon settle into his new role. He was sixty-two now; time he slowed down a bit. Anyway, he'd have more time for his bird-watching between showing round visitors, which was pretty much a seasonal job in this part of Cornwall.

As he reached the bottom of the hill he turned the corner and walked past the Roundhouse. Primrose had called it 'the heart of the village' and Will noticed that it had been smartened up since he last set eyes on it a couple of weeks ago. The window-frames were glossy white, and the clapboard exterior was now a soft blue. The slate roof sat on top like a coolie hat, and the double doors were crowned with a sign proclaiming 'Roundhouse Studio', framed by bleached lengths of silvery driftwood.

Will mounted the steps to take a closer look inside. He pressed his nose to the glass of the door and started when he saw a face inside looking directly back at him. He lurched back and one of his carrier-bags gave way, spilling an assortment of produce from wild rice to apples, tinned sardines to biological toilet cleaner.

"Sorry! I didn't mean to make you jump." The voice was a mixture of amusement and concern. Will looked up. Standing in the now open doorway was a woman in her late twenties. She wore jeans, a white T-shirt, and a mass of auburn curls cascaded over her shoulders. Her face was pale and expressive, and the corners of her mouth were doing their best not to allow themselves to turn upwards into a grin.

She knelt down and helped him retrieve his shopping. "I'm sorry. What a mess. Aaah!" She looked at the oozing eggs in their battered box. "I'm so sorry!"

"Don't worry. I shouldn't have been so nosy."

"I'm glad you were. It proves the place looks interesting."

"Are you open yet?" he asked, retrieving a tin of soup from the gutter.

"It's my first day today."

"Well, I hope you do well." He smiled. "The place certainly looks a lot better."

"I've done my best, but it's taken a while. It's a couple of months since I started on the inside. The outside was much easier. I only hope it works."

The shopping was back in the bags now and Will stood up, cradling one in his arms and hoping that the handles of the others would last until he made it back to the boat. "What are you selling?" he asked.

"My paintings." And then, belatedly, "Hi . . . I'm Amy Finn. I'm a painter. Sort of."

"Will Elliott. Lighthouse keeper. Well, until last week." He made to shake her hand, then realised he couldn't so grinned apologetically.

"What will you do now?"

"I'm living on a boat over there," he jerked his head in the direction of the Crooked Angel, "but it needs a lot of work doing."

"Well, you've got the summer to come."

"Yes." He found he was staring at her. She was quite small, with fine features and a dusting of freckles on her pale skin. She wore no jewellery, and there was a freshness about her that took his breath away.

"Do you . . . er . . . would you?" He hesitated.

"Yes?"

"Would you consider exhibiting work from other artists, or will it be all your own work in the gallery?"

"Oh, I'll have to take stuff from other artists. I can't paint fast enough to keep the place full – if my work sells, that is. And, anyway, I think people want to see lots of different styles – they might not like mine." She shrugged.

"How will you decide what to sell?"

"I'll keep my eyes open locally and see what I can find. And other artists will hopefully drop in and offer me stuff."

"Just paintings?"

"No, sculpture. All art forms, really." She looked at him inquisitively. "You sound interested."

"Well, it's just that . . . I make these model boats, you see, not Airfix, wooden models of Cornish cobles. Traditional rowing boats. Do you think you might have a look at one . . . just to see? I have to make a bit of cash somehow and—"

"Love to. Why don't you bring one round?"

"You sure you don't mind?"

"As long as you don't mind me turning you down if it's not the sort of thing I think I could sell."

"No. Not at all."

"Are you free tonight? I'll be closing at five. Why don't you come round then? If you'd like to?"

He felt a brief sense of elation. "Yes. Fine." He nodded nervously, a touch embarrassed, then walked backwards for a few paces down the lane before realizing that he must look silly, at which point he nodded again and turned. He began to whistle. He couldn't remember the last time he'd felt like this. He took a deep breath and headed for the boat and breakfast.

The cup of coffee revived him. Gryler had supplied him with a cylinder of propane and Primrose had sold him a twin burner. He also had a kettle, a saucepan, a single set of cutlery and some plastic plates, bowls and mugs.

The plumbing would have to be his first priority,

along with a mattress. He found a pencil and pad in one of his boxes and drew up a list of things to do.

He was at the bottom of page three when he heard a call. "Halloo? *Hallooooo?*"

A bearded face was peering above the rail of the boat. "Halloo?"

"Yes?" Will got up and ducked through the door of the wheelhouse.

"Permission to come aboard, skipper?"

It was the first time Will had been given the rank and it made him laugh. "Yes. Er . . . do."

His visitor clambered over the rail, a gangly man with long, thin limbs, grubby corduroy trousers that had once been green, and a navy-blue Guernsey threadbare at the elbows. His sandy whiskers matched the hair on his head – an unruly thatch unused to a comb.

"Utterly," said the man, offering his hand. Will looked about apologetically.

"Yes, it is a bit, I'm afraid."

"No!" The man threw back his head and laughed, displaying a mouth full of uneven teeth. "Aitch Utterly – I live in the boat next door." He scratched his head. "Good to have you with us. Not that there are many of us, but we're a jolly bunch."

Will noticed that the man hardly stopped smiling. He had one of those faces that probably smiled when he was asleep.

"You're the lighthouse keeper, aren't you? The last

lighthouse keeper. Read all about it in the paper."

Will's heart sank. Suddenly the prospect of living in a community once more – albeit a small boating community – filled him with dread. He'd imagined that on his own boat he could enjoy his own company. He'd not taken into account that he would have neighbours.

"Now, look," Aitch had seen the panic in Will's face, "you've probably come here for a quiet life so don't worry. Everybody on these boats does their own thing. We don't live in each other's pockets but we're good company when you want it. Well, most of us. We stick together. Great community spirit, but most of us know where to draw the line. Sorry to go on a bit. Spend a lot of time on me own. Think it makes you a bit of a chatterbox when you get in company. Sometimes." He chuckled. "Depends whose company it is, of course. One or two folk round here wouldn't give you the time of day. Can't be doing with them. Life's too short. Mmmm. Too short." He became introspective, as if transported to a different time and a different place. Then he was back. "Anyway, there I am, in my boat – *Florence Nightingale*, the yawl." He pointed to the other side of the narrow pontoon. "Bit close, I know, but I think we'll get on. I won't get in your way. Mmmm. No. Leave you in peace now. Let me know if you want anything – tools or whatever – only too pleased to oblige. Till then, cheerio." And he leapt over the side, on to the pontoon then back into his own boat, disappearing through the hatch with a wave.

"Well," said Will, to his cat, "I think we've just met our neighbour." For the second time that morning he felt unusually happy.

Chapter 5: Coquet

Getting clean is not easy when all you have is a bucket. Will arranged a carpet of pages from the now unwanted *Boats and Planes For Sale* in the middle of the wheelhouse, put the bucket in the centre and added a kettleful of boiling water to the chilly contents. He had a bar of Wright's Coal Tar soap and a flannel, a bottle of frequent-use shampoo, a throw-away razor and some shaving gel.

He set to work removing his stubble. He squinted into a small mirror and caught Spike's eye. "I know it's not what you're used to but at least you've got your own bit of blanket." The cat blinked. Will finished shaving, shampooed his hair then set about washing himself in the bucket. The absurdity of the enterprise suddenly struck him. He laughed. "The sooner we get that bath and shower sorted the better," he said to Spike, as he towelled himself dry.

"If Gryler wasn't too mean to have a shower block we'd be OK. Thank goodness he's got a loo." Spike ignored him: he was trying to remove the margarine from his paws.

Will dressed as tidily as he could in a clean pair of jeans and a sweatshirt, and brushed dried mud from his deck shoes. Then he went to the boxes at the sharp end of the boat to fetch out one of his models. It was carefully wrapped in tissue paper, and he eased it out of the box. He told Spike he wouldn't be long, then he closed the door behind him and locked it. It was safer than leaving Spike loose on what was only his second night as a sailor.

A meal was being prepared in Aitch's boat as he passed, and he could hear shipboard voices on pontoon number two, accompanied by the gentle lapping of water at the bows of an old speedboat named *The Slapper*. In the sunset the water of the boatyard glowed a dull orange. The cry of a single gull echoed across the glassy water. It was, he thought, as he walked down the jetty towards the gate, not a bad place to live.

He tapped on the glass of the gallery door. There was a pause, then the sound of feet, and Amy unlocked the door.

"Hi!" She flung back her arm to invite him in. He felt himself blushing. It surprised him. He was thirty-seven, for God's sake. He cleared his throat. "Hi.

How was your first day?"

"Oh, a bit slow. Quite a few people came round but I didn't sell much – it's early in the season."

She dropped the latch behind him and pulled down a linen roller blind. "So what do you think?"

He looked around. "Wow!" The Roundhouse consisted of a circular space on two levels, linked by a spiral staircase on the far side. The floor was of ancient oak planks that had been scrubbed clean of the nautical detritus of a century or two. The walls were white and lit with tiny bright spotlights fastened to wires that criss-crossed the room. On the floor, towards the middle of the room, stood half a dozen different artworks made from 'found objects' – lumps of driftwood, rusty old nails and chains. There were a couple of erotic sculptures of abstract figures, but it was the paintings that caught his eye, canvases of Cornish beaches with burning white sand and sky of the most brilliant azure. Each radiated a freshness and energy that amazed him.

"There's hardly anything here yet. There'll be more over the next few weeks, I hope, but I don't want to fill it with too much."

"No." He was gazing at one of the paintings, transfixed.

"Do you like them?"

"Yes." It seemed lame. "Very much." Then he found his breath. "I think they're wonderful."

"Oh, that's a bit strong."

"No, I do. I can take or leave the driftwood but the paintings, wow!"

"Well, that's honest!"

"Whose are the sculptures?"

"Oh, a friend. I want to get more smaller things for a sort of plain wooden counter over there. I'll have to sell little souvenirs, too, but I want them to be good. Anyway, come upstairs and have a drink. I've got a bottle in the fridge." She walked towards the staircase. "It's a bit spartan, I'm afraid."

Amy's spartan was not Will's spartan. The floor was covered in coir matting, the walls were washed pale blue and a vast cream linen curtain was hauled back at one end to separate the sleeping and living areas. Will noticed a large double bed with white pillows, and in the living area two blue and white striped chesterfields faced each other across a low, scrubbed-pine table.

A cello lay on its side on the floor, near a music stand and a pile of music. A few pictures were propped up against the wall.

"The bathroom is through there if you want it."

A single white-painted door was sufficiently ajar for Will to see an ancient iron bath with ball and claw feet and brass taps. "It's better than my plumbing. All I've got at the moment is a bucket." He put the boat on the table between the sofas as she came towards him with a bottle of Chardonnay and two glasses.

"Could you do this? Do you mind? I'll put some music on."

As he peeled off the foil she pressed the buttons of a small stereo, which eventually produced the soft sounds of a Bach string quartet.

The cork came out with a loud plop and he tipped the wine into the glasses as she returned.

"Mmm, that looks good."

"Well . . . here's to you and your gallery."

"Studio, please. Gallery sounds a bit posh. Cheers!"

They sipped and she motioned him to sit on the sofa. She sat opposite, tucking her bare feet under herself. "Now, then, show me the boat." He put down his glass and carefully undid the tissue paper to reveal the Cornish coble.

She slid off the sofa on to the floor, and studied it seriously. He began to believe it was not really her sort of thing. "I don't mind if it's not suitable," he said.

"What?" She was preoccupied.

"I don't mind if you feel it won't really fit in."

"It's beautiful." She spoke quietly. "Absolutely beautiful."

He sat still and quiet, filled with unexpected pride as her eyes ran over the boat's lines.

"I don't usually go much for model boats. They seem phoney, somehow. But yours has life. How long does it take you? Oh, God! I hate it when people ask me that about my paintings and here I am asking you."

"I've no idea. I've never timed myself. But a long time, I suppose."

"So often models like this are . . . well, numb. But yours isn't. I love it."

"I'm glad." He felt ridiculously pleased with himself.

"Can I exhibit it tomorrow?"

"Fine. Great." He could hardly believe his luck.

She climbed back on the sofa. "What made you start making them?"

"Oh, I had time on my hands and needed to fill it with something."

"But you could have done anything. Why model boats?"

"Because I love the sea and the escape it offers. And I love the idea of escaping on a wooden boat. So a model wooden boat seemed appropriate. I could dream while I made it."

"About what?"

"Sailing away."

"From what?"

"Oh . . . life."

She looked at him and sipped her wine.

"Is that why you became a lighthouse keeper? To sail away from life?" She made light of it, smiling as she spoke.

"Yes."

60

She noticed his shuttered look. "I'm sorry. I'm too nosy. I didn't mean to pry."

"No. It's OK." Will always felt self-conscious when conversations took this turn, but she looked at him with a combination of gentleness and concern that made him feel secure rather than threatened. He felt under no pressure to speak, but found that he could without the usual burning desire to run away. "It's six years ago now. I know it's stupid but I still find it hard to talk about."

"Sorry. Typical of Finn. Barging in. I'm sorry."

"No, really, it's fine. I should be used to it now."

She sensed the echoes of grief. "It is and it isn't. Some things stay raw and others fade. I know."

He looked at her open face. She didn't seem to be prying.

"I was working in Oxford. I was a clockmaker. I'd been married a year, to Ellie. We met at college – went out for ages." He smiled to himself. "Two days after our first anniversary she was killed. Hit-and-run driver. Just like that. Gone. She was expecting a baby. I lost the two of them in one go."

Amy sat looking at him, shocked, as he continued in a calm, measured voice. "I didn't know what to do. I just knew I wanted to be on my own. I don't mean I don't like company – I'm better at it now – but I still need space and time on my own. I find it difficult to be in a room full of people."

He was sitting on the edge of the sofa, his arms

resting on his knees and his pale blue eyes gazing into the middle distance. "I'm so sorry." Amy wanted to put her arms round him and tell him he was a lovely man and that it would be all right. "Did you ever think of seeing anybody about it?" she asked.

"Not for long. Didn't want to admit to anybody that I couldn't cope. I wanted to sort myself out. Share your troubles and they just keep being brought back to you. I didn't want that. Didn't want somebody else getting involved."

"So you shut yourself away?"

"Yes. I thought that way I could get over it in my own time. Cry myself silly. But I still haven't." He smiled. "Funny, isn't it? My world fell apart and I couldn't even cry."

"It's more common than you'd think. "

"I didn't feel I could be a monk." He brightened and she took the joke. "Anyway, Ellie wouldn't have wanted that. And I didn't know what I believed in, which was a bit of a drawback, so I looked for another solo occupation. As a lighthouse keeper I could be remote, solitary, have time to reflect. Then I found I'd be working with two other people, but our watches were solo so that meant I could be alone a lot. And I like Cornwall. It's out on a limb. Like me."

"No family?"

"No. Mum and Dad both died when I was young. I was brought up by my granny and she died ten years ago. Sorry story, isn't it?"

"I'm glad you told me. Pleased you felt you could."

"Thanks for listening. I'm sorry to go on. Talking about myself."

"Don't be silly." She moved across to sit nearer to him. "I did ask you – you didn't volunteer it."

"No, but when you spend so much time thinking about yourself and your own problems you have to be careful not to forget other people."

"It's not the easiest thing to get over, is it? Losing the person you loved most and your unborn child at the same time. It's the most devastating thing imaginable. I think anyone would understand that."

"Like you? I'm not sure they would."

"Oh, I'm not that special."

"Special enough to come here all on your own and open your own place. That's special. It takes courage." He paused, anxious to move the conversation on to a happier subject. "Have you always been a painter?"

"No." She looked up. "Like you, I'm an escapee, except that it was my career that was taken away from me."

"Oh?"

"I was with the Ballet Rambert. Then I moved to Ballet d'Azur. I was doing quite well. Principal dancer. And then my knee went. Lateral meniscus." She rubbed at the offending joint. "That was it."

"God. How awful."

She laughed sardonically. "Yes, it was a bit. Life devoted to my art and wham! Finished overnight."

"Do you miss it?"

"Like hell. It nags away all the time. Like unfinished business. I still do a bit of barre work every day" – she pointed to a rail along part of the wall – "but my career is finished."

"How can you be so sure? Won't it get better?"

"Oh, it is better. But there's always a danger it will go again."

"And you don't want to take the risk?"

"I wish I could. The trouble is, it's not just the knee. It's the nerve. I haven't got the guts to carry on, if I'm honest. I try, but I keep feeling this nagging doubt. Some days I think it'll be fine, and then others I know it's over. To be perfectly honest I'm terrified it'll go again and that I won't even be able to walk."

"So you decided to paint?"

"I'd always dabbled. I needed to find another way of earning a living so I thought I'd give it a go. I managed to sell canvases to friends and the time came when I had to get away from London. So I rented this place and here I am." She got up, picked up the bottle and came back to fill up his glass. She sat closer to him than before. He admired the clearness of her complexion.

"What about the cello?" He gestured towards it.

"Oh, I'm not very good, but it lets me get rid of the pent-up frustrations I have when I do a crap painting."

"I know what you mean. It's like me and boats. Stay off the water too long and I get withdrawal symptoms."

"Is that why you're living afloat?"

"Yes."

"For ever?"

"I wish. But for now anyway. I've always had this nagging idea about sailing around Britain. I kept telling myself it was daft but it's become a sort of personal challenge. I've learnt how to sail. I can navigate. And now I've bought a boat with two engines and no sails because I fell in love with it. Crazy!"

"How did you come to fall in love with it?"

"It turned out to be one of the little ships of Dunkirk, and I'm just a sentimental old fool."

"How old?"

"Thirty-seven."

"It's a dangerous age – fast approaching the big four-oh."

"How old are you?"

"Never you mind." She paused and looked him in the eye. "Oh, all right, then, twenty-nine."

"Not a dangerous age?"

Amy laughed. "What about supper?"

"Oh. No. I couldn't. I'm holding you up."

"You're not holding me up at all. It's nice to have someone to share things with. I've been on my own for a few weeks now."

"Well . . ." He hesitated. "Only if you're sure."

She smiled her relaxed smile. "I'm sure."

Will wondered about her attachments, but told himself it was both too soon and too obvious to enquire.

They talked on. She made supper – simple pasta with olive oil and broccoli – and they drank the rest of the wine.

It was after midnight when he left. They parted at the door of the studio and she kissed his cheek lightly. For a moment he was unsure how to leave.

"Thanks," he said. "I'll see you soon."

"Hope so."

"Thanks for listening," he murmured.

"It was a pleasure." They stared silently at each other, and then he was gone into the night.

Chapter 6: Smalls

"Jump, then! Go on, jump." Will heard the commotion and felt the bump from the engine room of *Boy Jack*. It was an East London accent, male, and more than a little irritated. Friday afternoon and the weekenders had arrived.

"Get it nearer, then! I can't jump that far." A female voice responded to the shouted order.

"Bladdy hell, woman. I'm as near as I can get it! Jump bladdy off." There was a loud bang followed by "Christ! Tie the bladdy thing off, then."

Will swung up from the engine room, arms smudged with black oil, and stuck his head tentatively out of the doorway. The speedboat whose name had intrigued him on his first visit to the boatyard – *Sokai* – was at right angles to his own pontoon, her engine burbling and her bows nudging one of the wooden piles. A long smudge of paint along the transom of

Boy Jack showed where contact had been made, and a blonde, fluffy-haired woman in a blue-and-white-striped Breton jersey and white pedal-pushers lay spreadeagled on the pontoon, a length of rope in her hand. On the foredeck of the boat, his legs surrounded by jumbled coils, was a man in white jeans and a white Arran sweater, a fat cigar-stub clamped between his lips, his face getting redder by the moment.

"Stupid bladdy woman. Tie it off, we're drifting." The pile of fluff in the pedal-pushers scrambled unwillingly to her feet and tied her end of the rope in an elaborate knot to a cleat on the pontoon.

"Now the other one. *Now the other one*," he bellowed as she tottered along the pontoon in her high-heels. He hurled at her a tangled web of rope, which dropped into the water just inches from her reach.

"Jesus wept! Where's the boathook? *Where did you put the boathook?*"

The woman, now on the verge of tears, answered in a quiet but frustrated tone: "You're standing on it."

Her tormentor looked down, swore silently to himself and pulled it from beneath his deck shoe. Then he poked and slashed at the water, as though he were stirring a gigantic pot of stew, and eventually hooked out the rope. This he tossed at the woman. She threw up her arms to catch it and received a faceful of muddy seawater as the rope looped itself around her neck.

Screwing up her face, she picked it off and held it at arm's length.

"Pull it, then!"

The woman's patience snapped. "I am pulling it, Jerry MacDermott, and if you don't think I am you can sodding well pull it yourself." Her voice cracked and a tear rolled down her cheek. "Now look what you've made me do! I've broken a nail and I only had a manicure yesterday. Bugger!"

"Have you done? Is that it? Are we tied off?"

"Yes, we are. Tied off and pissed off. I've had enough." And she teetered away down the pontoon in the direction of the jetty and the village, leaving the man to tidy up after her.

He switched off the engine then leapt unsteadily on to the pontoon and caught Will's eye. "'Allo, squire! Sorry about that. Not much of a sailor, my missus." He laughed, without dislodging the cigar, and continued to fasten a tonneau cover over the cockpit of his boat. "She enjoys a glass or two when we've anchored but she's not so hot on the ropes. Wants a bigger boat where she can entertain 'er friends. She'll 'ave one soon but she gets a bit uptight about 'andling this one."

He looked at the transom of *Boy Jack*. "Sorry about the bump. Not that it shows much. 'Ere, 'ang on a minute."

He disappeared below for a few seconds, then emerged with a bottle of whisky.

"Cop 'old of this. Goodwill gesture." He leapt off the front of *Sokai* and walked towards *Boy Jack*.

"No, really. It's OK. I haven't started painting her yet."

"Take it, take it. Sort of welcome present." He offered his hand. "Jerry MacDermott. Live at the big 'ouse – Benbecula – up on the 'ill. Come down at weekends. The missus misses London but it does 'er good to 'ave a change of air."

The missus was now sitting in a Mercedes on the lane by the jetty.

"You're new 'ere, aren't you, squire?" Will agreed that he was. "Thought so. 'Aven't been 'ere that long ourselves but we know a few faces in the boatyard and the village. Didn't think we'd seen you before. Stayin' long?"

"For a while," admitted Will.

"Lovely spot, ain't it? Olde-worlde charm. Wouldn't mind livin' 'ere full time but the missus wouldn't wear it. Too much of a townie. Likes 'er social life. Still, we've plenty of room to entertain down 'ere and I like gettin' away from it all."

Will smiled, not knowing quite what to make of the East End wideboy who didn't appear short of a bob or two. He was around the fifty mark, sharp as a razor, with dark brown hair that owed its colouring to something in a bottle. His wife was younger, perhaps by twenty years. Probably married him for his money, Will thought.

"You've got your work cut out."

"Sorry?" Will came back to earth.

"With this thing. Bit of a state, ain't it?"

"Yes." Will's pride in his old boat was momentarily bruised, but he found it difficult to disagree.

"As long as you're not thinking of sailing round the world – heh-heh!"

"No, not quite."

"Plenty of character, though, eh?" Jerry MacDermott eyed the boat up and down, seaching in vain for some redeeming characteristic. "Funny name. *Boy Jack*."

"She came originally from Yorkshire."

"Bloody cold up there. Went to Yorkshire once. Couldn't understand a bladdy word they was sayin'."

"What about yours?"

"Eh?"

"Your boat, *Sokai*. What does it mean?"

"'Aven't you guessed?"

"Something Japanese?"

"Nah. It stands for 'Spending Our Kids' Anticipated Inheritance'." He chuckled. "Not that they're *our* kids. My kids. She's my second wife, is Trudie. Got rid of the first one. Couldn't cope with the success. Wanted to stay in 'Ackney. I couldn't wait to get out. We just grew apart. Well, you've got to enjoy your success, 'aven't you? Can't 'ang around livin' like you used to when funds 'ave improved. Nah. Enjoy it, that's what I say. That's why we're goin' for a bigger boat. If you've got it, flaunt it. That's my motto." He looked around him at the picturesque decay. "Wouldn't mind gettin' my 'ands on this place. Gold mine if it was run proper. Gryler 'asn't a clue." Will could see that Jerry MacDermott was visualizing a fleet of floating gin palaces tied up in a West Country version of Monte Carlo. "Yes. A bit of imagination and you could transform this place. Not a bad idea."

He cast a glance at the Mercedes and the beckoning arm of the blonde inside it. "Well, better be off. She wants to 'ave a look in that new art gallery. Plenty of walls to fill at the big 'ouse. Be seein' you. Keep at it!" He unscrewed the cigar butt from his mouth, tossed it into the water and lurched off down the pontoon in the direction of the gleaming car.

Will shook his head, then turned back to *Boy Jack* and slapped the side of the wheelhouse. He stepped inside and was about to lower himself into the engine room once more when Aitch's head appeared from a hatch on *Florence Nightingale*. "What was all that about?"

Will turned round. "Hi. Oh, just some husband and wife having a disagreement about how to berth a boat."

Aitch looked in the direction of the speedboat. "Ah. Mr MacDermott and his floating bathtub."

"You know him, then?"

"Well, I wouldn't say I know him, but I've

encountered him a few times. Bought Benbecula when Hugo Morgan-Giles moved out. Keeps talking about buying the boatyard and sorting it out. I rather hope he never gets round to it. Made his money in mobile phones apparently. Rolling in it. Ha-ha. Lucky man. Think of all the books you could buy if you had that sort of cash."

Will grinned. He'd hardly encountered Aitch in the previous few days. *Florence Nightingale* had been shut up, the curtains inside her port-holes drawn and no sign of her skipper.

"Books?"

"Yes. Wonderful things, books. Never mind all this technology. Who wants to sit and look at a screen when you can turn pages that were printed centuries ago? Look at this . . ." He dived from view inside his vessel, and returned with a mighty leather-bound volume. "Been shopping. Had a few days in Dartmouth. A bit naughty, I know . . ."

Will jumped down from *Boy Jack* and walked across the pontoon to where Aitch was standing with his prize, his eyes shining with excitement.

He opened the large volume, about the size of a family Bible, reverentially, exposing marbled endpapers. He turned several pages to reveal the title: *The History of Devonshire* by the Reverend Richard Polwhele. "Look at that," he instructed, as though he were guiding a party of tourists around ancient ruins. "Been hunting for a good copy for years. Promised it to myself one day." He closed the book and stroked its spine with a loving hand. "All of Devonshire within my grasp." His eyes had a faraway look.

Will was struck by the look of pure pleasure on his face.

"And," said Aitch, "listen to this." He thumbed through the pages. "I thought of you when I read it." He found the page he was looking for and cleared his throat. " 'The storm that marked the twenty-seventh of November, 1703, was attended with awful consequences to the western counties . . . Daily intelligence of shipwrecks arrived, whilst great numbers of dead bodies were washed upon the coasts from Hull to Land's End. But the destruction of the *Eddystone Lighthouse* will long fix the memory of this dreadful night. Its architect, Mr Winstanley, had often wished to contemplate a storm from his lighthouse, imagining that the stability of his fabric was proof against the elements. He had his wish; but the violence of the weather increasing to a wonderful degree, his resolution forsook him and he made signals for help. No boat, however, could venture off the shore: and neither lighthouse nor its architect were any more seen. The morning opened on bare rock!'" Aitch closed the book. "What about that?"

"Quite a story, isn't it?" agreed Will.

"You know about it, then?"

"Yes. They replaced it with a lighthouse built by a man called Rudyerd, but that one burned down in

1755. Then came Smeaton, a Yorkshireman who built his lighthouse on the principle of the trunk of an oak tree. You can still see the stump of it, and the one that's there now was built by James Douglass in 1882 – it's the fifth. Winstanley lost his life in the second one he built."

Aitch scratched his head "Well I never. I should have known you'd know."

Will felt guilty at stealing his neighbour's thunder.

"Wonderful thing, knowledge," Aitch went on. "This book's full of it. Amazing chapters – 'The Air and Weather', 'Indigenous Plants', 'The Religion of Danmonium'."

"The what? As distinct from C of E?"

"Danmonium is what the Romans called this part of the world."

"Oh, I see. Which shows that I don't know as much as you thought I did!"

Aitch laughed. "Coffee? I'm just brewing up."

"I'd love some. All I can taste is oil at the moment. It's filthy down there." He indicated the engine room.

"They're fine when they're working," Aitch said, "but when they're not they're a pain in the nether portions. Come on board." And then, seeing that Will was concerned about his state of cleanliness, "Don't worry about the mess. It's not exactly spotless in here."

Will pushed his head through the hatch of

Florence Nightingale's wheelhouse and was startled by what he saw. It was like a shrunken Victorian study. The walls of the wheelhouse were almost totally lined with books. A long seat down one side was covered with a threadbare red plush cushion, on which were tin boxes full of artefacts and hanks of rope crafted into Turk's head knots. Bits of brassware gleamed here and there, and there was hardly room to put a foot down for clutter, most of it ancient nautical gear. On an old mahogany table a tarnished sextant tumbled from a broken wooden case. A couple of telescopes were in the process of being fitted with new lenses from a box filled with circular bits of glass and brass ferrules. A stuffed cormorant in an advanced stage of moult surveyed the scene from its glass case perched on a shelf, and plates of half-finished food sat on top of piles of books and periodicals. This was the domestic equivalent of Primrose Hankey's shop.

"Excuse the stuff. Can't seem to stop picking it up. I should have enough of it by now but, well, when you see it looking forlorn at a boat jumble you can't really leave it there, can you?"

"Er, no." Will looked about in vain for somewhere to stand.

Aitch took the kettle off the hob of the tiny stove and poured it into a jug, releasing the pleasing aroma of coffee. "Tell you what, let's have it out there – more room than in here. I'll clear it up soon and show you round properly."

Will backed out of the doorway and on to *Florence Nightingale*'s rope-strewn deck. Aitch thrust a mug of coffee into his hand and asked, "How's the restoration coming on, eh?"

"Slowly. I've had a plumber in to sort out the water, and I'm just cleaning up the engines. I reckon I can do some of the work myself – I've found an old manual. I'm trying to save as much as I can for the hull repairs."

"Mmm." Aitch cast his eye over *Boy Jack*. "She'll clean up well. Good lines. I probably won't be here by the time you finish, though."

"Oh?"

"No. Got to set off soon. Moving back to Devon. 'S where my family came from. Going to Dartmouth or Salcombe. Spend a while there."

"And then what?"

"No idea. Mr Micawber had the right attitude. Something'll turn up." He sipped reflectively at the coffee, his eyes misty. "Well, I'll let you get on. Chuck the mug back when you've done. I've got a telescope to fix. Early one. Probably used by Nelson!" He winked at Will and disappeared whistling 'Rule Britannia'.

Back on *Boy Jack*, Spike, who had been absent all morning, returned with another fish. "If you keep pinching the fishermen's catch we'll be thrown out of here. Go and eat it where no one can see you." Spike rubbed along Will's legs, then lay down in a coil of rope in the pulpit and began to chew off the head of his prey. "You know, you're really quite disgusting," Will muttered. "How we're going to live together in this old wreck I have no idea."

A mooring warp groaned. "I'm sorry. I didn't mean it. You might be a wreck now but in a few weeks – or months – you'll be fine." The rope groaned again under the wash of the tide. "Honest."

Chapter 7: Lizard

A my Finn's first week at the studio had been quiet. She'd had a few locals sniffing round, but more to find out what this girl who had rented the old capstan house was really like than to invest in her works of art. Some had politely taken their time, going to the trouble of feigning an interest in her work, others had darted in and out in the space of a couple of minutes. She'd had one or two enquiries about her paintings, a few tuts from village matrons at the erotic sculptures, and a few more from those who thought her sea views were overpriced.

Three hundred, thought Amy, is not a lot. Really it isn't. By Thursday night the cello was singing out the Elgar concerto, and by Friday afternoon she was feeling dispirited.

The arrival of a middle-aged London spiv with his candy-floss-haired floozy in tow did nothing to cheer her, and she busied herself quietly with a spot of framing while they looked around, surprised when the floozy made nice noises about the driftwood sculptures. Trudie persuaded her other half that one of them would look good in the hallway of their house up the hill and Jerry MacDermott pulled out a wad of notes, peeled off three fifties and handed them to Amy with a flourish.

"About the paintings . . ."

"Yes?" Amy was hopeful of a sale.

"A word of advice."

"Yes?" She was less hopeful.

"Get a few in that really look like the sea, eh? Might be interested then. Bit simple, these. Bright. But simple. Still, we'll pop back and see how you're goin' in a week or two. We'll need some pictures and it's nice to patronize local talent. Take care, sunshine. Ta-ta."

Amy stood open-mouthed as they departed, then looked at the notes in her hand and walked over to the cash desk. As she slipped the money into the drawer she admonished herself: "It is not up to you to tell them what they like, Amy, just provide them with what they want." She looked up at one of her paintings. "Get a few that really look like the sea . . ." Then she laughed, a brief, ironic sound, before going back to her frame, expecting to be undisturbed for the next half-hour.

She cleaned a pane of glass, cut a new cardboard

mount with a craft knife and was just about to frame a print of Lamorna Cove when the door opened again. She turned round to offer a greeting to her customer, but as soon as she saw his face she found herself lost for words.

He looked at her with a casual smile, exuding a mixture of self-satisfaction and arrogance. "Hallo, Ame!"

The hairs on the back of her neck bristled. She could not find her voice.

"Surprised?" He looked at her with one eyebrow raised.

She tried to answer but could not, then managed, "How did you . . . ?"

"Know you were here? Find you? I asked a few questions. Simple really." He was dressed entirely in black, his chiselled features emphasized by a polo-neck sweater under a black jacket. He leaned casually against the side of the door.

"You shouldn't be here."

"Yes, I should. I wanted to see you. And, anyway, you've got my sculptures." He pointed to the two erotic figures in the centre of the floor.

"I'm selling them. I don't want them any more."

"You can't sell them. They're us." He looked irritated, his pride wounded.

"That's why I don't want them." Having turned pale at the sight of him, the colour now rose in her cheeks and fire leapt into her heart. "How dare you

81

come back? How dare you find me here? You have no right to come barging in . . ." She ran out of words.

"I opened the door. It wasn't locked. I didn't barge, I stepped." The words were heavily overlaid with sarcasm.

"But why?" Her voice cracked. Desperation and sadness were now mixed with the anger: desperation at not being free of the clutches of the man she had tried to wipe from her life, sadness at his continuing interference, and anger at her own feeble response to his persistent harassment.

"What do you mean, why? It's obvious, isn't it?"

Her eyes rose heavenward. "Please go away, Oliver. Please, *please*, go away."

He walked towards her and placed his hands on her upper arms. She turned her head away from him.

"Look at me."

She strained her head even further away.

"Look at me, Ame!" He shook her, pressing his fingers into her flesh, and she turned to him. His nearness made her heart beat faster. His face had a strength and beauty that made her weak.

He spoke softly now. "I want to see you. I need to see you. Come on!" He shook her again. "Why did you run away?" He sighed impatiently. "Your knee will mend, you know. Why won't you believe in yourself? If you really want to we can dance again. You just have to want to. Why won't you?" He lifted a hand and stroked her hair. She turned her cheek and winced.

"We can't . . . I can't find it . . ."

"Why?" Oliver Gallico was even more insistent.

"Because – because I've had enough." He pressed himself closer to her and a wave of fear overwhelmed her. "I don't want this any more. I'm so tired of . . . being tired. Hurt and tired." She let out a sob. All strength seemed to be leaving her. She was trying hard not to resign herself to the usual course of events. The trying to escape and the failure to get far enough away. Her inability to shake him off. His inability to understand that she really did want to escape. She thought that down here, at the edge of the world, she might at last have eluded him but she should have known he would find her, would persuade some young dancer desperate for promotion to wheedle Amy's whereabouts out of her friends.

She felt so hopeless, so fatigued by it all. Perhaps unhappiness and frustration were to be her lot. The prospect shook her. She lifted her arms and flung off his hands. "Just go. It's too late. I'm not here for you any more. You can't keep behaving like this."

He looked at her disbelievingly, and had begun to approach her again when a rattling sound surprised him.

Amy turned and saw Will standing in the door-way. "Can I come in?"

"Yes. This gentleman was just going."

"I'm not," he said defiantly.

"Yes, you are."

He looked hard at her, but Amy stood her ground. Gallico shrugged and walked to the door. "Your loss." At the threshold he turned. "I'll see you later." He glanced expressionlessly at Will, then back at Amy before stepping out into the street and closing the door silently behind him.

Will watched him go, then turned to Amy. Thoughts whirled around in his head. What had happened? Who was the man? What had he done to Amy? He blurted out, "What was all that about? Are you OK?"

"No, I'm not OK." There was anger in her voice, then apology. "I'm sorry. Yes, I'm fine. I think. Funny, I thought I could make a new life here and my old one has just caught up with me." She sniffed, and tried to smile, feeling in her pockets for a tissue. Will handed her a slightly oily one. She thanked him and blew her nose.

"Do you want some tea?" he asked. It was feeble, but it always seemed to work in *The Archers*.

"No, thanks, I couldn't." And then, "Oh, yes. Why not."

"Come on. Upstairs." He motioned her to the staircase then stepped to the door, shot the bolt, turned round the Open sign to read Closed and pulled down the blind before following her to the apartment above.

"You picked a good time to come in." She smiled at him.

"I'm not sure I did." He filled the kettle and switched it on, then gathered together the cups, milk and teabags.

"Oh, you did. I don't know what would have happened if you hadn't."

"So you do know him?"

"Oh, yes. All too well. He's been in my life for eleven years. Eleven years," she repeated, as though she could not believe it herself. "Eleven years of torture, one way or another."

She made the tea, and then, as she carried a mug over to him, she explained, "His name is Oliver Gallico. He's the artistic director of the Ballet d'Azur."

"I should have guessed that. He looks the part."

"And acts it. He'd be funny if he wasn't so serious. He's so up himself it's not true. When I first met him he was with Rambert. A soloist. Brilliant. Drop-dead good looks, an amazing dancer. He took a shine to me. We started dancing together and then we became lovers, off and on – more off than on for me. He was arrogant – *is* arrogant – but I could cope with that. He has such a tremendous talent. I tried not to love him but you know what it's like." She looked at Will, half smiling and almost apologetic. "You can't always love the people you feel you should love."

"No," he said quietly.

"Anyway, it was pretty intense. But he started getting violent. Nothing serious at first, just heavy-handed. He's very strong – beautifully made," she said, ruefully, but Will caught the sparkle in her eyes. "Then it began to get out of hand. He'd really hurt me when we were . . . you know. He never struck me or anything, it was just a sort of rough brutality. I wasn't physically strong enough to stand up to it. I used to hurt for days afterwards."

Will was appalled and saddened by what he was hearing. "The bastard," he said softly, his face suffused with fury.

"Then he'd say things about me that really hurt. God, it sounds so pathetic. He'd tell me about other dancers in the company. About what they had that I hadn't got. It was clear that I wasn't the only woman in his life." She paused and sipped her tea, leaning against the wall.

Will looked at her incredulously. "Why didn't you leave?"

"I was trapped. Mesmerized. Under his spell – whatever you want to call it. I wanted to dance with him – had to dance with him. Then he decided to leave and set up his own company. Couldn't bear to be told what to do by other people. He asked me to go with him. I said no, that I wanted to stay with Rambert. I think I knew by then that I had to get away. Finally I saw my opportunity. But he wore me down. Pitiful, isn't it? Why didn't I just tell him to sod off? I wish I knew."

"So you went with him?"

"Not at first. Only after a few months. I didn't seem to be getting anywhere with Rambert. My dancing had lost its spark. To tell the truth I missed the excitement of his company. We were great together. Some kind of telepathy, two people dancing as one. You can't make that happen, however good a dancer you are. Either it's there or it isn't. The technique can be brilliant, but if there's no chemistry the result is soulless. I've never felt elation – exhilaration – like I felt when we danced together." Her cheeks were colouring, her eyes glowed. Then she talked of her injury, the evaporation of confidence that followed and his unbearable lack of feeling and disdain at her inability to dance with him. His suggestion that her weakness had ruined his career.

"But he's still in your life?"

"He wants to be. He doesn't believe my career is over. Says that a meniscectomy isn't the end. That I could come back if I believed in myself enough to work it through. Other dancers have had the same injury and gone back. I also think he feels I owe him something. He still directs Ballet d'Azur but he rarely dances. He says he doesn't want to dance with anybody else. Instead he sculpts. Those two are his." She pointed to the writhing figures in the centre of the studio. "They're supposed to be him and me. I can't bear to look at them so I thought I'd try and sell them to make some money. But I think I'll just cover them up and stick them in a back room. They don't seem to have brought me much luck."

"Do you think he'll come back?"

"Oh, I know he will."

He put his hands on her shoulders. She noticed the difference in touch between his hands and Oliver's. The strength was there, but the contact was lighter. "You know where I am. If you have any trouble come round whenever you like. You shouldn't have to feel like this."

She looked up at the slight, dark man before her, whose own life had been torn apart by tragedy. There he stood, in a fisherman's sweater several sizes too big for him, his bare feet showing above the deck shoes beneath a worn pair of sailing trousers.

"Thank you. You're very kind." She smiled into his eyes. Yesterday she had almost believed she had finally escaped the past; today she seemed manacled to it.

"I'll go," he said gently. "Thanks for the tea. Just let me know if I can do anything."

"I will. Thanks." She shot him another smile and he felt a surge of protectiveness.

"By the way, what did you come for?" she asked.

"I brought the rest of the boats. There are five." He picked up the bubble-wrapped parcels from just inside the door where he had left them. "I thought they'd be safer here than with me while all the work's going on. Has anyone shown any interest in the other?"

"Not yet, but they will. It's only been a few days, and we've the weekend ahead of us now. Just watch this space."

"I will. And don't forget, you know where I am."

Chapter 8: Mumbles

Saturday lunchtime in the Salutation was not the time for a quiet, contemplative drink. While not exactly heaving this early in the season, it was still thronged with locals aware that soon their time would not be their own. Pencurnow Cove fell short of being a tourist honeypot in summer, but it relied more heavily now on day-trippers than it had in the past, thanks to its dwindling fishing fleet.

Over the past couple of years the number of ships in glass cases inside the pub had grown as the fleet declined outside. The place had seen an influx of decorative glass floats, fishing nets, binnacles and brass telegraphs, but it had still not shed the seediness of a former life. The ashtrays were too full and the lavatories too malodorous for the ladies, which meant that the clientele in the off-season was predominantly male.

Ted Whistler leaned over one end of the bar, ordered his customary pint and lit his Camel cigarette, drawing the rich mixture deep into his perished lungs. The reason for Ted's profound personal sorrow was lost in the mists of time. He'd probably even forgotten himself. He was, and always had been, a miserable sod whose glass was always half empty rather than half full.

A trio of fishermen muttered in desultory fashion at the other end of the bar, while the landlord Alf Penrose attended to the wants of an increasing number of customers, his pint pulling only slightly impeded by the size of his gut, the legacy of a lifetime spent drinking ullage.

By the time Len Gryler arrived he had to shoulder his way to the bar. "Pint of best, landlord," he shouted, over the swelling din. "And a lager for the lad." Christopher Applebee slouched over to the pin-ball machine.

The landlord looked round, nodded to acknowledge the order, while serving a cycling couple who had rashly committed themselves to one of his cholesterol specials, extravagantly described on the menu as Mixed Grill.

Had each of his creations carried an indication of the amount of saturated fat they contained this one would have warranted a public health warning. He pushed a note of the order through the hatch at the back of the bar, from which steam, the noise of an impatient cook and the fragrance of burning oil emanated in rich mixture, then waddled over to the pumps and pulled Gryler his pint.

"How's trade?" he enquired of his maritime regular.

"Not bad, not bad."

"I should think you're quids in, aren't you, after selling that rotting hulk?"

"What do you mean, 'rotting hulk'? That's a seaworthy vessel of historical importance, that is. Rescued hundreds from Dunkirk during the war. Only wish I'd known that at the time. Might have got a bit more for her."

"More? Dream on!" Penrose smiled.

"So how's the ex-lighthouse keeper?" Gryler asked of the hunched figure next to him at the bar.

"No better for you asking," replied Whistler, pulling on his pint.

"Your mate's a damn sight more cheerful than you are."

"Huh. I don't know why. He's got no reason to be."

"Well, at least he's keeping himself busy doing that boat up. Can't let yerself slide." Whatever accusations were levelled at Gryler (and there were a goodly number) indolence was not on the list. A rogue he might be, but he was a busy one. " 'Ere! Sunshine! Yer lager's ready!" he roared across the bar. Young Applebee waved acknowledgement without turning round, evidently at some crucial point in his pin-ball wizardry.

"Want to get yourself a job," offered Gryler.

"What, like yours?"

"Why not?"

"Couldn't risk being found out."

"What do you mean?"

"You know what I mean," muttered Ted, into his receding pint. He was well aware of Gryler's reputation as a dealer in all things shady and a purveyor of goods of doubtful provenance.

"Just you be careful what you say in here," whispered Gryler. "Them fishing floats has ears."

"Anyway, I've had a job," countered Ted. "Having a rest now."

"Suit yerself. Elliott obviously doesn't agree with you. Working like a Trojan. Seems to be getting on with Aitch, too. Couple of oddballs together, if you ask me. Nutty as a fruitcake, Aitch. He's been setting off for Devon every week for the past three years, and he's still here. But at least Elliott looks as if he's enjoying himself."

"Just because he's busy it doesn't mean to say he's happy," said Ted. "Everybody has their way of coping – his is to keep busy."

"Is that why he enjoyed lighthouse keeping?" Gryler winked at the landlord. "I thought you only worked for a month and then had a month off. And when you were on duty you were on shift work. More time off than the rest of us put together."

"Aye, well, you keep busy. Well, *he* did."

"What doing?"

"Making his boats. Writing up his diary."

"Not much going on round here to write about."

"Nature diary – birds. Staring out to sea most of the time, then writing up notes of what he saw in the evening."

Christopher Applebee came over and took his lager. "Ta," he said, before going back to his machine.

"Every day?" Gryler sounded interested, but there was also a note of unease in his voice.

"Every day."

"Sounds a bit boring."

"I suppose it does to you, but you notice things when you're a lighthouse keeper."

"What sort of things?" He was fishing, and probably not for the first time that day.

"Anything out of the ordinary. Weird weather. Movements of shipping. Bird migration."

"Sounds bloody boring to me."

"Aye, well, it would. It bored me in the end. Glad to get out of it."

Gryler drained his glass and thumped it back on the bar. "This conversation's depressing me. Give us a couple of pies, Alf, and I'll be off. Might as well sit in me shed and eat 'em." He tossed a couple of pound coins on the bar, then retreated with his lunch, leaving his assistant to play with his balls.

She might have known he wouldn't come back

straight away. Oliver had always liked to keep her waiting, to make her nervous. He had succeeded. Since the previous evening she had been on edge, hardly sleeping, making sure the door was properly locked, alternately sweating and shivering.

In the morning she had showered and put on a clean pair of Levi's, some canvas shoes and a pale blue shirt. She tied back her hair and opened the studio at nine thirty, determined to carry on her life and not be threatened by his impending return.

Thankfully, customers had been in and out all morning, taking her mind off the situation a little. Late in the afternoon her spirits had lifted with the arrival of a smartly dressed middle-aged man, who was interested in buying a painting. Hugo Morgan-Giles introduced himself and welcomed her to Pencurnow Cove. "We've had quite a few artists in the past but I'm sure you'll make a go of it. I think your paintings are wonderful. Where did you study? St Martin's?"

"No. No . . . I wish I had. I haven't studied anywhere. I'm self-taught."

"Really? Remarkable!" He looked closely at her work, leaning forward with his arms held behind his back and making appreciative noises.

He was the epitome of the English gentleman, she thought, from his highly polished brogues to his neatly brushed receding fair hair. He was in his early fifties, she guessed, corduroy trousers of good cut, and a bottle-green cashmere sweater with a touch of cravat showing above the checked shirt at his neck. Even the signet ring was in place on the little finger of his left hand.

"Did you paint these down here?" he asked, gazing at one seascape with intense interest.

"No. From memory. But I want to paint from life now that I'm here."

He turned and smiled at her. "I hope it doesn't spoil your technique!"

"Me, too!"

"Look, I rather like this one. Is it for sale?" He pointed to the scene of an azure blue bay, surrounded by a white curve of sand.

"Well . . . yes. Would you like to take it now?"

"Could I come back with my wife to make sure she likes it? I think it will be OK but I really ought to check. Could you put a red spot on it, or whatever it is you do?"

"Yes, of course."

"I'd say yes straight away but I don't want to be told we haven't the space for it. There was always plenty at Benbecula, but since we've been down at the Moorings it's a bit tighter." He looked slightly embarrassed.

"I'm happy to reserve it for a few days."

"Marvellous. Well, I've enjoyed meeting you, Miss . . . er . . ."

"Finn. Amy Finn."

"I'll be back, Miss Finn. And very good luck with your enterprise. I'm sure it will work." He walked to the door, then paused as something caught his eye. "That's nice." He pointed at Will's Cornish coble, then walked over to it. She had stood it on a solid chunk of oak just inside the door. "I haven't seen one so well fashioned for a long time. Did you make it?"

"No. Will Elliott did. The lighthouse keeper that was."

Hugo picked it up and examined it. "This is excellent." He looked closely at the cut of the planking, the intricate copper riveting and the flawless varnish. "I'll have it."

"Goodness."

"Well, you see, I don't have to ask about this. It's for my study and that's my domain!" He looked at the price tag. "Are you sure this is right?"

"Yes. I think so."

He pulled a chequebook from his back pocket. "I'll round it up." He gave her the completed cheque.

"Do tell Mr Elliott that he really ought to price them a little higher or he'll never keep pace with demand. They must take so long to make that he should be well recompensed."

"I'll tell him. I'm sure he'll be pleased."

Amy wrapped the coble in its original tissue paper and a square of bubble wrap then put the cheque in the back compartment of the cash drawer.

"Well, thank you again. And I'll be back at some point with Mouse – sorry, my wife – and I'm sure we'll have the painting, too. Goodbye!"

As the door closed she could not resist a loud "Yessss," and she punched the air. For a few seconds she forgot her troubles and felt a flush of satisfaction, even thrill, at her first sale. She had sold a painting, and that must make her a painter. For the first time in her life she had earned money from something other than dancing, and she glimpsed a chink of light in the gloom that had lately surrounded her.

She looked at her watch. Five to six. She would close the studio, have a long soak in the bath then find Will and give him his money. She would also tell him the good news about her own painting. Nervously she opened the door of the studio and looked out. Behind Bill's Island there were clouds on the horizon – prophetic, she thought – and a gentle breeze was blowing in off the sea. But the lane was empty. There was no sign of the expected dark figure hovering in the shadows. She stepped back inside, flipped the sign to Closed, pulled down the linen blind and locked the door.

Oil was in his hair, underneath his fingernails and his clothing reeked of it. Even the cat had begun to turn up his nose. It was time to have a break from the sordid confines of the engine room and think about supper. He replaced the hatch, cleared up the assorted bits of oil filter and rubber hose then set about washing in the hip-bath. It made a change from the bucket, and he'd perfected a way of using very little water and even less soap in deference to the plumbing on the boat and the marine life in the boatyard.

He was drying himself, concealed from the outside world by a newly purchased shower curtain, sporting seahorses and starfish (the least garish that Primrose Hankey could supply), when he heard Aitch's now familiar "Hallooo." He wrapped the towel around himself, clambered up into the wheelhouse and stuck his head out of the door.

"What are you doing for supper tonight?" enquired Aitch.

"Hadn't thought. Too busy with my heaps of metal."

"Right, then. Dinner will be served in one hour. Aperitifs in twenty minutes. Does that suit?"

Will was taken aback at the offer of hospitality, then suddenly realised how hungry he was. "I'd love to."

"Fine. I'll see what I can rustle up from the gastronomic Aladdin's cave that purports to be my larder. Most of it will be unidentifiable, but it should at least be edible." With that he vanished and a clattering of pans and crockery ensued.

When Will emerged from *Boy Jack* twenty minutes later, with the punctuality born of six years' shift work, he was welcomed aboard *Florence Nightingale* with enthusiasm.

"Come in, come in! Ah, yes, and you can come, too."

Will looked round in the direction of Aitch's gaze and saw Spike peering at them. Slowly he sauntered towards *Florence Nightingale*, trod tentatively over the threshold. He pummelled the red plush seat cover with his paws, his whiskers twitching as they took in the rich aroma of cooking. Then he saw the stuffed cormorant. The hair on his back became vertical and he spat wildly at it before leaving the cabin without touching the floor.

"Oops. I don't think he's taken to Draculus."

For the rest of the evening Spike sat and stared at them through the cabin window.

Aitch had gone to great trouble for his guest and it occurred to Will that the invitation had not been quite as spontaneous as it had seemed. For a start there was space to sit among the nautical para-phernalia, and the table was laid with a deep red cloth, cutlery and glasses. Nothing matched – there was one plate of this pattern and one of that – but the effect was welcoming, especially when lit by the glow of paraffin lamps as the sun set.

They were sipping a glass of sherry apiece – Aitch's recommendation – and Aitch was poking and prodding at a clutch of pans on the stove, in a galley lined with bottles of spices and chutneys, when they heard footsteps on the pontoon outside and a polite "Is anybody there?"

Will looked up to see Amy peering into his boat. "Hi!" he called. "I'm over here!"

"Hallo! They told me this one was yours." She pointed at *Boy Jack*.

"She is, but I'm over here for supper."

Aitch put his head out of a hatch. "Company?"

"Aitch, this is Amy Finn. She's running the Roundhouse Gallery – sorry, Studio. She's trying to sell my boats."

"Not trying to sell them. Selling them." She took an envelope from her pocket and waved it in the air.

"Crikey! Have you got rid of it, then?"

"Yup. And a painting – I think."

"Good for you!"

Aitch endeavoured to continue stirring his culinary creation while leaning out of the hatch. "Have you eaten, Miss Finn? Would you like to join the sailors for supper?"

"Oh, I couldn't. I'd love to but I only came to give Will his money." Then she added guiltily, "Minus my ten per cent."

Aitch dropped his spoon and clapped his hands together. "Well, stay, then. There's plenty for three. A spot of female company would be very pleasant. I promise we'll have no salty sea talk!"

"Oh, what a shame! But I'd love to, if you're sure."

"Come aboard, then."

Amy picked her way among the coils of rope, the lowering sunlight glinting on her curls now freed from their daytime ties. Will was relieved by the change in her from the previous day, although she seemed tense at his proximity. He moved along the red plush seat to make room for her. It was a tight squeeze, in spite of Aitch's clearing up, and he found himself closer to her than he had been before. He felt a sudden thrill.

She pushed the envelope of notes into his top pocket, almost afraid to touch him, as Aitch passed her a sherry.

"Cheers."

"Cheers!" she responded, and sipped at the tawny liquid from the dainty engraved glass. 'Trafalgar – 21st October 1805', it read, and there was a depiction of the *Victory* firing its cannon.

"This is lovely!"

"The sherry or the glass?" asked Will.

"The glass."

"Probably used by Nelson," quipped Aitch.

"Along with the telescope," added Will.

"Well, you never know," said Aitch, and winked at him.

They dined more lavishly than Will had anticipated from Aitch's invitation: crab bisque was followed by seafood risotto, then crème brûlée.

They sat and drank and talked as though they were old friends. The dry white wine gave way to a full-bodied red, and the faces of the three, flushed with warmth and wine, became more animated.

"Oh, I've forgotten Auntie Betty!" exclaimed Aitch. He leapt to his feet and out of the hatch. He reappeared rolling up a red ensign on its staff. "Left her out after dusk. Bad form. Sorry, Auntie Betty." He laid the furled flag on the long, narrow shelf that was clearly her nocturnal resting place.

The two onlookers laughed and Will noticed that Amy now seemed happy to be sitting close to him, comfortable and relaxed in his company. Occasionally she would rest her hand on his arm to make a point. He was acutely aware of how good it felt. He wished that the evening would never end.

Aitch was recounting one of the more outrageous episodes of his life at school when Amy complained, "But you still haven't told us what the Aitch stands for."

"Oh, my dear girl, you don't really want to know that."

"I do!" She leaned back against Will.

"Come on!" Will said. "We need to know. We deserve to know! It can't be that bad!" He put his arm around her shoulders and she leaned into him.

"Oh, it is," replied Aitch.

"Well, my full name is Amaryllis," confessed Amy.

"Amaryllis?" Will spluttered.

"Yes." She giggled. "Grim, isn't it?"

"Oh, I don't know. It has a touch of class." He

pulled her close again and she giggled.

"Amaryllis is as nought compared with mine," mused Aitch, with just a hint of moroseness.

"Come on, then."

He blustered some more, then eventually drew a large breath. "You need to understand a bit about my background. The Utterly family come from a long line of retailers. Retail. Not wholesale. Tut-tut. Below the salt." He took another sip of the rich red wine. "My father followed his father into the bakery and he hoped that I would do the same, continuing the Utterly tradition of baking loaves for the gentry. That was why he generously bestowed on me a name that he hoped would spur me on my endeavours. But it had the reverse effect. It put me off for life. I was christened in honour of my father's favourite loaf. My name is Hovis Utterly."

Will and Amy wanted to be polite. They tried to be polite. They sat holding one another for at least fifteen seconds before dissolving into fits of laughter.

At first Hovis regarded them dolefully, but eventually joined them in wild hilarity. From then on, he knew they would never call him Aitch again, but for the first time in his life he didn't really mind.

It was twenty past twelve when they left. She'd looked nervous suddenly at the prospect of departure and he saw the fear in her eyes. "I'll walk you back."

"It's OK."

"No, I don't want you walking there on your own." The words came naturally and she made no further protest.

They went along the jetty towards the lane, his arm around her shoulders, keeping her close, and her fear subsided. They talked casually, about Aitch and about the meal, then stopped by the railings of the jetty and looked out over the sea, the moon streaking the water with silver, and the clouds shot through with orange and purple.

She caught her breath. "Isn't it beautiful?" she said softly.

"Beautiful," he agreed, but for once his mind was not on the sea. They stood quietly for a while, then she shivered a little and they walked on up the lane.

At the door of the studio she turned to face him. "Thank you for a really lovely evening."

"No. Thank *you*." He looked at her face. Before he knew it she had wrapped her arms around his neck, drawn his face to hers and kissed him with a tenderness he had all but forgotten. They paused briefly and he put his arms around her, held her even closer, stroking the back of her head and kissing her again.

Eventually they drew slightly apart, and she rested her head on his chest. He inhaled the fragrance of the soft skin at the nape of her neck and rocked her for a while. At last she lifted her head and said, "Thank you for being there."

"I'm always here. Just let me know when you need me." He squeezed her to reassure her. "I'd better go. You've the studio to open in the morning and I've a boat-builder to see about my planking."

"How romantic."

He smiled at her, then realised with a profound shock that this had been his first intimacy since Ellie's death. The pleasure of the moment was replaced by a stinging sensation of guilt, which he did his best to mask.

She saw it. "Are you all right?"

"I'm just a bit out of practice."

She pulled him to her again and held him close. "I'll see you soon, I hope."

"Yes. Are you sure you'll be OK?"

"Sure. Go now. And take care."

"*You* take care."

She nodded silently. He turned as she reached the bottom step. "Lock it."

"I will."

He heard the mechanism click home as he walked back down the moonlight-washed lane. For the first time in six years he felt alive. His fingers seemed to be tingling, his head reeling with an intoxication not wholly due to the wine. Yet the guilt deep inside him gnawed at his heart.

He paused by the railings where they had stopped on the way up, and looked out across the moonlit waves. His mind swam with conflicting emotions.

Below him the sea toppled on to the loose pebbles, sucking them away then flinging them back. He gripped the cold iron railings as tears filled his eyes, and he shook uncontrollably as his words spilled out over the sea. "I have to go on. I have to live. I can't stay, Ellie. Don't make me stay. Please . . . let . . . me . . . go." For the first time since her death, he looked to the heavens and sobbed.

Chapter 9: Inner Dowsing

The boat-builder had good and bad news. The good news was that the state of *Boy Jack*'s hull was better than Will had feared. The bad news was that for the duration of the work – around two weeks – she would have to come out of the water and would be uninhabitable.

The prospect of having to find a temporary home threw him into confusion. It had not occurred to him that he would have to live elsewhere while the work proceeded, but the builder was adamant. The clearer the decks, so to speak, the faster the work could be done.

The whole scheme had not been without its ups and downs. Gryler, anxious for as much profitable work as possible, had been less than pleased when,

out of courtesy, Will had asked if another boat-
builder could come to the yard to work on *Boy Jack*.

"Is he accredited?" he asked, officiously. The irony
of the remark was not lost on Will, but he felt it best
to play along.

"Yes. He advertises in *Classic Boat*, and he's well
established as a restorer of wooden craft."

"Only I don't want any old Tom, Dick and 'Arry
comin' in 'ere and givin' the yard a bad name."

"No. Quite." It was the best response he could
think of under the circumstances.

"I suppose you'll be wanting to use my boat lift?"
asked Gryler, waving in the direction of the rusting
metal giant alongside the jetty.

"Please."

"It'll cost yer. It's free if I do the work but I have to
charge for it when I don't."

"That's fine."

"When do you want to get her out, then?"

"Some time this week – as soon as I can sort out
temporary accommodation."

"Aye, well, I suppose that'll be all right. It's
irregular, though. Do you know where you're going to
put her?"

"Er . . . well, I was hoping . . ."

"Hoping what?" Gryler was doing his best to be
tricky. He stood firm in his oil-encrusted boiler-suit,
his trademark wrench clasped in his right hand like a
sceptre.

"I was hoping that you could help me out by letting me put her over there." Will pointed towards an area of hard standing to one side of the yard.

"What? Just like that?"

"Well . . ."

Gryler was intent on extracting as much from this encounter as he could. "I shall have to charge."

"But you'll have the berth free while I'm out of the water."

"Not the same. I've had no chance to advertise it, and who's going to come and take it at this time of year? Specially on a temporary basis. I suppose you'll be wanting it again when your boat goes back in the water?"

Will remained silent, thoroughly miserable at the thought of having to grovel to Gryler every time he needed anything out of the ordinary.

"How long would you want to be there for?"

"Just a couple of weeks."

"A hundred pounds a week."

"What? But you agreed to three months' free berthing when I bought the boat."

"In the water, not out of it." He slapped the wrench in the palm of his left hand. "Call it a hundred and fifty quid for the fortnight and I'll throw in the use of my lift."

"A hundred."

"Hah!" He laughed derisively. "Oh, go on, then. I'm a fool to meself where boats is concerned.

Where's that lad got to? Better get him to grease the nipples." He beamed at Will, confident that he'd come out ahead.

Will watched him head back to the peeling hut and cursed under his breath at the loss of another hundred quid that he could ill afford. He tramped back to the boat, climbed aboard, and slammed the kettle on the gas burner. He looked around him at the squalor.

"Shit," he muttered, under his breath. He had just a few thousand pounds put away, five model boats to sell, and a voyage ahead of him. How was he going to survive? He looked across at *Florence Nightingale*. Hovis Utterly. Now there was a happy man. How did he make ends meet? He didn't seem to have any income. Perhaps he had a hidden legacy.

The kettle whistled and he made himself a mug of coffee. There was no sign of Spike. It occurred to him that the ship's cat had yet to meet Amy. He'd put her out of his mind during the encounter with Gryler, though she'd been in his thoughts constantly since the night before. But he hardly knew her – had met her just three times. How could she come even close to Ellie?

He'd tried to come to terms with the tragedy, to counsel himself rationally, but six years on he still could not bring himself to admit that Ellie was dead. He could not form the words, even in his thoughts. The reason was plain. Inside him she was still alive.

Every hour of every day she was with him. Her face was as clear as day – the short black bob of her hair, the wide almond-shaped eyes, the way her face crinkled when she smiled. He could still see her naked. He could still feel the touch of her skin, her hand in his, hear her teasing him and getting irritated when he was stubborn about something inconsequential. But last night a part of him had been trying to move on.

Amy had come into his life with all the force of an earthquake, rocking him to his foundations. The merest hint of resentment crossed his mind. He had had enough anguish already without falling in love. Yet he saw her face in his mind's eye and the resentment faded. He wondered where she was now, what she was doing and what she was thinking.

He drank his coffee quickly and looked through the port-hole at the morning. It was bright, and a stiff breeze blew from the south-west. He needed a walk. He would take the coastal path to the lighthouse and see how Ernie was getting on. It was time he called in. Ernie would think he had been forgotten.

Will pulled the sailing jacket around him against the force of the breeze as he rounded the corner from the boatyard. He looked across at the Roundhouse and saw that the blind was down on the door and the Closed sign in position. He checked his watch.

Five past nine. She must be having a lie-in. He looked for some sign that all was well. He thought about knocking but didn't want to alarm her. Nor did he know where to pick up the threads of the night before. He strode on, up the lane and past the little cottage known as the Moorings, where a middle-aged man in a tweed jacket and corduroys was looking out across the cove with a pair of binoculars.

Will looked in the same direction. The woman with the pea-brained Labrador was at her stick-throwing as usual, and a couple of fishing boats butted their way through the water, which was generously sprinkled with white horses.

"Good morning," Will greeted the man as he passed.

"Morning." The man was startled, then recovered himself. "Lovely day for a walk."

"Hope so. I think I'd rather be on land than out there today."

"Yes. Bit choppy, isn't it?"

Will carried on up the hill.

The top of the lane petered out into a rough footpath that led across the cliffs. Benbecula was the only house that remained above him now. He gazed up at it on its lofty eminence and thought what good views it must have of the bay.

Sitting down on the tussocky grass through which the thrift was pushing its flower spikes, he took out his binoculars and watched as the boats at sea headed off in different directions, one to the east, and the other westwards towards Bill's Island. This, he reflected, was what he would be doing in a couple of months' time. The prospect thrilled and frightened him at the same time.

The boat heading towards Bill's Island looked familiar. He took in the markings on the bows – PZ 291 – it was Gryler's, an old fishing smack he had obviously bought for a song from a redundant fisherman. Christopher Applebee was at the tiller in yellow oilskins and there were lobster pots and fishing lines in the bottom of the boat. A bit of poaching, like as not, thought Will. He put away the binoculars and continued his climb.

The path levelled out on the cliff top and, on the promontory of Prince Albert Rock, he could see the lighthouse. Three sandpipers wheeled overhead, buffeted by the breeze, and as he rounded the cove he noticed a small figure ahead of him, seated and looking out to sea. As he came closer he saw the easel, and instantly realised it was Amy.

Fearful of startling her he began to whistle.

She turned round, irritated at first by the intrusion then pleased to see him. "Hi!"

"Hi, yourself. You're up early."

"I thought I'd have a breath of fresh air and see if I could get any inspiration." She remained seated, the wind blowing strands of coppery hair across her face.

He leaned down and kissed her cheek. She put her arm around his leg as he stood beside her, and he felt a surge of warmth in spite of the breeze.

It was a brief touch, but reassuring. He crouched beside her as she continued to paint.

"How do you stop everything blowing away in this wind?" he asked.

"Clothes-pegs and will-power." She grinned.

He studied the beginnings of the painting. "It looks good."

"Oh, it's only a quick daub. Just a few ideas. I can't stay long – I'll have to open up in half an hour but I thought a breath of fresh air would do me good." She began to pack away her brushes. "Where are you off to?"

He stood up. "I'm on my way to see my old boss. Haven't dropped in on him since I left and I'm feeling a bit guilty."

"Well, don't get blown away."

"I won't. I'll see you later." He was unsure whether or not to kiss her again. He settled for stroking his hand across the top of her head, and felt again the texture of her hair. They both recognized the awkwardness of the moment, neither quite sure how to pick up the threads. Will smiled and walked on across the clifftop, leaving Amy to pick up her bag and her chair and set off towards the lane.

"We thought you'd forgotten us." Ernie Hallybone

was only half serious, but Will apologized for his long absence.

"How's the boat coming along?" May asked, as she ferried the kettle from the stove to the table.

"Slowly. I've got to get her out of the water for a couple of weeks while the hull is sorted out and that means I'll have to find somewhere else to live." The moment he had said it he realised it might sound as though he were angling for accommodation.

May jumped in immediately. "Well, you'll be welcome here. Your old flat has been turned into part of the visitor centre but we've a spare room at our end. Your odds and ends are stored there, anyway. Why don't you come here?"

"No, really, that's not why I came. I mean, that's not why I said it."

May laughed her free and easy laugh, and her plump cheeks reddened even more than usual. "I know. But it's up to you. There's always a room here for you if you want. Now, then, are you joining us for breakfast? Eggs from the Marans, bacon and sausage from the pig, and beans from Mr Heinz."

Will did his best to decline, but the sound of the bacon and sausages sizzling on the old stove and the sparkle in May's eyes meant that he hadn't a chance. Ernie brightened at the prospect of company, and Will sat down at the table, as his old boss gave him chapter and verse on the current developments at Prince Albert Rock.

"*The Gull*'s been useful."

"I'm glad."

"Caught a couple of mackerel off the back of her for tea last night. Made a change from pig."

"Don't you go knocking my pork and bacon, Ernie Hallybone. Keeps us alive it does," May scolded from her position by the stove. She stood there, every inch the farmer's wife, errant strands of hair escaping from the bun at the back of her head.

"How's the farm?" asked Will.

"Lambs aren't worth a penny piece but folk still wants bacon and sausages," May replied, "but I do it for us, really, rather than anyone else."

They tucked into a hearty breakfast, catching up on local news. May was still running her smallholding single-handed, though she'd cut it down to five acres now and sold the rest to a local farmer. Ernie was OK, he said, but a bit bored. Still, that would improve when the tourists started coming in a month's time. "You sold any of them boats yet?" he asked Will.

"One of them. Somebody called Morgan-Giles."

"Hugo Morgan-Giles?"

"That's him. Do you know him?"

"Not exactly, but I know of him. With May's relatives being out St Petroc way we tend to know more folk over in that direction than in Pencurnow, but the Morgan-Giles family has been around for years. Used to live in the big house up at the top – Benbecula. Now they lives in the little one lower down. The Moorings,"

May brought a pot of coffee over to the table. "Yes. Been there for a few years now. Sad business."

"This Morgan-Giles," said Will, "is he in his fifties, sandy hair, Army type?"

"That's him."

"I think I saw him this morning. I didn't realise it was him. I should have said thank you. What's so sad about him?"

"Well, not so much him," explained May, "more the family situation. He was one of them Names. You know, the ones that lost a lot of money. Something to do with insurance."

"You mean Lloyds?"

"That's it," confirmed Ernie. "Family money. All tied up. Then it all went pear-shaped, didn't it? Lost the lot. Well, almost everything. They'd owned Benbecula for generations and Morgan-Giles had to sell up and move into The Moorings, which they used to let. Bit of a come-down. I don't think his wife was too pleased. Kids at public school an' that."

"And those folk from London now live in Benbecula," added May.

"That's right. Some East End tycoon, by all accounts. Made his money in televisions."

"Mobile phones," corrected Will, and told them about his encounter with the MacDermotts. He did not mention Amy, but filled them in about Hovis, and Gryler's penny-pinching ways.

"You shouldn't be surprised." Ernie mopped up his egg-yolk with home-made wholemeal bread. "You be careful in your dealings with Gryler."

"Oh, I know he's a rogue," admitted Will. "But I think he's a straightforward rogue."

"Just don't cross him," Ernie continued. "There've been funny goings-on at that boatyard over the years."

"What sort of funny goings-on?"

Ernie continued with his mopping. "Rumours of smuggling and the like. Don't you get yourself too involved."

"Smuggling what?"

"Dunno. I choose not to ask. Ted Whistler knows more about it than I do, not that you heard me say."

"Are we talking serious stuff or just the odd bottle of booze?"

Ernie looked at him earnestly. "I wouldn't know."

Will thought back to his walk across the cliff and the fishing smack helmed by Christopher Applebee. He felt a sharp thrill at the prospect of being surrounded by illicit trading, and worried at the implications.

He kissed May and promising Ernie that he would not leave it so long before he visited them again, Will began the return trip along the clifftop path, his mind whirling with the events of the previous few days and the news gleaned over the past couple of hours.

Chapter 10:
Anvil Point

The sight of Len Gryler scuttling into his blue hut reminded Will of a rabbit running into its burrow. He wondered what the old rogue was up to now. He took off his sailing jacket as he walked along the jetty and down the pontoon, refreshed after his walk and his mighty breakfast. Halyards pinged in the breeze and the gentle slapping of water against hull reflected the state of the tide. He stepped on to *Boy Jack* and stopped short. The port-side door was slightly ajar. He could have sworn he'd locked it when he left. He felt in his pocket for the key, and there it was, still firmly attached to the lump of cork that would make sure it floated were it ever to fall into the briny.

He slid open the door and stuck his head inside.

Nothing seemed amiss. The place was apparently exactly as he had left it. He stepped down into the wheelhouse and walked through into the forward cabin, calling for Spike as he did so. There was no sign of the cat. He turned and walked aft, noticing a long, oily smudge on one of the cabin windows. He stopped and cursed himself. Then he realised that he had not made the smudge. The pathological tidiness that had been instilled in him during his days as a clockmaker, then as a lighthouse keeper, had made it impossible for him to endure what many would consider normal signs of wear and tear. That oil stain was not his. Someone had been on board the boat. Perhaps it had been Hovis, looking for him. But Hovis never had oil on his hands: his engine room was not a venue to which he was especially attached.

The sinking feeling in the pit of his stomach abated at the sight of Hovis walking down the pontoon with a shopping bag on one arm and a baguette under the other. Will ducked through the door of the wheelhouse and hailed him. "Hovis!"

"Ssh, dear boy. Our little secret. Aitch in public, please."

"Sorry. You haven't been on board, have you? On *Boy Jack*, I mean."

"Today?"

"Yes."

"No, I've just been up to see Primrose." He gestured in the direction of his provisions. "Why?"

Will knelt down on the deck, the better to explain without broadcasting to the entire boatyard. "Somebody's been on board. The door was ajar and there's oil on the wheelhouse window."

"Could be Gryler. Oil is his equivalent of aftershave. Did you ask him about letting you have a dry berth while your hull's being done?"

"Yes."

"Maybe he was just eyeing her up."

"From the inside?"

"That's a point. Are you sure?"

"Somebody's been here, I know it. I can feel it."

"Anything missing?" asked Hovis.

"Nothing obvious."

"Mmmm. Odd. Well, perhaps he was just having a nose. I caught him sizing up my binnacle once." He pointed in the direction of the brass compass sitting atop its varnished pillar. "He was looking at it just a bit too covetously for my liking, so I had a go at him a few days later about security here. I thought that might let him know I had my eyes open. He talked about installing video cameras. I knew he wouldn't do anything but at least I'd made my point."

Will looked thoughtful. "Are you here for a bit?"

"Yes."

"Can you keep an eye? I've some phone calls to make so I need to go up to the village."

"All right, dear boy. I'll keep the beadies open. Mmmm."

123

"Thanks." Will walked back up the pontoon, checking that the piece of paper with the telephone numbers on it was in his pocket, along with a handful of change.

"Give her my love," shouted Hovis.

Will turned to protest, then smiled. "I will."

He made two phone calls from the box outside the Post Office: one to the boat-builder Harry Gwenver, telling him that *Boy Jack* would be out of the water by the day after tomorrow, and the other to the Association of Dunkirk Little Ships asking for more information about his boat. The voice at the other end asked him for details of *Boy Jack*, explaining that brass plaques bearing the legend 'Dunkirk 1940' were not uncommon on ships that had played no part in the evacuations. Will quoted the information Gryler had given him, along with various keel markings, and was pleased when his interlocutor confirmed that *Boy Jack* had indeed played her part on the Normandy beaches, though at that time the vessel had been known as *Graceful*. He would be sent a membership application form, and would he like a pennant that could be flown from his jack-staff on entering and leaving port, and when in the company of other Dunkirk Little Ships? Will, rather proudly, said he would. He also enquired about how many of the Little Ships had survived. "There are around a hundred and seventy still in existence and we have a hundred and twenty-four registered with us as members. We'll be glad to add you to the list."

Will put down the phone, feeling better disposed towards *Boy Jack* than he had recently. Perhaps the old girl was worth persevering with, after all.

He walked down the lane again and as he approached the Roundhouse he saw Amy on the doorstep. She saw him, waved and called him over. He worried at first that something was the matter, but then, as he walked into the studio, he saw the man he now knew to be Hugo Morgan-Giles, with a well-dressed woman in a tweed skirt and sweater, whom he assumed to be Mrs Morgan-Giles. Amy effected introductions.

"You really are quite a craftsman, you know," offered Hugo, once the pleasantries were out of the way. "I was telling Miss Finn that I thought you were rather selling yourself short."

"I'm just happy that someone likes them enough to buy them," demurred Will.

"Yes, but you might as well get as much as you can for them in recompense for your effort, eh, Mouse?"

Mrs Morgan-Giles half smiled.

"I've just brought Isobel in to see the painting I fancied. I think we can find room for it, dear, can't we?"

"Well, yes . . . if you think . . ."

"Oh, I'm sure we can afford it. Can't keep

economising all the time. Have to allow ourselves the occasional treat, you know!"

"Well, if you're sure, Hugo. It *is* a lovely picture . . ." She looked wistfully at the blue sea and sky, the white sand, almost as though she were trying to spirit herself into the idyllic landscape.

Will thought she looked deeply sad. He suddenly felt sorry for this couple who had once been the lord and lady of the manor in all but name, and who now had been relegated to the Dower House while some East-End-barrowboy-made-good had taken over their old family home. It must be galling. But with a staunchness imbued in them since childhood the Morgan-Gileses had mucked in and carried on.

"Can we take it with us?" asked Hugo. "I'd love to hang it today."

"Yes, of course." Amy lifted the painting from its hook and took it to the counter.

Their painting was wrapped and handed to them, and the Morgan-Gileses left. Will watched them go.

"It's a shame, isn't it?" Amy broke in on his thoughts.

"Mmm?"

"Such a sweet couple. It's a terrible shame about all their troubles."

"You know, then?"

"Primrose told me."

"Ah, so you've been talking to the human tele-scope."

"Don't be rude. She's a poppet."

"Just don't tell her any secrets, that's all. She's better than the BBC at spreading the news."

"Well, she did tell me a bit about the Morgan-Gileses."

"How much?"

"Oh, that they lost a lot of money in the Lloyds fiasco, and that they're living in the little house now and not the big one, and struggling to keep their kids at public school. The boy's at Eton and the girl goes to St Mary's, Ascot."

"So how does he earn his living now?"

"A couple of consultancies in the City, according to Primrose. Goes up to London two or three times a month."

"You did get a lot of information!"

"Well, I was curious. And he's the first person to buy one of my paintings so he must have exquisite taste!"

"Just a bit biased I should say!"

"Cheeky!" She came and stood in front of him, looking up at him. "Thank you very much for last night. It was so lovely. I hope you don't think that–"

He butted in, anxious for neither of them to spoil the moment by analysing too much too soon. "It was a pleasure. *Is* a pleasure. I really enjoyed it."

She took his hint, disappointed. "I thought Hovis was sweet. Funny, too. Another lovely man."

"He's turning into a good mate. Haven't known

him long but he seems to know when I want company and when I want to be alone."

"You sound like Greta Garbo."

"Oh, you know what I mean."

"I know exactly what you mean." She looked at him hard and struggled for words. "Look . . . I was wondering if perhaps you might like to come to supper?"

"I'd love to." Will had the strangest sensation that she seemed able to see through the outer Will Elliott and the veneers and defences he had spent so long building up. What shocked him was that he didn't mind. It seemed the most natural thing in the world.

He stared at her and felt a deep inner warmth and security that he had almost forgotten existed.

They didn't hear the door of the gallery open, only the words, which struck like a bolt of lightning: "I seem to have lost my sense of timing."

It was Oliver Gallico. He removed his dark glasses, to look Will up and down. "This is getting a bit tedious." He regarded Will with the sort of displeasure that most cat owners reserve for a regurgitated fur ball. "Who is this?"

"This is Will Elliott. Will, Oliver Gallico."

He stood squarely in front of them, arms folded, and nodded carelessly in Will's direction. "When is he going?"

Amy was recovering herself now. "He isn't going."

"Oh, come on, Ame. Let's sort this out. Tell him

to piss off."

Amy interrupted, "Look, just leave, will you?"

"You can tell me to leave as many times as you want. But I'll come back. I'll keep coming back. I'm not giving up, you know." He smiled insolently. "You know you'll have to come. Why pretend that you won't? It's only a matter of time. You always come in the end." He tapped his foot repeatedly against the white wall, leaving black marks on the once pristine paintwork.

Amy tried hard not to appear rattled. "I'm not going to leave all this."

"Why not? What are a few paintings compared with what we have? You're prepared to give all that up for this?" He looked around him at the vibrant Cornish seascapes.

"Yes," she said firmly.

He walked towards them but Will stood his ground. "I think you should go now," he said.

Gallico looked him directly in the eye with undisguised contempt. "Piss off."

Will persisted, "It's time you left."

"Or else what?" He sounded cold and threatening.

Will reined in his emotions and spoke steadily. "Just leave."

Gallico moved closer to Will, who could now feel the heat of his breath on his cheeks. "What's it to do with you?" He looked towards Amy. "Tell him about us. Go on, tell him who we are!"

"We're nothing, Oliver. Not any more." Amy looked frightened. "Please, just go. It's too late. It's all over."

"You stupid bitch!" he said. "It'll never be over. Not what we have. You hear? Never!"

He paused, waiting for something else to push against. It did not come.

He turned to Will. "All right, I'll go. But I'm not giving up. I'll be back."

"No, you won't." Will fixed him with a steely gaze. "You'll go now and you'll stay away. Amy's had enough, and you don't belong here."

"I'll–"

"No. You won't. Come on, out."

He took great care not to touch Gallico, but walked round him to the door and held it open. "Goodbye."

The arrogant dancer made to speak, but thought better of it. "Shit!" he sneered at Will, cast a backward look at Amy then strode out.

Will hoped he had also swept out of their lives, but felt it unlikely.

Amy stood perfectly still, the gamut of emotions she had run during the past few minutes robbing her of the power of speech.

As Will walked towards her the door of the gallery burst open again. "Will! Come quickly!"

Will spun round to see Hovis in a state of breathless agitation. "What's the matter?"

"Fire at the lighthouse. Engines on their way. Thought you'd want to know." Hovis leaned against the door frame, doing his best to catch his breath.

Will shot a look at Amy and said, "I'll call you," then bolted out.

She shouted after him, "Take my car!" But he was too far away to hear, running up the lane towards the cliff path as fast as his legs would carry him.

Chapter 11:
St Anthony

He could see the smoke billowing from the buildings behind the lighthouse as he ran along the cliff path. Above the sound of the breaking waves he could hear the sirens. His pounding footsteps took him round Pencurnow Cove and along the headland towards the lighthouse, but it was still impossible to see which part of the building had caught fire. It was only when he finally leapt up the steps towards the tower and rounded the corner that he saw flames licking out of a downstairs window adjacent to the rooms occupied by Ernie and May. He could see neither of them in the confusion.

His lungs felt as though they, too, were on fire, and he rested his hands on his knees for a moment, lowering his head and catching his breath. The journey had taken him the best part of twenty minutes, during which the fire had taken hold. Where were Ernie and May?

Then he saw them, on the other side of the veil of grey smoke that was now blowing across the craggy rocks and out to sea. Ernie had his arm around May, who was wringing the corner of her apron in her hands. They were watching as the firemen worked, directing their hoses through the window from which angry flames licked upwards towards the roof.

"Are you all right?"

Ernie was surprised and relieved to see him. "We're fine. I think."

"What happened?"

"Don't know. One minute we were in there minding our own business and the next minute the place was ablaze."

Fifteen minutes later, the flames had died away, to be replaced with a gentle hissing as red-hot timbers cooled under their saturation. The visitors ambled off, the spectacle over and the acrid smell of charred wet timber biting into their nostrils. The firemen rolled up their hoses while Will comforted May.

The two policemen were with Ernie, fixing up a time for him to attend the station in St Petroc to make a statement. They warned him not to touch anything until Forensic had been out to examine the scene. Plastic tape was fastened to slender poles driven into the ground with the intention of keeping out trespassers, not that anyone would have wanted to get near the blackened, sodden mess, thought Will.

"Lucky," commented Ernie, though the expression on his face did not accord with the word.

"What do you mean?" asked Will.

"It's only damaged one room. It could have been much worse."

"What's gone?"

"Just some old furniture. We were using it as a store . . ." He stopped short as he was saying it, and looked at Will, his face etched with regret. "Oh, Will! It was where we'd put your stuff. Your books and things."

The three of them gazed at the blackened window frame. There was little likelihood of anything being salvageable. What the flames had not destroyed, the water would have finished off.

Will gazed at the yawning hole almost in a trance. Why had he not taken all his things with him to the boat? His books, his charts, the few CDs, his old boating magazines all gone. His Trinity House certificate – well, that could easily be replaced – and his diaries. His diaries. His legs weakened and he flopped down on the grass beside Ernie and May. His life was between their covers. The record of his existence since he had lost Ellie. He felt sick. It seemed as though he had lost her for a second time.

Events of the last episode of his life swam in his head, from his arrival on this spot six years ago, to the building of the *Gull* and the maturing friendship with Ernie. He had put down between the covers of the twenty or more exercise books his daily thoughts and observations, his feelings about Ellie and his feelings about himself. Now they were all gone up in smoke.

"I'm sorry. I'm really sorry."

He looked up at Ernie. "No, no." He didn't want to add to their misery. It would be better to appear unconcerned. "It's not your fault. It's not anybody's fault. It's just one of those things." He shrugged and tried to look as though it were no great tragedy.

"We can still put you up if you want somewhere to stay," offered May.

"No. I mean, don't worry."

"Oh, but your things . . ." May looked agitated.

"Just books and stuff. It's all replaceable." He remembered them individually. The pilotage books, the navigation manuals, and the five volumes of Cowper's *Sailing Tours* that he had so looked forward to taking with him on his voyage. Now all gone.

"I expect the insurance will pay up," remarked Ernie.

"Yes. I suppose so." It had taken Will a long while to find each of the five volumes of Cowper. He expected it would take him even longer to replace them. But right now what did it matter? He snapped out of his introspection. "Look, the important thing is that you two are safe. Who cares about a few books? What are you going to do now?"

"Can't really do anything until the police have given us the say-so. It's a good job that the room is a bit out on a limb. The rest of the place should be OK, even if it is a bit smelly. Trinity House will want to come and have a look. I suppose I'll have to leave it up to them as to what happens next. But I'll tell them about your stuff. You'd better give me a list of what you think you've lost."

Will ducked under the streamers of police tape to take a look inside the window. The small room looked like the black hole of Calcutta. It was about twelve feet square. The iron bedstead against one wall was intact, in shape at least, but everything else had coagulated into an amorphous charred mass, dripping with water. The door on the far side had remained shut. Will heaved a sigh of relief that Ernie's assiduousness at closing doors behind him had prevented a small conflagration from turning into a major blaze.

"There's nothing salvageable in there." Will dodged back under the tape to where Ernie and May stood. "Is there anything you want me to do?"

"No, you get off. I'll let you know what happens." Ernie put his arm around May's shoulder. She dabbed at her eye with the corner of her apron and Will saw she was crying.

He stared at the pair of them, standing on the grassy knoll with the gigantic white tower rising up behind them, and thought how small they looked.

*

Boy Jack looked massive from this angle. Will stood under her bows as she sat on the concrete hard to one side of the boatyard, supported by a flimsy-looking rank of wooden poles, secured with slender wooden wedges. It was the traditional way of propping up a boat when it was out of the water, but he always marvelled that such a Heath Robinson approach could be effective.

A ladder leaned up against her side, fastened with rope at the top, and Will shinned up the rungs to fetch a wire brush and have a go at the barnacles on the propeller while he waited for Harry Gwenver to turn up. He liked this kind of work: his mind could wander while he scrubbed. He'd returned to the Roundhouse after the fire to explain what had happened, but had been called away yet again to supervise the lifting out of *Boy Jack* when Gryler had finally succeeded (probably courtesy of a few smart clouts with his monkey wrench) in getting the boat lift to work. He'd spent the night on board, high above the jetty, with Spike looking puzzled about their sudden elevation.

The day had dawned bright and clear, but the prospect before him was still cloudy. Early in the morning he strode up the hill and fixed up accommo-dation at Mrs Sparrow's B and B for two weeks, hoping that that would be long enough. He also hoped he could carry on working on the boat during the day, if he didn't get in Harry Gwenver's way.

"You!" The voice startled him. It was old, male and Cornish. Harry Gwenver, sixty-something, in brown overalls, a tweed jacket and a tweed cap stood, with his hands on his hips regarding the boat. He was tall and angular, the opposite of Len Gryler, and he had a quizzical look on his face, which gave way to a broad smile. "You ready for us?"

"Er . . . yes. I think so. But I can't be out of her just yet. I'm still sorting myself out." Will saw the smile on Harry Gwenver's face replaced with a frown. "I'll keep out of your way, though – but I can't promise about him." He gestured in the direction of the furry face surveying the scene from the rail above the transom. It would take more than a refit to get Spike away from a home that provided such a rich supply of fish suppers.

Harry Gwenver laughed. "Oh, we'll cope with him. Is he friendly?"

"Nothing much worries him. Except stuffed cormorants," he added.

"Right," said Harry, "we'll make a start."

He returned to his van, parked at the end of the jetty, to fetch his tools, while Will climbed the ladder to reassure the cat that he wasn't about to be made homeless. The two sat, on the wheelhouse roof, looking out to sea, and Will was engulfed in a wave of self-pity. His books had gone and his diaries were no more.

He felt like a man whose history had been taken away. But they were only diaries. Only a record of things gone. They were not of now and although they had vanished the memories were indelible. Through the sense of loss and desperation came a new feeling: release.

Chapter 12: Casquets

Mrs Sparrow was a decent sort. She let Will have the front bedroom of Myrtle Cottage because it had the sea view, though she did explain that, should he stay longer than anticipated, he might have to move when the holiday season arrived.

Will's biggest problem was breakfast. Persuading Mrs Sparrow not to cook him a full English every morning was no easy matter. She was tiny and bird-like herself and clearly assumed that her guests also ate like birds – seven times their own bodyweight daily. As a result Will found himself wading through egg, bacon, sausage, fried bread and black pudding for the first two mornings of his stay. Finally he managed to convince her that a bowl of what she called 'rabbit food' would do very nicely during the week and he would save his fry-up for weekends.

He breakfasted early – at around seven thirty – and

tried to be 'on site' at the boat soon after eight when Harry Gwenver turned up. The old man didn't seem to mind Will pottering around doing his own thing, provided he kept out of his way, and Will was gradually getting used to the peppering of Cornish language that decorated Harry's speech. He now understood that "You!" meant "hello", *durdathawhy* good-day and *benetugana* goodbye, but it had taken him a while to work out that *durdaladawhy* was thank you. He'd asked Harry why he used such expressions, only to be told that someone had to keep the old Cornish language going, and that he didn't see why it had to die with Dolly Pentreath in 1777.

Will watched Harry disappear into the hold of *Boy Jack* and set to work himself removing the old antifouling with a paint scraper and a wire brush. He was surprised when Ernie turned up.

"You all right, then?" enquired Ernie, looking up at the towering hull.

"I'm fine. How about you?"

"A bit shocked."

Will stopped scrubbing and looked at him. "What do you mean?"

"Police think the fire was started deliberately."

"What?" Will was stunned.

"They found traces of a bottle and petrol. Reckon it was lobbed through the window."

"But why?"

"Blowed if I know." Ernie looked troubled.

"Have you told May?"

"No. I thought I wouldn't."

"You'll have a job keeping it from her."

"I suppose so. I just don't want her worrying." Will saw the fear in his friend's eyes. "It can only have been some yobs, can't it, having a bit of mischief? Couldn't be anything else, could it?"

"No. I shouldn't think so." Will hoped Ernie was right. What other reason could anyone have for torching the lighthouse?

"Do you want a look round?" Will tried to cheer him by showing him over the boat, but Ernie was preoccupied. After ten minutes or so he made his excuses and left. "Got to get back to the rock. May's nipping over to her pigs and I can't leave the place unattended."

Will watched as the older man walked round the jetty to his van, got in, started up and drove off. He put down his brush and scraper, walked along the jetty and down the pontoon towards *Florence Nightingale*. Hovis was bending down and attending to his mooring warps. He looked up at the sound of Will's footsteps. "You look a bit fed up," he offered.

"Confused, more like."

"What's the problem?" Hovis stretched.

"Ernie says the police think the fire at the lighthouse was started deliberately. They found glass and petrol. Reckon it was a fire-bomb."

"Good grief. Who'd want to do that?"

"I wish I knew. Local oiks, probably."

"First time ever if it is. I know we've a few tearaways round here but rollerblading down the middle of the road from Primrose's to the jetty is about their limit. They've set fire to a few litter bins in their time but I wouldn't have thought they'd have touched the lighthouse. Too much a part of their lives. And their dads'."

"But who else would have done it?"

"Can't imagine. What does Ernie think?"

"Hasn't a clue. I think he's in shock."

"And Whistler? What about him?"

"I haven't asked him."

Hovis looked at Will. "Don't you think you should?"

"Yes. I suppose so. What time is it?"

Hovis glanced at the marine chronometer through the glass of *Florence Nightingale's* wheelhouse. "Half past nine."

"He's probably still having breakfast at the Salutation. I'll nip over and see if I can catch him."

Ted Whistler was just coming out of the door of the Salutation as Will turned up on his doorstep. "What do you want?" he asked plainly. He had never held the social graces in high regard.

"Just coming to see you."

"Oh? That's a turn-up for the books."

Will ignored the gibe, and asked Ted if he had

heard about the fire.

"Where do you think I've been living for the past month? Course I've heard about the fire. The talk in there," he gestured over his shoulder, "has been about nothing else since it happened."

"What do you think caused it?"

"Somebody must have been careless. Fag end or something." That reminded him that he had not lit up his post-breakfast Camel, and he rummaged around in his donkey-jacket.

"It wasn't an accident."

"What?" Ted was looking for matches and asked the question absentmindedly.

"The fire was started with a petrol bomb."

This time Ted Whistler heard. He stopped what he was doing and asked for confirmation. Will explained about the storeroom and his belongings, about what the police had found and the conclusion they had drawn.

"I wondered if you had any idea who could have done it. Or why?"

"Why me?" Ted was defensive.

"Just asking, that's all. Ernie and I can't figure it out."

Ted leaned on the iron rail at the edge of the pavement across from the Salutation, the wind temporarily knocked out of his sails. His hunched but lanky figure with his thinning grey hair swept back from his face, gave him a cadaverous appearance.

— *Alan Titchmarsh* —

"Was it only that one room that was damaged? The storeroom where you had your stuff?" he asked.

"Yes."

Ted shrugged. "Funny that."

Will wondered what he was getting at.

"What do you mean?

"Maybe they want to make sure you don't keep any more records."

"Who?"

Ted shrugged again.

Will faced him squarely. "What's going on?"

Ted looked out to sea. "I don't know. I'm sorry you lost your diaries, but it's none of my business."

He turned away from Will and walked back along the sand towards the Salutation, leaving his former colleague determined to get to the bottom of a mystery that seemed to be deepening by the hour.

It had not occurred to Will that the police would want to question him. The statement was taken at St Petroc police station by an apologetic detective sergeant sympathetic to his loss. Providing a list of possessions that had gone up in smoke lowered his spirits again.

"Is that it, sir? You're sure that's all?" The portly sergeant, his Brylcreemed head bent low over the statement sheet, proceeded in his methodical longhand.

"Yes. I think so." Then he remembered the

146

photograph album. He had forgotten about that. A sinking feeling in his stomach. Then a brightening of spirits. He had not put the album into store at Ernie's. He had meant to, but something had made him wrap it in polythene and put it at the bottom of a canvas holdall filled with clothes, which now sat in the bottom of the wardrobe at Mrs Sparrow's. He still had a reminder of Ellie.

"You all right, sir?"

"Mmm? Yes. I just remembered something I didn't lose. That's all."

"I'm afraid I have to ask you where you were, sir, when the fire started."

Will filled in the officer on his movements that morning.

"So you did visit the lighthouse, then?"

"Yes. I had breakfast there."

"And then you left?"

"Yes. I walked back over the clifftop path to the boatyard. Then I made some telephone calls and then I went to the Roundhouse Studio."

The sergeant asked questions about the phone calls and precise details of timings. He asked if Will thought there was a reason why such a fire had been started. Will said he had no idea. He had already mentioned his missing diaries and what they contained. If the police thought this had some bearing on the case they would no doubt follow it up. It struck him as unwise to mention Ted Whistler's conjecturing and, anyway, he was not sure he believed it. It seemed sufficient to say that he had kept diaries during his time at the lighthouse and that he had made no secret of it.

The policeman beavered away with his Biro. He might be slow and steady, thought Will, but he's thorough. His questioning over, and his painstaking calligraphy completed, the sergeant asked Will to check his list of lost possessions and confirm that it was correct.

"Have you any ideas at all who might have done it?" asked Will, curious to know the detective sergeant's take on the case.

"We have our suspicions, sir," replied the officer, "but as yet there's nothing to go on. We think it might be something to do with your diaries, sir."

Will was surprised that the sergeant was so candid. "Do you?"

"Yes, sir. They could pose a threat to someone who didn't want their movements known. But, then, you'd probably guessed that, sir, hadn't you?"

Will looked suitably abashed. "It just seems so far-fetched."

"Not at all, sir. You'll hear all sorts of rumours about romantic notions of smuggling and the like. But it's not romantic, sir. It's against the law and we have to make sure that those who participate in it are brought to account."

"And you think that . . ."

"I can't really tell you what we think, sir. I would just tell you to be careful. It's unlikely that anything else will happen now, sir. The diaries are gone and that's probably all they were after. I should think you're quite safe now, sir. But it might be a good idea not to keep another diary."

Will smiled weakly. "Yes. I suppose you're right."

Chapter 13: Varne

The next few days Will spent in a daze. Dispossessed of his living quarters, his concern for Ernie and May jostled in his mind with confusion about his feelings for Amy. He had deliberately stayed away from her, though he yearned to see her again, and to add spice to his jumbled brew of emotions there was now the possibility that somebody in the village had it in for him.

Mrs Sparrow cleared away the breakfast dishes from his little table in the front bay window at Myrtle Cottage, flicking the dust off the aspidistra with her tea cloth as she passed. "Dinner at seven thirty then, Mr Elliott."

"Thank you. Yes." Will got up from the table and walked through into the hallway. He grabbed his sailing jacket from the mahogany coat stand, unconsciously straightened one of the flying ducks that was doing a nose-dive towards the skirting board, and left the house to begin another day of restoration.

Harry Gwenver was already lost in the bilges of *Boy Jack* when Will arrived. It seemed a shame to interrupt him. The poor man was getting used to being watched as he worked. Not that he seemed to mind.

Will looked up at the sky – pasty and pale – then down when he felt a familiar rub on his leg. Spike was gazing up at him, silently miaowing.

"Hallo, old lad! Where've you been?" He had neglected his old shipmate for the better part of a week. "Come on. Do you fancy a walk?" Leaving Harry in peace on *Boy Jack,* Will went along the jetty and out towards the cliff path. Spike followed, trotting behind him as obediently as any spaniel. They reached an outcrop above Pencurnow Cove and Will clambered up it. The cat reached the top in a couple of light bounds.

They sat together looking out to sea and across to the lighthouse, still white as chalk in spite of the fire.

"Oh, Spike! What are we going to do, eh?" The cat rubbed his head along Will's arm, purring. He smiled. Sometimes the silence of animals was their most attractive quality.

"People, Spike. Sometimes I think I don't do people." It dawned on him, now that he was here, how much he had needed to get away from the boatyard, the village and dear old Mrs Sparrow. How much he had missed solitude.

The sea lapped at the sand below them, and whispered across the nearby shingle. A pair of black and white oystercatchers were probing the shore with their scarlet bills, fluttering out of the way when the incoming waves interrupted their scavenging. Among the tussocky grass that surrounded their lump of granite, slender drumsticks were pushing up from the tufts of sea pinks, and a watery sun did its best to cut through the clouds.

A fishing boat bobbed gently on the waves half a mile from the shore, its crew hauling up their lobster pots, emptying them, then tossing them back overboard. Tiny orange floats marked their position, dotted across the surface of the dull green sea like a sparsely beaded necklace.

Man and cat sat and watched as the tide receded, leaving the beach fresh-washed, the colour of fudge, and unsullied by footprints.

As the waves advanced and receded Will remembered the Cornish holiday he and Ellie had enjoyed the year before they married. It was on the north coast, even more rugged than Pencurnow. They had walked, and eaten, slept and made love in the front bedroom of a boarding-house not unlike Mrs Sparrow's.

He felt a rush of sadness. From the blissfully happy days of being together, living for each other, he had returned to being a man happiest in his own company. Until now. He stroked Spike, and remembered the night on Hovis's boat, with Amy sitting close to him, the kiss in the doorway, the looks between them. The tears that had finally come after six years.

Was he wrong to want to start again? To be happy? When he thought of how happy he and Ellie had been together, it seemed impossible to imagine that he could ever feel the same about anyone else. And yet he could not deny his feelings for Amy. That, in its way, would be as wrong as betraying Ellie's memory.

"Oh, Spike!" He leaned forward, resting his hands on his knees and looking out to sea. A freighter edged slowly across the horizon and he remembered, with a sickening feeling, his diaries. "What to do?"

"Come on, then, Spike." He chucked the cat under its chin, caressed the white bib that ran like a starched shirt front across its breast. The cat chirruped. "Let's see how far you can walk. I'll carry you if you get tired." He got up, stretched his legs and set off in the direction of Land's End, striding out and breathing in the salt air. The cat was never more than a couple of paces behind him.

They stopped for lunch at a pub near Logan Rock, where the sight of a man with a black and white cat in tow was greeted with good humour by the laconic landlord. Will got himself the other side of a Cornish pasty and a pint of bitter, while Spike tucked into mackerel pâté and a saucer of milk before they retraced their steps on the return journey.

The cat walked almost every inch of the way, even though Will offered him a lift from time to time. He would sit in Will's arms for a couple of minutes before letting out a brief harrumph, bounding down and off in the direction of home. Spike took the lead all the way back, sometimes running fifty yards ahead, until the Crooked Angel boatyard came into view and he sat on a rock and curled his black tail around his white feet with a smug expression on his face.

Will scooped him up and walked down to the yard. When they reached *Boy Jack* there was no sign of Harry. Will looked at his watch. A quarter past five. Their walk had taken them the best part of the day, and he felt better for it. Spike leapt up the ladder and on to the deck. Will followed, keen to see how Harry had got on in their absence.

He fished in his pocket for the spare key for *Boy Jack*, opened the wheelhouse door, found a torch by the hatch and shone it down into the hold. Harry was making good progress: the once gappy planking now looked uniform and watertight, and part of it was even painted. With any luck he would finish on time and *Boy Jack* would be back in the water where she belonged.

He swung up from the hatch, replaced the torch on its narrow shelf and came out on to the deck. The early evening was still, bathed in a soft light. A movement caught his eye. A distant figure was running down the lane. He watched as it rounded the corner of the jetty and continued towards the boatyard. He could see now that it was Primrose Hankey, clad in a baggy navy blue tracksuit, her long plait bobbing from side to side as she jogged across the yard.

"Mr Ell-ee-ott," she panted, her face the colour of smoked salmon, perspiration running off her chin.

"Primrose! What's the matter?"

She was unable to speak. Instead, she bent forward from the waist (not an easy movement for a woman of such unusual weight distribution) and plunged her head between her knees. Will wondered if she would be able to straighten up again.

"Nothing wrong. Just getting a bit of exercise," she gasped. "Letter arrived for you this morning. Thought I'd drop it off. This the boat?" In the battle of curiosity versus exhaustion, the former now gained the upper hand.

"Yes."

"Mmm. Lot of work."

"Yes."

"Still. I'm sure she'll look nice when she's finished." She held the letter aloft, having checked out the ladder and decided against a precarious ascent. "I didn't know you were old enough to have been at Dunkirk," she quipped, as Will came down the ladder and took the letter from her.

"Not quite." He looked at the postmark and the frank of the Association of Dunkirk Little Ships.

"Is this boat one of them, then?" asked Primrose, her breathing almost back to normal.

"Yes." Will felt guilty at not offering more information after her exertions, but suspected that Primrose already knew more than she was letting on.

"What a week you've had, Mr Elliott. We've all felt very sorry for you."

We? thought Will, wondering just how far round the cove his tale of woe had spread.

"Yes. It's been a bit tricky," he said,

"I can imagine." Her complexion had now returned to normal. "But it's so nice that Miss Finn has been such a good friend."

"Sorry?" He was unnerved at Primrose's conjecture.

"Miss Finn. I gather you've become quite friendly."

Will was staggered at her candour. "Er . . . well, friendly, yes."

"Lovely. Very nice for both of you."

"Yes. Well. Thanks for bringing my letter." He felt irritated at her intrusion and didn't mind if she knew it.

Primrose realized she'd overstepped the mark, and seeing that he was not about to share the contents of the envelope with her she flapped her arms a couple of times and said, "Yes. Well. Must be off, back up the hill. The hard bit now."

Will felt a pricking of conscience. "I didn't know you jogged."

"Oh, yes. Got to keep fit. Once a week. Vary the route. Always out for a good fifteen minutes. Gets the circulation going. Keeps me trim. Back home for supper. 'Bye, then." She lumbered away up the jetty.

Will took out his pocket knife and slit open the envelope. Out fell an assortment of papers. There was a membership form, some general information about the Association and a covering letter explaining that the enclosed document had been sent to them by *Boy Jack's* previous owner in case they were interested in the boat's history. They had retained photocopies but were sending him the original as the new owner of the boat. Will's heart leapt. He unfolded the yellowing piece of paper and read:

To whom it may concern:
'Boy Jack' (originally 'Graceful')
Built 1931 Staniland & Company, Thorne, Yorkshire.
Length: 36ft
Beam: 9ft 6in
Displacement: 8 tons
Draft: 2ft 6in
Engines: 2 × 30 h.p. Perkins M30
Hull: Pitch pine on oak.

The following history is what I have been able

to piece together during the thirty years I have owned the boat. She was brought down from Yorkshire by a Thomas Cherry in 1937 and moored on the Thames at Oxford. At that time she was called 'Graceful'. In the middle of May in 1940 she must have been moored further down the Thames as she was used in the evacuation of Dunkirk. She broke down twice on her first crossing but is credited with saving the lives of 246 men.

Her life immediately after the war is not well documented, but I found her in a poor state of repair on the Thames at Oxford in 1962 and decided to take her on. My wife and I sailed her down to Dartmouth that summer, where she was used very happily for summer holidays and weekend excursions. We lived in Totnes at the time. She became a regular cruiser up and down the river Dart and along the Devon coast.

I endeavoured to keep 'Graceful' in good repair, and to this end the hull was refurbished and new stringers put in place in 1967. I also replaced the deck planking. We then moved to Falmouth so that we could enjoy boating in Cornwall and live by the sea which is what we had both dreamed of. Sadly, in 1969 my beloved wife died while giving birth to our son. The boy himself died a week later.

I planned to sell the boat and move away, but she was the one thing that we had shared and I could not bring myself to part with her. For this reason I renamed her 'Boy Jack', after our son. I have continued to use her ever since, and more restoration work was carried out in the 1980s. Now, in my later years, I do not get out on her as often as I would like and my circumstances make the cost of repairs difficult.

I explain these facts in the hope that the person who next owns 'Boy Jack' will remember her history, and mine, and take good care of her. She saved the lives of many British soldiers during the war and gave me, and my family, many hours of great pleasure. She deserves to be looked after.

Yours sincerely,
Walter Etchingham

Will folded the piece of paper and put it back into the envelope. For the second time in a week he was in tears.

Chapter 14:
Hartland Point

Amy looked at the old station clock on the wall of the studio. It was ten past one. The morning had dragged by. A few customers had turned up. One had even shown a passing interest in one of the erotic sculptures and she hoped at last that it might pass out of her life. But no, the customer left with the familiar "I'll have a think about it", which meant that she'd never see him again.

She set up a canvas on her easel in one corner of the studio and made a start on a rich blue sky, spreading the azure acrylic paint with her palette knife, all the while wondering where Will was and what he was doing. Had she been too pushy? Perhaps she had frightened him off. And who could blame him? Here was a man who had not known female company for six years, who had sought the solitude of a lighthouse. What made her think she could snap him out of his introspection in a matter of a few days' acquaintanceship. But it was more than that, wasn't it?

She wiped clean the palette knife on a piece of rag, replaced the cap on the tube of paint and climbed the spiral staircase for her jacket. She came down, threw a purple woollen scarf around her neck, and pulled the blind over the door. She needed a walk. A twenty-minute tramp along the beach would be just the thing

The salt tang in her nostrils filled her with renewed energy. The brisk breeze blew through her hair and made her scalp tingle as she waded down through the tussocky grass alongside the clifftop path towards the sand. She ambled along the waterline, looking down at the bubbles that erupted from the sand as the white waves retreated, stooping occasionally to pick up a razor shell or a whelk, and looking at the indentations in the sand that were instantly washed away by the next thin sheet of advancing tide.

She thought of him, and tried not to think of him, then threw back her head and breathed in deeply.

"Had enough shop-keeping for one day?"

The voice surprised her and she jumped. Hovis was walking towards her.

"Oh! It's you!"

"You look as though you've just escaped from prison."

"I have. In a way. Just needed some air."

"Me too. What have you got?" He nodded towards Amy's fistful of shells.

"Oh, just some razors and a whelk or two. And one large mussel."

"I think that's what Will needs."

"Sorry?" She tried to look unconcerned.

"Large muscles. His boat looks bigger out of the water than it does in. I think he's a bit daunted by all the work."

She tried a smile. Hovis watched as she turned and looked out to sea. Then he said, gently, "Shall we go and see how he's getting on?"

Amy looked at her watch, half wanting to make an excuse.

Hovis offered her a way out. "Oh, I forgot. You'll be opening up again soon."

Suddenly her way was clear to her. "No. I'm going out. But I've time to see how he's doing. Will you walk with me?"

"Happy to."

They strode back along the beach, where the receding tide had left the sand firm, and Hovis showed her his treasure trove – a rusted metal ring from a boat; a length of silvery driftwood and a dogfish's egg, the black purse equipped with wispy handles at each corner.

They found *Boy Jack* sitting on the concrete hard, propped up like Noah's Ark waiting for the flood, with wooden shores sticking out from the hull like the legs of a gigantic insect.

"I've brought a visitor," Hovis yelled up at the deck, dwarfed by the massive hulk.

Will stuck his head over the side, his face smeared with white paint. "Hi. How are you?"

"I'm fine. Just wondered how you were getting on." She leant on one of the shores.

"Don't lean on that! I mean, be careful. I always get nervous when boats are propped up."

"Sorry!" She looked crestfallen.

"So am I. I didn't mean to snap. I just can't believe that these things can ever stay upright when they're out of the water." He climbed down the ladder, grinning, and the uncomfortable moment passed.

"She looks huge."

"I know. Frightening, isn't it?"

Hovis made his excuses. "Must dash. Got to get some stuff from Primrose's. See you later." He executed a slow pirouette and shambled off.

Amy walked around *Boy Jack* and looked up past the propellers at her stern. "She looks like the *Titanic* from here."

"Well, with any luck, when Harry's done his job she won't suffer the same fate."

He took a piece of sandpaper from his pocket and began rubbing at a propeller blade.

"Have you got enough lifeboats?" she teased.

"I'm getting a raft."

"Big enough for all the passengers?"

"It depends how many there are." He looked at her steadily.

"How many are you thinking of taking?"

"Oh, just a couple." He looked upwards past the towering topsides and a small black and white face peeped back at him over the rail.

"There's him . . ."

"A cat?"

"That's Spike. We've been together a couple of years now."

"Just you and him, then?" She posed the question jokingly.

"Well, it all depends."

"On what?"

"You do ask a lot of questions."

"Only because I'm interested."

He turned to face her. "I'm very glad you're interested." He bent down and kissed her forehead.

She looked at him steadily. "You've got paint on your nose."

"I've got paint everywhere."

"I was just wondering . . . You said you'd come round for supper."

"I will when I'm asked." His eyes danced.

"Well, I'm asking. Tonight, if you like. I'm shutting up shop this afternoon. There's an arts and crafts exhibition in St Ives and I want to see if I can find some new stuff for the studio. I'll be back around six. Come round at about eight?"

"Sounds fine to me. It'll take me that long to get this paint off."

"OK, then. Don't get tangled up in your propeller. Oh, and don't lean on those props. It always makes me nervous." He started, aware that he was, indeed, leaning against one of the shores.

She laughed. "Take care!"

"And you."

He watched her go, the purple scarf trailing behind her like a pennant.

She returned just after six, happy but exhausted, with promises from four artists that they would call in during the week and bring some of their work. As she opened the door of the studio the first things that greeted her eye were Oliver's sculptures in the middle of the floor.

"Enough!" she shouted, then walked to the storeroom at the back of the studio and wheeled out a sack barrow. She wrapped old blankets around each of the sculptures, eased them on to the barrow and trundled them into the store. Now she would not have to stare her past in the face every day.

She took a shower, then pulled on a pair of jeans and a baggy sweatshirt and began to prepare supper.

*

It was only supper, he told himself. Nothing more. She had asked him for supper. There was no reason to feel so apprehensive.

He walked up the lane towards the studio. The blind was down. He tapped lightly and tried the handle but the door would not yield. He tapped again.

Footsteps approached and the door opened. They looked at one another, he leaning against the wall, a bottle of wine in his hand, she barefoot, her hair, fiery in the studio lights, tumbling over her shoulders.

"It's cold out here, you know."

"I'm sorry." She came out of her daze. "Come in."

They kissed, then Amy led the way up the spiral staircase to the living area.

"I've brought you a bottle. I think it's chilled enough."

She rummaged in the kitchen drawer and eventually found a corkscrew.

"Here, let me." He took it from her, opened the bottle then handed it back to her. She poured the wine into two blue glasses, and handed him one.

"Cheers." It seemed such an innocuous thing to say, devoid of real sentiment. Her eyes told him how she felt.

"Cheers," he replied, and they sipped, all the while staring at one another. Will noticed the flickering muscle in her upper lip and the nervousness in her eyes.

He set his glass down on the table then took Amy's

glass and put that beside it. He folded his arms around her and she laid her head on his chest. "I'm so glad you came."

"And me."

"I thought you wouldn't."

"So did I."

She eased away from him and looked up into his eyes.

"But then I knew I had to." He stared at the floor, discomfited by his own admission. "I knew I wanted to."

"Are you hungry?"

"Starving."

"Good. There's masses. I thought a boat-builder might have a good appetite."

They dined by candlelight at the small round table, sharing the day's news. Amy told Will about the artists who would bring their work over the next week – an ex-headmistress who made stunning New England patchworks, a potter who worked in vivid ceramics, another painter, and a Bohemian jeweller who had BO and probably fancied her. Will told her what he'd discovered about *Boy Jack*. Amy's eyes shone, and she held his hand as he recounted the story of the old boat and her owner.

"How sad. But how lovely."

"Why lovely?"

"Because you know now that she was meant for you."

"Do you think so?"

"I know so. He even had the same initials."

"I hadn't noticed," he said in surprise.

They dawdled over lemon mousse, laughing and chattering like old friends. Will could not remember when he had felt so rested and happy. The meal finished, they rose and moved towards the sofa.

"Coffee?"

"I'm fine. It was lovely." They kissed, longingly and tenderly as though they had been waiting for the moment when they could let go. Her tongue darted in and out of his mouth and he felt an intensity of passion that took his breath away. He broke from her momentarily, his heart pounding.

She looked at him anxiously, longingly, searching in his eyes for the love she knew must be there, then took his hand and gently led him towards the bed. He stood quite still, as though time had stopped, then slowly began to undress her. He pulled off her sweatshirt and her amber hair tumbled over freckled shoulders. Her breasts were rounded and firm; he stroked them lightly with the back of his hand. She unbuttoned his shirt, pulled it off and kissed his forearm. He began to kiss her body and she threw her head back with pleasure before they tore away each other's remaining clothing and made love beneath the covers. The tension Will had lived with for so long slipped away, and that night he slept more soundly and peacefully than he had for years, with

Amy curled up alongside him, and his arms cradling her. He felt as though he had come home.

A scream awoke him. He sat upright with a jerk. It was a gull. His heart was beating wildly in his chest, but it subsided, and the inner calm returned. He lay back on the pillow and Amy stirred. He watched her surface, beaming from ear to ear, her eyes not yet open. He stroked her hair, breathing in her fragrance.

She laid her head on his shoulder and touched his arm. "You have lovely arms," she murmured. "I'd like to paint them."

He studied the look of contentment on her face with deep pleasure. He wanted to keep this moment going, to stop the clock and let it always be like this.

Amy opened her eyes. "Hallo."

"Hallo."

They said no more for several minutes, then he kissed her and they made love again. Eventually she slipped out from under the covers and made her way to the bathroom. He watched her go, her lithe body almost floating over the floor.

After a few moments he slid out of bed and followed her, into the bathroom where she was turning on the brass taps above the iron tub.

She poured essence into the steaming water, then stepped into it and looked at him with one eyebrow raised. He walked across the room and got in after her.

Later, over breakfast, they said little but smiled a lot. The thing that struck him most was the serenity. Until he remembered the fire, the break-in on his boat, and that it was no longer in the water. Spike would need feeding, his books had been lost and . . . Ellie.

"Hallo?" Amy said.

"Sorry. Just remembering."

"Don't."

"No." He smiled apologetically. "I'd better go. You have to paint. And I have to . . . paint."

She looked at him across her bowl of cornflakes, a droplet of milk balanced on her lower lip. He reached over and wiped it away with his finger, and felt a wave of love envelop him. "See you later, then?" he asked.

"Yes."

He kissed her lightly on the cheek and spiralled down the iron staircase. He could not remember when he had last felt so unassailable, so powerful and so alive. The guilt that had gnawed for so long at his soul seemed to be relaxing its grip.

Chapter 15:
Strumble Head

Primrose Hankey was having a high time of it all. On a scale of one to ten in terms of quality gossip, Pencurnow would normally struggle to reach two. But the past few days had yielded rich pickings, which she gleefully retailed along with the paraffin and Pampers. Not that her face betrayed any pleasure in passing on the information: it was all done with an innate sense of duty.

Will had avoided the shop for the best part of a week, but eventually had to call in for provisions. Mrs Sparrow's hospitality did not run to lunch, and a boat-builder, as Amy had discovered, had quite an appetite. His curiosity also encouraged him to acquaint himself with the lie of the land as Primrose saw it.

Will hated himself for falling prey to her desire to inform and be informed, but something inside him told him that she might have some knowledge, however scanty, that would give him a better overview of what was going on. And he felt guilty at not having shown more appreciation of her athletic personal delivery service.

Primrose was up a ladder, which was unfortunate, not only because the view of her from ground level was less than flattering but also because when she set eyes on Will Elliott her excitement was so great that she almost lost her footing. In the event, she descended to the concrete floor with greater speed than was good for her, and a shelf stacked high with tinned goods vibrated dangerously on impact.

"Mr Elliott! How nice to see you. Come for your magazine, have you? Lovely to see your boat. So glad I was able to help!" She reached under the counter for *Classic Boat*, anxious to ingratiate herself after their last meeting.

"Yes." It was as good as Will could manage, and a considerable accomplishment, bearing in mind the short space that Primrose allowed between sentences.

"About Miss Finn . . ."

"Have you any Cornish pasties?" Will waded in to change the subject.

"Over there in the cool cabinet. She seems such a nice person. Very genuine. I'm sorry if you thought I was interfering."

Will delved among the chicken and mushroom slices and sausage rolls, seeking vainly for a pasty and wishing he'd shopped elsewhere.

"Sorry to hear about the fire. It must have been dreadful."

"Yes. Terrible."

"Poor Mr and Mrs Hallybone. Are they both all right?"

"I think so. A bit shocked but I hope they'll get over it. It's just a good thing that the fire was fairly contained."

"I'm sorry you lost your diaries. All those memories gone."

Will had finally located a battered pasty. He closed the cabinet and came over. "No. Not the memories. Just the diaries. But you have to move on, don't you, Primrose?"

Primrose was unsure whether or not this was delivered as a reproof. She paused to consider. Will felt that the best form of defence was attack. He became the inquisitor rather than the one who was being quizzed.

"What do you make of it all, then, Primrose?"

Primrose was an old hand at being pumped. If anything, she enjoyed dispensing information even more than discovering it. What was the point in having theories and bits of intelligence if you didn't spread them around? Every now and again her conscience niggled, but she invariably failed to restrain herself. This made her popular with the ladies of the village, except when the piece of gossip being retailed concerned them personally. Under these circumstances Primrose was regarded as an interfering busybody.

"Very strange." She looked conspiratorially to left and right. "There's something very unpleasant going on, I think. I reckon we've not heard the last of it yet."

Will leaned on the counter and did his best to sound casual. "What sort of something?"

"The sort of something that goes on by the sea. Things coming and going, if you know what I mean."

"What sort of things?"

"Oh, not for me to say, Mr Elliott. Gracious me. I mean, if the lighthouse has been burned down on account of your diaries it would be very silly of me to start saying things, wouldn't it?"

"I'm sorry, I shouldn't have asked. I'm just rather confused about it, that's all." Will was amazed that Primrose had cottoned on to the significance of his diaries.

"I think it's been going on for quite some time, Mr Elliott." She was whispering now. "Ever seen *Whisky Galore?*" she asked.

Will nodded.

"Well, you know what I mean, then. Them folk from the city like to think they have a hold on us down here in Cornwall, when they don't have a hold on us at all. It's a sort of gesture of defiance, if you know what I mean."

Will could not help but show a little surprise, and Primrose read his reaction. "Oh, don't you go thinking that we're all at that game!" She pointed to the bottles on the shelf behind her. "My stocks come from the wholesaler!" She chuckled.

"But you could get some that didn't if you wanted to?"

Perspiration was forming on Primrose's upper lip. She clearly thought she had said more than she should and changed the subject. "Anyway, how's Mr Utterly?"

"Hovis?"

"Sorry?"

"Hovis. Bread. I need a brown loaf. Have you got one?"

"Yes." She looked at him as though he had had a brainstorm.

Will recovered himself with commendable and unusual speed. "Mr Utterly. Yes. He's fine. Says he's leaving in a few weeks, though. Going back to Devon. Salcombe or Dartmouth. I shall be sorry to see him go." The moment he had said it he bit his lip: in covering up his slip about Hovis's name he had revealed different information, which Primrose would now impart to the rest of the village.

"Oh, don't you worry about that. Mr Utterly has been leaving for Dartmouth or Salcombe every month for the past three years to my certain knowledge."

"Sorry?"

"It's a dream he's always had. Going back to his roots. Where his family used to live. But, so far, he's never made it. They do say," she leaned over the papers on the counter to speak more confidentially, "that he hasn't a clue how to sail that boat of his. Wouldn't even know which way to turn out of the harbour to get to Devon."

"Really?"

She nodded. "Nobody likes to push him, though. Lovely man. Very good family. Bakers, by all accounts."

"Really?" Will said again. He fished in his pocket for money and scooped up the carrier-bag into which she had deposited his goods. "Must dash, Primrose."

She called after him, "Not a word now!" But it was too late: he was already on his way down the lane, feeling strangely excited about the prospect before him, and even more warmly disposed towards his whiskered neighbour.

Chapter 16: Breaksea

"Wight, Portland, Plymouth, south-westerly five or six, increasing seven or gale eight. Occasional rain. Good becoming moderate . . ."

The sound from the radio on board Hovis's boat seeped out of the port-holes and Will heard the unfavourable forecast as he approached. "Doesn't sound too good."

"No." Hovis was sweeping his decks and looked up. "Sounds distinctly grim. Batten-down-the-hatches time. I think I shall have to put off my voyage for a bit. No point in setting off if there's a gale threatening."

"No." Will didn't like to say any more. "Have you seen Gryler or his lad?"

"He was around half an hour ago. Probably in the pub by now. The lad's gone off in his boat."

"He spends a lot of time in that boat, doesn't he?"

Hovis stopped sweeping. "You think he's up to something?"

"I don't know." Will looked thoughtful.

"How's *Boy Jack* coming on?"

"Better than I'd hoped. Harry reckons he'll be done by tomorrow. That means I can finish painting and antifouling the hull and have her back in the water some time next week, weather permitting."

"Well, it might not. You heard the forecast."

"How imminent?"

"Pretty imminent. And talking of pretty, how's the lady?"

"She's fine, thanks. Fine."

Hovis chuckled as Will's eyes grew misty. "Well I never."

"Mmmm? Sorry?" Will realized his momentary lapse.

Hovis grinned. "What have you got planned for the afternoon?"

"I want to nip over to the lighthouse and see if Ernie and May are OK. If that weather is as imminent as you say it is, though, I'd better get a move on or I'll get a soaking."

Their conversation was interrupted by the throaty rumble of a powerboat and they turned in unison to see a white gin palace bearing down on them, with Jerry MacDermott at the helm. The boat, almost fifty-foot long, was slewing precariously towards the pontoon, and Will, anxious to avoid a repetition of the MacDermotts' last berthing exercise on a vessel barely a third the size of their new model, dashed along the pontoon to fend it off before it could do any damage. Hovis followed.

"You OK?" Will asked the helmsman, before laying a hand on the boat.

There was a look of panic in Jerry MacDermott's eye, as though he knew that this time he had bitten off more than he could chew. He lobbed his cigar butt into the water, the better to grind his teeth and bite his lip. "Bit tricky, son. Could do with a hand. The missus is on her way down by car. Thought I'd surprise her."

"You on your own up there?"

"Yes. Broker said it could be 'andled by one at a pinch."

Yes, but not this one, thought Will. "Put your rudder amidships then go astern on your port engine," he said.

"Sorry?"

"The left-hand engine. Ease it into reverse. Keep your starboard engine – the right-hand one – in neutral."

"Right." The port engine gave a rich, deep growl, and the water churned at the stern of the boat.

"Not too much. Now go ahead gently on your starboard engine."

The boat did a stately pirouette.

"Put them both into neutral and throw us a rope."

Jerry MacDermott did as he was told and threw ropes to both Hovis and Will.

"Just ease back on both engines now – very gently," instructed Will. "That's it. A little more. Fine. OK. You can switch off." He fastened the new black mooring warp around a rusty cleat on the pontoon and Hovis did the same. The one thing Hovis knew how to do was keep a boat in port, thought Will, watching his companion deftly wind the rope around another corroding cleat.

"You're a gent, squire." MacDermott tossed the compliment with a note of relief in his voice.

Will read the name on the transom of the new boat: *Sokai Again*. Jerry MacDermott had pushed the boat out in more ways than one.

"Like her?" asked her new owner proudly.

"She's . . . er . . . very big," said Will diplomatically.

Hovis stood perfectly still, eyeing her up from stem to stern, scratching his head and wondering just how much money had been spent on the largest piece of Tupperware he had ever set eyes on. He didn't have to wonder for long.

"Two hundred and fifty grand," boasted her owner. "Only a year old. Barely run in."

"How big?" asked Hovis, his eyes like saucers.

"Forty-eight feet," replied MacDermott. "Got everything. Radar, GPS, generator, two TVs, CD player, cocktail bar, twin staterooms – both with *en suite* showers – two fridges, fly-bridge, bathing platform. It's even got a gangplank."

"Passarelle," supplied Will.

"And one of them as well," confirmed MacDermott. "The missus will love her."

"Are you sure you've got enough fenders out?"

"Not blown it up yet."

"No. Not your tender. Your fenders – to stop it scraping."

"There's some in that crate thing at the back."

"I'd tie a few more of them down the pontoon side, I think. And your springs and your head and stern lines will need to be strong. Some high winds are forecast. You'll want her secure." Will hated dishing out orders, but the prospect of that amount of money at the mercy of the impending elements drove him into offering unsolicited advice.

"Are you going to leave her here?" asked Hovis, still in awe of the stately hulk.

"For a bit, squire. Thought she'd give this place a touch of class." MacDermott had recovered and was back to his swaggering ways. He hopped down.

"Are you sure she'll be safe?"

"Oh, I think so. With the likes of you on site I shouldn't have too much to worry about."

"Yes, but it's a lot of money."

"Nah. Bit of fun, really. Take us along to Brighton in a jiffy. Trudie'll like that. Likes Brighton. Good shopping."

"Brighton?" Hovis was musing on how long it would take a Cornish yawl to get from Pencurnow to Brighton, with a favourable wind. Pencurnow to Falmouth. Falmouth to Salcombe. Salcombe to Weymouth. Weymouth to Lymington. Lymington to Brighton. He reckoned on a good five days, allowing for overnighting in port.

"How fast does she go?"

"Thirty-odd knots."

"Good grief. It's not natural."

"No. But it's the business, squire. Anyway, mustn't 'old you up. Old Gryler around?"

"Pub, I think," murmured Hovis.

Will had been watching silently. MacDermott and his boat seemed so out of place in this tiny Cornish boatyard. Perhaps it was a sign of the times. A sign of the way things were going.

"Old bugger. I'll go and tell 'im 'e's got a new charge to keep an eye on. Be seein' you."

"Yes." Hovis stood, entranced. "Two fridges," he muttered. "And a cocktail bar."

"Yes", said Will, "but once he plugs into shore power just think of the size of his electricity bill."

Hovis brightened. "That's a point. There's a lot to be said for a locker below the water-line. Let nature do the cooling. And anyway . . ."

Will looked at him quizzically. "Yes?"

"I've never liked Brighton. Not a patch on Salcombe."

*

Amy turned the envelope in her hand and ran her fingers over it. She had put off opening it, half afraid of its contents, half annoyed at its encroachment on her life. The handwriting was assured, over-elaborate. At least it meant, hopefully, that Oliver was now some distance away. That much should have been a relief, but it was not.

She walked to the counter and picked up a pair of scissors, sliced neatly through the top of the envelope. She pulled out the single sheet of crisp white paper and unfolded it.

The message was written in black ink.

Ballet d'Azur

Dear Ame,

I didn't mean to upset you, angel. You know I wouldn't do that for anything. [Amy threw her head back and let out a single sharp laugh.]

I just want you back. Need you back. You know what it's like – the not dancing. The not being near you. You must miss it as much as I do. I only get angry when I think we won't be together again. I have so many plans for us. We *can* get back what we had. You know we can. Trust me and it will all work out.

I'm planning to take the company to Nice – the

place where we thought up the name. Remember the hotel? The room over the terrace? Five times a day? Again perhaps?"

She winced, half at the painful memory, half at the cloying sentiment shot through with arrogance that Oliver seemed to think would override everything that had happened since.

Don't shut me out. Give me a chance to show you that we can do it again. We have so much together, you know that. We shouldn't waste it.

I'll come and see you again, soon, and this time I won't take no for an answer. You must come. We can make a fresh start. There is nothing else for either of us. Believe me. O

She dropped the letter on the counter. Then she picked it up, tore it into little pieces and threw it into the wastebin.

The walk along the clifftop was not pleasant. His thoughts of Amy warmed him, but the sky was threatening and the wind building in gusts. He wondered what she was doing. He saw the *Gull* pulled up on the patch of shingle to one side of the lighthouse. Ernie was coming out of the door below the tower and hailed him. "Not looking so good."

"In there?" Will was concerned about the lighthouse.

"No. The forecast. Blowing up."

"I know. I thought I'd nip over and see you before it bucketed down."

"Nice of you. They reckon we're OK for a few hours yet."

"How's May?"

"Oh, coming along. Getting over it. She was a bit shocked, you know. Nothing like that's ever happened to her before. Not to either of us."

"I know."

"Still, got to carry on. Look forward, not back. That boat of yours," he pointed at *The Gull*, "good at catching mackerel. Hooked another two this morning. Reckon I'm on to a winner there." He patted Will on the back. "Fancy a cup of tea?"

The two men walked through to Ernie's kitchen and he brewed up.

"Seen much this morning?" asked Will.

"Not much. Quiet, really. *The Scillonian* pushing out to St Mary's. Young Applebee out there with his lobster pots but that's about all."

"Still out, is he?"

"Reckon so. Motored off behind Bill's Island an hour or more ago. Haven't seen him since. Time he was getting back in." Ernie searched for clues in the sky.

"Strange."

Ernie stared at him. "You think he's up to something?"

"Might be. Not sure."

"Best not enquire. Not after . . . you know."

"I know." Will was anxious to avoid worrying Ernie. They chatted for a while, about *Boy Jack*, about May's livestock and the lighthouse, the visitors who would come with the warmer weather. Will was relieved to see Ernie cheerful at the prospect of his new job.

"I'm getting used to the idea. Got all me patter off. Listen to this, see what you think." He stood up and cleared his throat. "Prince Albert Rock Lighthouse was constructed in its present form by William Tregarthen Douglass, the same engineer responsible for the construction of Bishop Rock Lighthouse, which is positioned on rocks beyond the Isles of Scilly. It was completed in 1873 and is now one hundred and twenty-six years old. The lamp is hand made and for almost a hundred years nothing has been replaced except the bulbs. It floats on a bath of mercury and weighs three and a half tons. The beam is 1.2 million candle power and is visible for twenty-six miles."

Will stayed silent, anxious to be as encouraging as possible.

"There are four 'bull's-eyes' in the lamp and one revolution takes twelve seconds, which therefore means that there is one flash every three seconds –

the signature of Prince Albert Rock Lighthouse." He paused for a reaction.

"Very clear."

"You've heard it all before, haven't you?" He looked crestfallen.

"But you won't be telling it to me. I think you're doing well."

"It's a real bugger trying to stop it sounding too technical."

"Well, why don't you weave a few stories in?"

"Like what?"

"Oh, you know. The story about the lighthouse keeper on Smalls. The one who died and his mate had to hang him over the side to stop the smell."

"And that's why there are always three keepers not two, so that the third one can provide . . ."

"The alibi," they said in chorus.

"That's it. And the three keepers on Flannan Isles who just disappeared."

"The *Mary Celeste* of the lighthouse world." Ernie's eyes lit up. "That would be a spicy one, wouldn't it? Perk things up a bit."

"You're a good story-teller and you've got all the yarns. Use them."

"So long as Trinity House don't mind."

"Oh, I can't see them bothering. Enjoy yourself."

Ernie looked across the table at him. "You know, I think I just might!"

*

By the time Will had walked back, the wind had strengthened and banks of ominous-looking purple-grey clouds were building to the south-west. *Boy Jack* sat on her shores. She looked as if she was itching to get back into the water. "It won't be long now, old girl." Will patted her hull and noticed an envelope from Harry Gwenver pinned to the planking. He pulled it off, tore it open and read the note it contained: "Fatlagena whye? Have done my bit. Over to you now. Hope you are pleased. Will send my bill when Mrs Gwenver has worked out the sums. Darzona. Harry Gwenver."

He looked at the note and frowned. *Fatlagena whye* he remembered as meaning 'how are you?' but *Darzona?* He'd not heard that before.

He wandered down towards *Florence Nightingale* and called Hovis, who emerged towelling his beard. "Caught me at my ablutions, young man."

"Sorry. Just wondered how you were at Cornish?"

"Ropy. Very ropy. What sort of Cornish?"

"*Darzona.*"

"Ah. Emphasis on the second syllable to rhyme with gone. *Dar-ZON-a.*"

"Meaning?"

"Very simple: God bless."

Chapter 17: Blacktail

Towards mid-afternoon the wind had built up to force five or six, and Will studied the props supporting *Boy Jack*. They would hold, he convinced himself, protected by the high jetty wall, which offered some shelter from the worst of the south-westerlies.

Halyards in the boatyard rang against the alloy masts with the insistence of unanswered doorbells, and Hovis was at work lashing down anything on his deck that was in danger of moving. Even the water in the boatyard was choppy, and the sea was becoming decidedly lumpy.

Will climbed the wall of the jetty and looked out towards Prince Albert Rock. White crests topped every wave. It would soon be an uncomfortable passage home for anyone not yet in port.

His thoughts turned again to Amy. The previous

night seemed so far away now. Would she want to see him tonight?

His introspection was interrupted abruptly by the arrival of Len Gryler. "Your boat-builder finished, is he?"

"Yes. Down to me now."

"When do you want her back in the water, then?"

"Probably by the end of next week, if that's all right."

"Should be. But I'll need a couple of days' notice. Need to make sure the machine's up to it. Busy time coming now. Boats going in and out of the water. New shower block going up." He tossed his head towards a small portable building being craned from the back of a truck alongside his peeling cabin. "That should please the punters." But his entrepreneurial tone lacked its usual relish and he seemed distracted as he looked out to sea. "Bit rough out there. Getting worse, too." He was edgy. Uneasy, thought Will. He wasn't carrying his monkey wrench, and his hands were stuffed into his pockets. He seemed to be clenching and unclenching his fists.

"Is your lad still out there?"

Gryler's gaze raked the waves for a sign of his boat. "Yes."

"In this?"

"He should've been back an hour or more ago. Don't know where he's got to. Must have broken down."

"What are you going to do?"

"Dunno. Wait and see, I suppose. He might have put in further along the coast and be walking back. Can't see him on the water."

"There's not much of a view from here. I'll climb the cliff path and have a look," Will suggested.

"No. He'll be back. He'll have put in further along. Probably waiting for the weather to calm down." Gryler looked at Will with a stubborn glare, then rolled off down the jetty to his shed.

"You sure she'll be safe in this?" Will turned to find Hovis at his shoulder, looking up at *Boy Jack*.

"I hope so. I've checked all the shores and the wall's offering a fair bit of shelter. Nothing else I can do now. How's *Florence?*"

"Oh, she'll be fine. I've stowed everything that might blow away, and what I can't stow I've lashed down so she'll just bob about a bit until it's over."

"You look a bit pasty. Fancy a walk?"

"In this?" Hovis looked at Will as though he were off his head.

"Young Applebee hasn't come back. Gryler reckons he's put in further along the coast. I reckon he's still out there."

"Once a lighthouse keeper always a lighthouse keeper."

"I suppose so."

"I thought it was the coastguard who kept an eye on the movements of shipping?"

"I know, but old habits die hard. Anyway, the lad might be in trouble."

"In more ways than one by the sound of it. You sure you want to get involved?"

"I can't just mess around here if he's out there."

Will remembered his first encounter with Christopher Applebee, giving him the magazines. It was hard to think of the indolent youth as a smuggler. He was more than likely poaching lobsters. Nothing more.

"Well, I'm nipping up there for a look."

"Let me grab my oilskin. It's starting to rain."

While Hovis went back to *Florence Nightingale* for his waterproof, Will nipped up the ladder on to *Boy Jack's* deck, grabbed his sailing jacket and secured the hatches.

They met at the end of the jetty as heavy rainclouds passed overhead. The two men braced themselves against the strengthening wind as they climbed up the sandy cliff path between the tussocks of grass. They could make out a figure with a dog walking towards them as they crested the first knoll. It was Hugo Morgan-Giles.

"Good afternoon. Not going out in this, are you?" He was holding on to his flat tweed cap and reining in the yellow Labrador. "Steady, Elsie."

Hovis began, "We're just–"

"Out for a breath of air," Will interrupted. "Before it gets too bad."

"Bit grim, isn't it? Even mad dogs don't enjoy this," agreed Hugo, trying to remain upright in the face of a stiff breeze and a strong dog. "Don't get blown away." He carried on past them, hauled by the Labrador in the direction of the Moorings.

The rain became heavier, and as the two men breasted the highest point of the cliff the full might of the sea came into view below them. There was a ten-foot swell, and white spume flew in the air to twice that height as the breakers crashed on to the rocks below. The thundering of tide on granite was deafening, and the rain stung their faces. Hovis reached into the pocket of his grubby yellow oilskin, pulled out a matching sou'wester and clamped it on his head, pulling the strap firmly beneath his chin. "You look like the man on the tin of pilchards," teased Will.

"Yes, but at least I'll be dry."

They walked across to the edge of the cliff, planting their feet carefully on the uneven turf, strewn with rabbit droppings, and peered out to sea, scrutinizing the water between the boatyard, Bill's Island and Prince Albert Rock as rain and salt spray blew into their eyes.

On the horizon a container-ship ploughed its course doggedly. "That's about the only thing I'd want to be on in this weather," shouted Will, his hair soaked and clinging to his head like a tangle of black serpents.

"I wouldn't even want to be on that," countered Hovis.

It was fully five minutes before they saw the boat, tossing like a cork on the heaving waves between Bill's Island and the lighthouse.

"Christ!" Will reached into the pocket of his sailing jacket for the binoculars. It was difficult to hold them steady in the near gale-force wind, and impossible to keep them clear due to the lashing onshore rain. He tucked his elbows into his sides, the better to keep the glasses steady, and tried to focus on the small boat between the massive rollers.

"He's still in there! Look!" He handed the binoculars to Hovis who finally located the buffeted fishing smack.

"Good God! His outboard must have packed up." Hovis rubbed the lenses clear of rain again. "He's got no oars, as far as I can see. We'd better call the lifeboat. Where's the nearest phone? Pencurnow or the lighthouse?"

"Pencurnow's nearer. You run there and call them out, I'll get round to the lighthouse."

The two men set off in different directions, Will unsure why he was heading for the lighthouse, but knowing that he needed to be there. He ran as fast as the gusting wind and rain would allow, keeping his eye on the little boat as it pitched and tossed ever nearer the rocks strung out like jagged teeth at the foot of Prince Albert. The nearer he got, the more clearly he could make out the tiny figure spreadeagled in the bottom of the boat, one arm braced against each side, clinging on amid a tangled mess of lobster-pots, fishing-nets and rope.

The rain was torrential now, flung sideways by the wind. Will reached the end of the path and began to pick his way over the rocks at the base of the lighthouse, spray thrown high above his head.

At first he thought he was seeing double and rubbed his eyes to clear them of salt water. Then he knew that his eyes were not playing tricks: there were now two small boats on the water: the fishing boat PZ 291, containing Christopher Applebee, and a smaller rowing boat manned by an oarsman negotiating the waves and travelling in the direction of the stricken craft. It took only a moment for Will to grasp that the second boat was *The Gull* and that the oarsman was Ernie Hallybone.

Rooted to the spot, rain running off his chin, he watched as Ernie, now a hundred yards from the rocks, rowed towards the other craft, which was still fifty yards away. The fishing smack tilted alarmingly from side to side and Christopher Applebee clung to the port side as the boat heaved to starboard. His right leg was entangled in the fishing net, which had been dragged from the boat by the waves. He fought to disengage himself, then lost his grip and slipped rapidly from view. The boat turned turtle and the outboard motor parted from the transom.

Will's heart was pounding and he spotted Christopher Applebee's head bobbing between the waves, then disappearing as he was dragged down by fierce undercurrents.

Ernie pulled rhythmically on his oars in spite of the towering waves, cresting one as though he were on the back of a heaving whale, then hurtling down into the hollows between the watery mountains.

He was barely twenty yards from the youth now, and closing, but all the while the two of them drifted towards the rocks at the foot of the lighthouse. As he watched Ernie battle against the water, Will could barely breathe, praying that he would reach Christopher Applebee in time and that he would be able to stay clear of the rocks until help arrived.

The head above the water seemed nearer to the boat now. Ernie was in with a chance. Without warning *The Gull* twisted in the water, pulled by the current and pushed by the wind, and a rolling breaker caught her beam on, flipping her over and tossing Ernie into the water like a crumb.

Will shouted, "No!" as the oars were flung aloft like matchsticks, only to tumble back into the sea and be swallowed up. *The Gull* righted herself, then caught the crest of a roller and was propelled toward the rocks. Under the thunder of the waves and the scream of the wind, Will heard the cracking and splitting of timber on rock as she was riven into splinters against the jagged granite below the lighthouse.

Fear seized him as he leapt from rock to rock, searching for Ernie amid the spray and spume. He scanned the water for him, hoping with every passing second that his friend would appear, but the only thing visible was the upturned hull of PZ 291, slewing and tumbling ever nearer to the rocks.

He tore off his waterproof and shoes, then breasted his way into the oncoming tide. Where was Ernie?

The waves slammed into Will as he tried to swim, sweeping him towards the rocks. He was powerless to resist their force as he somersaulted headlong into the next wave, which seemed to be coming from a completely different direction. Deafened and gasping for breath as the water swirled around him, he heard it echo thunderously in his ears. His head bobbed up, only to be submerged again by a towering roller.

His arms aching from useless exertion, he pulled even harder towards the spot where it seemed Ernie had been tipped out of the boat, only to be flung with violent disregard against a rock. He felt the sharpness of limpets against the side of his head and saw the redness descending in front of his eyes.

He held on to the image of Ernie, willing him with every fibre of his body to appear from the waves, and praying that the sea would give him up. Again and again Will dived forward. He wanted to let go, but struggled to keep his mind on what he was trying to do. The vision of the craggy face became fuzzy and another took its place: a younger face, framed with amber curls; a smiling, loving face. Another gigantic wave broke over his head, pushing him deeper into the sea. His body was willing to be taken now; Ernie had gone and he could feel the life being pounded out of him, sucked from his feeble grasp. But with Amy's image shining like a beacon in front of him, and with one final burst of energy, he raised his head above the waves and looked for the shore, before another mighty wall of water picked him up, turned him round and scooted him like a surfboard towards the edge of the rocks.

Dragging himself upright in the few seconds between waves, he hauled himself clear of the tide as it sucked back the crushed shells and pebbles with a threatening roar. With the last of his energy he scrambled on to the grass above the granite outcrop.

As the lifeboat rounded the headland Will fell to his knees in desperation, his hands gripping the sodden grass until his knuckles turned white. He prayed pasionately for Ernie's salvation, but above the howling din of the wind and waves his anguished entreaties remained unanswered.

Chapter 18: Sunk

"What on earth's the matter?" She had opened the door and found him standing there, his face ashen, except for the bloody graze on his forehead. "Tell me."

He found it impossible to speak.

"You're soaking. Come in. What's happened?"

"Ernie." He sought for words. "He went after Applebee in *The Gull*. He'd lost his outboard. He just disappeared. Just went. One minute he was there and the next he wasn't. Washed over the side."

She wrapped her arms round him and held him. He shook with fear and cold. "Why did he go after him in a sea like that? In a bloody rowing boat?" He spat the words out angrily. "How could he even think of it?"

"Ssh. Ssh." She rocked him from side to side as he clenched his jaw and fought back the tears.

"It was my boat. My bloody boat."

She kept silent while his body went into spasms of shock. "Have they found him?"

"No."

She tried to hold back her own tears. "And the boy?"

"Yes. Lifeboat picked up his body. They're still looking for Ernie."

For several minutes neither spoke until Amy said softly, "Let's get you out of those wet things."

She led him upstairs and took off his clothes as he stood and shivered. His hair was matted with brine and she towelled him dry, found him a pair of baggy canvas trousers, then slipped a T-shirt and a thick sweater over him

"I have to get back to May. Her sister's come over from St Petroc but I said I'd go back."

"How is she?"

"Frighteningly calm. She's going to stay with her sister tonight. Doesn't want to be on her own."

"Poor woman."

"Yes. I have to go." Will looked distracted.

"Will you come back?"

"Yes. No. I don't know. I have to go to the police station at St Petroc. I'm not sure when they'll finish with me. I don't know what I'll feel like . . . if I'll want to . . ."

"Whatever," she said, masking her disappointment. "I'm here if you want me."

He looked at her absently. "Thanks. I . . . I'm sorry." He walked to the door, turned back hesitantly, then left her.

"I'm sorry you've had to come in again so soon, sir. And under such circumstances." It was the same detective sergeant who had taken his statement after the fire.

"Yes." Will sat on the hard wooden chair, slumped forward with his elbows on his knees. He could not remember feeling so low since Ellie had died. He seemed to be tumbling into a deep pit of despair, free-falling into misery. Ernie. Friendly, understanding, generous Ernie. The nearest Will had come to having a father. Only yesterday the old man seemed to have come to terms with his new life; now the tourists wouldn't hear his patter. His hand shook and he held on to the edge of the table to steady it.

"Are you able to answer a few questions, sir?"

"Yes."

"Can we start by finding out how you came to be there when the accident happened?"

"I was in the boatyard – the Crooked Angel – talking to Gryler, the owner. He said his lad had been out during the afternoon in his boat, and that he hadn't come back. I was concerned. Decided to go up the cliff path and see if I could spot him."

"Why did you feel a need to do that?"

"Don't know. Just did. I suppose it's what comes of

watching boats all the time from the lighthouse. You get used to things not being quite right. Develop a sort of sixth sense. Can't really explain it any more than that."

"Did you know the lad?"

"Not really. I'd met him a couple of times but I wouldn't say I knew him."

"How did you know he was in trouble?"

"I didn't know, I just surmised."

"I see."

The detective sergeant made occasional jottings on an A4 notepad.

"Did you go on your own – on the cliff path, I mean?"

"No. I went with Mr Utterly. He has the boat next to mine in the yard."

"Yes. I've already spoken to him. He called the lifeboat out."

"Yes. I went to the lighthouse."

"Why was that, sir?"

"Again, I don't really know. Sixth sense."

"And what did you see?"

Will filled in the sergeant on the events he had watched with horror earlier that afternoon, of Christopher Applebee clinging to his boat, of Ernie's attempted rescue and of the wave that washed him overboard. He did not mention his own attempt to rescue his friend. The sergeant listened intently as Will told of the Sennen lifeboat's arrival, its combing the sea for the bodies, and the discovery only of Christopher Applebee.

"Popular man, Ernie Hallybone. Sad loss."

"Yes."

The detective sergeant got up from the desk and walked to the window, where the rain was running down the panes.

"Any idea why the lad was out there?"

"None at all. Unless he was after a few lobsters."

The sergeant turned round. "Or something else."

"Sorry?"

"Lobsters might gain him a few bob but I don't think he'd have gone out in this weather for a few bob, do you?"

"I suppose not."

"Seen any sign at your boatyard of booze?"

The sergeant's direct questioning threw Will off-balance. "Booze?"

"Yes. You know – whisky, gin, vodka. Rémy Martin."

He regained his equilibrium. "No. Not at all. None."

"Not in a shed? Or being offloaded from boats? In boxes? They probably wouldn't say Famous Grouse on the side. Bit obvious, that. But if they'd said Golden Wonder you'd have noticed if they'd looked suspiciously heavy?"

Will was taken aback by the note of irritation in the policeman's voice. "Yes. There's been nothing.

It's very quiet down there." Then the implication of the question hit home. "You don't think . . ."

"What, sir?"

"You don't think *I* had anything to do with this, do you?"

"At the moment, sir, I'm keeping an open mind."

Suddenly Will felt the weight of the world upon his shoulders. The sergeant read his reaction and offered a placatory smile. "Using my sixth sense, sir, you're not high on my list of suspects, but I have to ask the questions. I also have to try to get to the bottom of this."

Will tried to smile back, but found it impossible.

When he had given precise details and times, the sergeant was seemingly satisfied, and brought the interview to a close. "I think that's all I need to know for the present, sir. You can go now."

Will thanked him, for the second time in a week, and wondered if this was to become a regular occurrence. Until this week he'd only ever been in a police station once to report his grandmother's lost Jack Russell, and now here he was every few days.

He rose to go, and the sergeant coughed. "Er, sir?"

"Yes?"

"I'd be grateful if you could keep our conversation to yourself for now."

"Yes. Yes, of course."

"Especially as far as Mr Gryler is concerned."

The rain had petered out to a light drizzle, and the

wind was no more than a gusty breeze in the dark, wet night. He glanced at his watch. Just after ten. Where had the day gone? The agonizing, dreadful day. He unlocked the door of Ernie's van, slid on to the driver's seat and slammed the door. Ernie's peaked cap, its white top fresh-laundered for his new job, lay on the passenger seat. He picked it up and looked at the marks around the inside of the headband where years of sweat had stained the leather. He studied the badge and its legend, TRINITAS IN UNITATE. Three in one. He couldn't bring himself to smile, but he hoped in his heart that Ernie had gone somewhere where the Trinity House motto would be appropriate.

Amy sat up in case he came. Ten o'clock, then eleven, then midnight. She hoped he would want to be with her to share his sorrow. At twelve thirty she slid into bed, keeping one small lamp on just in case, and listening to music on the stereo to keep her awake, until finally came the song that touched her soul.

"You may wish that he would tell you all the feelings in his head, and say that life's worth living when you're there."

Tears ran down her cheeks and soaked into the pillow.

"But deep inside your heart you know, when lying in your bed, he can never ever know how much you care."

Chapter 19: Blacknore

He thought he had reached a point in life where sadness could no longer affect him as it once had. He had been so deeply sad for so long, had become so used to battling through it. But Ernie's death was so unfair. It was not just the sorrow of losing a friend and father figure, it was the injustice. First Ernie had lost his job. Then he'd been given another that he hated. But he had soldiered on, determined to make a go of it, seizing the opportunity to forge a future for himself. He had a wife who loved him and to whom he was devoted. He should have been heading for a retirement in which he could have enjoyed his beloved Cornwall. Instead, life had been snatched from him.

Will had taken himself back to *Boy Jack* on the night of Ernie's death; had felt that old black cloak of despair rising up to envelop him once more. Half of him wanted to go to Amy, but the other half was gritting its teeth and battening down the hatches with a vengeance. What was the point in risking yet another attachment? Better to be in control of his own destiny than risk handing it over.

He lay inside the boat, wrapped in his sleeping bag, cold and stiff, the cat curled into him for warmth. He hardly slept, listening to the wind.

The morning dawned, not unusually after a storm, with a sly calm, weak sunshine slanting in through the wheelhouse port-holes. He stirred from shallow sleep and lay still, the events of the previous day replaying in his mind.

Spike lay still, purring in the curve of his body. Will raised his head and looked out at the yard and the sea beyond. He saw, with the bitter taste of irony, a perfect May morning. The first day of May. May's first day alone.

Amy woke to find the bedside light still on. She switched it off and looked up at the skylight and the pale blue sky. She wondered why it was blue when it should be grey; the deep, dark, threatening Paine's grey of a watercolour palette.

She lay still and thought of him, hoping he would call in. She knew she could not seek him out, that she must wait. She gazed up at the deepening blue of the morning and realized for the first time just how much she loved him.

*

It was nine o'clock before Will could drag himself out of his cocoon and brave the day. He walked up on deck and shivered in the cool, clear morning air, drawing the sleeping-bag about his shoulders. Spike looked up at him; then tumbled down the ladder and ran away along the jetty. Will was about to head back inside when he saw a figure walking along the hard standing towards his boat. Hovis raised his hand and walked up to *Boy Jack*. He climbed the ladder. "Need anything?"

"No. Not really."

Hovis cleared his throat. "I'm going to make myself unpopular."

"Mmm?" Will was looking out to sea, his eyes unfocused.

"You're going to go and shower in Gryler's new, if makeshift, facility and then you're coming on to *Florence Nightingale* for breakfast."

"No, really, I'd rather be—"

"I know what you'd rather be, but that's not on."

Will kept looking at the sea.

"It's not your fault, you know."

Will spoke quietly. "It was my boat."

"It was his choice. He chose to go after that lad. You can't blame yourself."

"But I do." He looked at Hovis for the first time, and the despair in his eyes was plain. "Everything I touch turns to dust."

211

"You mustn't do this." Hovis used none of the bluff brightness that normally characterized his conversation. Instead he spoke calmly, firmly. "You mustn't be so hard on yourself."

"But it's my fault."

"No. It is not your fault." He laid his hand gently on Will's shoulder. "It is a most dreadful thing to happen, but you have to get over this. Do you hear?"

Will looked at him, pleadingly.

"Come on." Hovis eased the sleeping-bag from Will's shoulders and stowed it in the wheelhouse, before ushering him down the ladder and propelling him towards the newly positioned shower block beyond Gryler's office. He walked back to *Florence Nightingale* for a towel and flopped it over the top of the cubicle door as the steam rose and the hot water did its best to wash away the troubles of the previous day.

Will returned to *Florence Nightingale* as though in a trance, the towel over his shoulder. The smell of bacon and eggs went unnoticed as he sat down at the table.

Hovis pushed the plate in front of him, along with a large mug of black coffee. He sat down with his own plate at the other side of the table and began to eat, noticing that his fellow diner was letting his breakfast go cold. He tapped his knife on the side of Will's plate. The ringing sound brought him to earth. "Sorry?" He looked at Hovis as though he had missed part of the conversation.

"Eat."

"I don't think I–"

"Eat!"

Hovis tucked in himself and watched as Will began to toy with a scrap of bacon and then his egg. He ate reluctantly at first, then more avidly – he hadn't eaten a meal for almost twenty-four hours. He cleared his plate before Hovis had finished.

"Better?"

"Thanks." He tried to smile but his face still had a distracted, hunted look. He made to leave.

"Where are you going?" Hovis asked.

"Just back."

"Wait for a bit. Don't go yet. More coffee?" Hovis offered the pot.

"No, thanks."

He put it back on the stove. "Can I say something?"

"Mmm?"

"Don't go there."

Will looked at him. "Where?"

"Where you've been before."

"What do you mean?"

"Don't go into yourself. Not now. It's not worth it. A waste of time."

"How do you know?" Will was surprised and a touch irritated by Hovis's plain-speaking.

"Because I've been there." He began to clear the

table. "Just try and see ahead, not backwards. That's all."

"It's just that I thought—"

"You thought that at last things were going right for you. You had a glimpse of something special. Something real. Then suddenly you're back where you started." Hovis was filling the sink with water and looking out of the port-hole.

"How do you know?"

"Because I see things. Things that people don't think I see. You see boats coming and going, I see people. People's faces. People's hearts." He turned to face Will, a cup in one hand and a dripping cloth in the other. "Sometimes their souls."

The two men looked at one another for a few moments before Hovis spoke again, very softly. "Some things in your life you have no control over. It is quite pointless worrying over them. They are the way they are, and they will be the way they will be. Call it fate. Then there are the other things, the things that are yours to decide. And one of the strangest and saddest things in life is that some people cannot differentiate between the two. They spend all their time punishing themselves for things that have happened and which they can't change, and while they're busy doing that they fail to see life's opportunities." He smiled. "Don't miss out."

"On what?"

"Oh. I think you know."

*

The talk in the Salutation at lunchtime was of nothing but the previous day's events. Alf Penrose dispensed his pints with quiet circumspection and listened as the fishermen and other locals chewed the fat. Ted Whistler, perched on a stool at the end of the bar, stared blackly into his glass.

Gryler had been carted off to the police station the night before and had not, as yet, returned. Speculation grew until, at half past twelve, the door swung open and he bowled in, his face like thunder.

"Usual?" Alf Penrose enquired.

"Usual," he growled.

The bar, exuding a low rumble before Gryler's appearance, was hushed as Alf pulled the pump. The beer gushed into the glass and the slooshing sound echoed in the silence.

Gryler looked around. "You needn't look so surprised." The customers studied their feet. "They didn't keep me in."

Alf broke the ice. "What happened then?"

"Asked me about the lad and his boat."

"Oh, aye? So what do they think?"

"The lad was out pulling up his lobster pots. Outboard packed in and he hadn't taken any oars. Storm blew up and he got thrown out. Drownded."

"Didn't he have any flares?" asked one of the three fishermen at the end of the bar.

"No. Daft sod. No flares. No oars. Shouldn't have

215

been out in that weather." Gryler took a sip of his beer. "Bloody lighthouse-keeper, neither. Bloody waste."

Ted Whistler pushed his stool noisily away from the bar, crossed the room and walked out.

"Taken it hard, has he?" asked Gryler, eyes on the disappearing figure.

"Must have done. Hasn't said a word. Hasn't even finished his pint." Alf gestured towards the half-full glass on the bar. "What happens now?"

"Dunno. Nothing, I suppose," said Gryler, taking another pull on his pint. "Misadventure, they'll call it. Misadbloodyventure."

One of the fishermen shot a look at Alf Penrose and Gryler caught his eye. "I'm telling you, it were nothing to do with me. I didn't even service the engine – he did it himself. I might have been his boss but I weren't his keeper. 'Ad a life of his own, you know." He registered the suspicion on the faces of those still at the bar. "Ah, bugger it. I've got work to do. On me own now, too." He slammed his glass down on the bar and stormed out, all eyes on him as he went.

Amy had not expected him so soon. She had steeled herself for a wait of a few days. Instead she looked up from her painting and saw him in the middle of the afternoon. She got up from her easel and walked over to where he stood. "Hi."

He put his arms around her, and kissed the top of her head. "I'm sorry. About yesterday."

She eased away from him and put her finger up to his lips. "Don't. No need."

"But there is—"

"Sssh . . . no." They stood, their arms around each other, gently swaying from side to side.

"I just felt so . . ."

"I didn't expect you. I knew you'd want to be on your own. It's OK, really it is."

"I just . . ."

"Just hold me, will you?"

He bent his head into her shoulder and sighed a long, deep sigh.

The door opened. "Anybody at home?"

The two sprang apart as Jerry MacDermott and his wife burst into the gallery.

"Oh. Sorry, squire. Didn't see you there. Didn't realize you were . . ."

Amy spoke first. "It's fine. Can I help you?"

"Well, me and the missus – don't want to interrupt or anything, but we've just come to look for something for the 'ouse. Sorry to 'ear what 'appened, though." He spoke to Will. "Sorry about the old man. Terrible thing, the sea. Very sad. Knew 'im well, did you?"

"Yes. I used to work with him."

"What would you like to see?" Amy tried to change the subject.

"You 'ad a couple of sculptures. They were 'ere . . ." He gestured to the middle of the floor. "Sold, are they?"

"Er . . . no. I just put them in the back room."

"Could you get them out again? I'd like Trudie to see them. She didn't notice them last time."

The blonde, clad in a bright pink sweatshirt, white leggings and stilettos, had been simpering on Jerry's arm. "Jerry says they're awfully sexy." She giggled.

Amy stood transfixed by the suntanned vision in pink and white. She looked like a slice of Neapolitan ice cream.

"Yes. I'll get them out." She turned to Will. "Can you give me a hand?"

"Sure."

The two writhing figures were brought out and stripped of their blankets so that Trudie and her squire could behold them in all their glory.

"Ooooh!" she half cooed, half giggled. "What do you suppose they're doing?"

"I dunno, love, but they seem to be enjoying it."

Amy looked abashed as Trudie MacDermott continued her eulogy. "Ooh! 'E's big, inne? Looks a bit like, you know, wassisname . . . That one we saw in Florence, Michelangelo's David."

"Well, sweetheart, if that's David, I'd like to see Goliath." Jerry guffawed at his own joke. "What do you think, then?"

"I think they're lovely," responded the blonde.

"Can we have them?"

"Course we can," replied her spouse, patting her bottom. And then, to Amy, "Can we take them with us?"

"Yes. Of course. If you're sure you can manage."

"Yes. We can, can't we, love?"

"Let me help." Will came forward and took the sack barrow towards the first of the sculptures. He put the blanket over it, not just for protection, eased it on to the wheeled trolley, and pushed it towards the door.

"Now then," said Jerry. "Five 'undred apiece, wasn't it?"

"Well . . ." She wondered whether she should offer a discount for bulk-buying but Jerry took a large wad of notes from his back pocket and peeled off twenty fifty-pound notes. He pressed them into her hand with rather more pressure than was necessary.

"Thank you. Thank you very much." Amy did her best to sound polite but not too grateful.

Will bumped down the steps of the studio with the trolley, one hand on the first sculpture to prevent it taking a nose-dive down the steps. He repeated the exercise with the second, and the two were loaded on to the back seat of the MacDermott Mercedes then driven off up the lane in the direction of Benbecula.

Amy and Will stood on the steps watching the car climb the hill.

"I really didn't expect that," said Amy.

"Why?"

"I don't know. I'd just given up hope of ever getting them out of my life."

"Well, you have. They've gone."

As the Mercedes purred around the corner and out of sight, she looked up at him, tired and pale against the blue sky. "Time to start again."

He smiled at her and nodded. "Yes." He sighed, gazing out over the calm blue-green water.

Amy only wished that she had not received Oliver's letter.

Chapter 20: Skerries

Mrs Sparrow had done her best to be pleasant about Mr Elliott's departure. As she explained to Primrose Hankey, he had not been home the night before the storm and she had sat up for a while, wondering if something had happened. The following day she would have dropped into the conversation a few pointed remarks about his absence, had it not been for the tragic events that put matters into perspective. She related these facts to Primrose when making her call for groceries, the bits and bobs she had run out of before her monthly shop at Tesco's in Penzance.

Primrose's pique at Mrs Sparrow's shopping habits was put to one side as she listened attentively. Even though Will Elliott had stayed with Mrs Sparrow for two weeks, the information Primrose had gleaned had been minimal. Now, with the death of Ernie

Hallybone casting a pall over the entire village, it was a relief to have something more spicy.

But Mrs Sparrow had few details – either that or she was keeping them strictly to herself – and the conversation turned, inevitably, to Ernie's funeral the previous day.

"A good way to go," Mrs Sparrow opined.

"What – drowning?" asked Primrose.

"No. With that sort of funeral. Uniforms and whatnot. Very smart. Gave it a sense of occasion." Mrs Sparrow added a packet of Bourbon biscuits to her pile.

"Mrs Hallybone looked tired," said Primrose.

"Worried, I suppose. What with the body being washed up three days later it must have taken it out of her. All that not knowing for certain. She'll have to find somewhere to live now." Mrs Sparrow sorted through the pickle jars and plumped for a bottle of Mrs Pengelly's lurid brew.

Primrose tried another gambit. "Miss Finn looked nice. She didn't sit with Mr Elliott, though."

"Why should she?"

Primrose decided that she was evidently in possession of more information than Mrs Sparrow. But, then, Mrs Sparrow was not the sort to trade in gossip; she merely handed out opinions. "Nice hymns. 'Eternal Father Strong to Save'. Even if it was a bit late. And 'I Vow to Thee My Country'. Good choice. Important, like."

Primrose put aside her newsmongering and re-called her feelings at the funeral. "I was all right," she said, "until they carried him out – Mr Elliott and the other keepers. That's when it was all too much for me. Seeing their faces. Their caps under their arms. Mr Hallybone's cap on top of his coffin." She put her hand into her tracksuit pocket, pulled out a man's handkerchief and blew hard.

"The lad's funeral was in Penzance, apparently. Family affair. Quiet."

"Well, at least Mr Hallybone had a good turn-out."

"Majestic," said Mrs Sparrow, reflectively. "My Arthur would've liked that, instead of just a service at the crematorium. It's not the same. I think a burial's preferable."

"Yes. Nicer, really. And they've put him in St Petroc churchyard where he can see the sea." She realized what she had said, and blew her nose again.

Mrs Sparrow asked for her goods to be totalled up. Primrose patted each item, her lips moving in time with her mental arithmetic. "Seven pounds seventy-five, please. So Mr Elliott's back living on his boat now, is he?" She delved in the till for change to Mrs Sparrow's ten-pound note.

"There or somewhere else. He left the day after the accident. Didn't say much. Just thank you. A bit quiet. Understandable, I suppose."

"Yes."

"Still, he was no bother. Apart from the one night.

And it'll soon be the start of the season. Only a few weeks to the May bank holiday."

"Yes." Primrose was lost in thought as Mrs Sparrow left, the bell on the door pinging behind her.

Will watched as *Boy Jack* swung out over the water. He was pleased with his brushwork; the newly painted white hull reflected the ripples below, although it was a dull day.

"All clear?" Gryler's voice asked, from the seat of the boat lift.

"I think so. Go ahead slowly." Will watched as the boat descended, the keel touched the water and the propellers disappeared from view.

Amy and Hovis observed from the safety of the jetty as the Dunkirk veteran took to the water once more, settling evenly as the massive straps of webbing slackened and she found her own equilibrium.

Gryler jumped down, extracted the straps, then drove the lift back along the concrete hard to its usual parking place.

Will watched him go, trying hard to control his feelings. He had no proof that Gryler had had anything to do with Ernie's death, or even Christopher Applebee's. Nobody had. It was all speculation. He tied off the boat alongside the jetty as Hovis and Amy approached.

"Round of applause and a bottle of champagne, I should think," suggested Hovis.

"Thought we'd celebrate on board tonight," said Will. "Time I repaid the compliment. Dinner at eight?"

"Sure?" asked Hovis, sensitive to his neighbour's feelings.

"Sure." Will winked at Amy. "Can you come round at about seven?"

"Love to."

"What about getting this old girl back to the pontoon?" asked Hovis.

"Gryler's going to tow me over with his dinghy. I've a few checks to make on the engines yet, but with any luck we should be able to try her out in a day or two. See how she runs."

"All very exciting," said Amy. "Anyway, it's all right for you two, but I've a studio to open. See you both later." She blew Will a kiss. He watched her walk along the jetty, and found it difficult to turn away.

They had not slept together since Ernie's death. Will had expected her to be hurt, but instead had been heartened by her understanding. Amy, determined to do the right thing, had given him space. They saw one another every day at some point – either Will would call in at the studio for coffee or a meal, or Amy would nip down to the boat.

She surprised herself with her own willingness to wait. Normally she would have given up by now, grown tired of being messed about. But she knew he was not oblivious to her feelings, that he was trying hard to rebuild his life. Letting him down was not an option. She had never felt this way about anyone. Yes, she had been in love before. And she was in love with Will – she could admit this to herself now, if not to him. But it ran deeper than that. She *cared* about him too. It was unnerving yet comforting. In his company she felt complete. Without him she felt more alone than she could ever remember feeling before. She would wait. And hope.

She had watched him at the funeral. He had looked so desperate. She could not take her eyes off him as he helped carry Ernie's body from the church. At the graveside he had stood beside her and slipped his arm through hers. She looked up at him. He had seemed taller somehow in his uniform, his eyes that piercing pale blue, the muscles in his jaw expanding and contracting as he fought to control himself. His hair had been cut. He looked older, weary.

That night he came back to the studio for supper and told her about the interviews at the police station. He thought it better that she knew, even though she might worry. She felt elated at his willingness to share it with her, but made no fuss, just sat calmly and listened as he told her about the police suspicions of illicit alcohol and Gryler's possible involvement.

They had parted after midnight. He had kissed her lips and held her for a long while, his cap under his arm like a polite serviceman going off to war.

So much had been spoken, but so much remained unsaid. Somehow it didn't seem to matter. She knew that he was mending, that she had to be patient.

At seven o'clock on the dot she left the studio, a cool-bag clutched in her arms.

He heard her approaching footsteps on the pontoon and jumped down from the deck of *Boy Jack* to greet her. "Just a minute. Don't come any further." He held up his hand like a traffic policeman. "It's here somewhere." He located an old wooden beer crate on the foredeck and picked it up. It was heavier than he had expected. Then Spike hopped out of it and stalked off across the deck with-out a backward glance. Will placed the crate in front of the gangway.

Amy's eyes followed the cat. "I don't think he likes me."

"Jealous, that's all. Never been keen on company." He checked that the crate was stable. "There we are, madam. Ready to be piped aboard!" He took the cool-bag from her and helped her climb on to the deck. She wore white jeans, deck shoes and a T-shirt that almost matched her hair. "You look stunning," he said softly.

"Don't drop that! There's something in it to christen your boat."

He came back to earth. "Sorry! It's just that you're so beautiful."

She stood on tiptoe to kiss him. "I'm glad! Do I get to see round this vessel, then?"

"Lucky timing. The evening tour is about to commence." He held out his arm, directing her into the wheelhouse, and she walked down the two newly varnished steps.

"Wow! I had no idea! So this is what you've been doing!" Amy gazed at the immaculate woodwork. "But you've had less than a month. How did you get it like this?"

"I didn't sleep much."

"I can believe that." She was amazed at the transformation. She'd only seen the outside of the boat before, but the condition of the interior had been obvious from the state of the carpets and curtains she had seen hauled away and dumped. She had feared it would never be fit for human habitation. Now the varnish on the deep mahogany timber gleamed, a new brass bell engraved 'Boy Jack' shone, and the wheelhouse smelt of polish and paint. There were no curtains as yet, but the wooden floor sported an Indian rug and the table-top shone like a mirror.

The propane cylinder and burner had been replaced with a small stove fitted among wooden worktops to one side of the wheelhouse; from the oven came an appetising aroma. A brass oil lamp dangled from the wood-panelled ceiling and another stood on the table. Every catch and knob, every hinge and bracket had been buffed to within an inch of its life.

She turned to look for'ard and saw the mahogany wheel with its brass cap, and the glittering instruments surrounding it. Positioned centrally among them was fixed a brass plate bearing the legend 'Dunkirk 1940'. She turned towards him, her eyes glistening. "You've worked so hard. Walter Etchingham would be proud of you."

"Oh, there's a lot to do yet, but at least now you can see that it'll look good when it's finished. Old Mr Etchingham looked after her well. She's as sound as a bell, really. She must just have been neglected after he died. Most of the work we've done has been cosmetic."

"What's left to do?"

"Oh, there's still a bit of rigging to sort out, the masts to varnish, anchor winch to repair, curtains to find, navigation equipment to put in. I'd like a fixed GPS but I'll have to settle for a cheaper hand-held one. Still, I think I can run to an autopilot."

"I thought it would be you doing the steering."

"Not all the time."

"You mean it can steer itself?"

"On a straight course, yes. And if it's a long passage I won't want to be stuck to the wheel the whole time."

"But if you're not looking where you're going you could hit something."

"Oh, I won't just go to my cabin and forget it. Not unless I decide to cross the Atlantic."

"No." Suddenly she remembered what the boat was for. It was the means by which he would leave her. She felt chilled.

He noticed her change of mood. "What's the matter?"

"Nothing. Just looking at the front bit."

He put a hand on her arm. "What's the matter?"

"I was just thinking."

"About what?"

"About you going away."

He said nothing at first; just turned her round to face him. She avoided his gaze.

"Look at me."

She stared at the floor, then at the wooden panelling to one side.

"Look at me." He said the words softly but insistently. She raised her eyes to meet his. "I'm here now. Don't think too far ahead. Please."

"I can't help it."

"I know. But try not to." He paused and stroked her cheek. "I'm trying not to."

"Are you?" She looked at him questioningly.

"I've got something else to show you." He took her hand and pulled her towards the hatch that led to the aft cabin. He bent down and flicked a switch. Two small brass lanterns, one to port the other to starboard, illuminated the previously dim interior.

"Oh!" She caught her breath.

The cabin, like the wheelhouse, was lined with

mahogany, and most of the space was taken up with a large double bed, covered in a deep red quilt with fat pillows propped up against the bulkhead at the aftermost end. In one corner the door of the bathroom stood open, revealing the marble basin and the now pristine hip bath. The old Blake's head had been restored, and while the effect was not quite up to Dorchester standards it had, on a miniature scale, undeniable charm.

He bent down and kissed her, wrapped his arms around her, then let one hand slide down to stroke her bottom. Then he pushed a stray wisp of hair from her cheek. "Shall we cook? We've company coming."

She nodded and he looked at her intently, then grinned and pushed her up the steps into the wheelhouse, trying hard to reconcile within himself the conflicting feelings of love and the anticipation of his impending expedition. What had Hovis said? "Some things in life you have no control over. Other things are yours to decide." He remembered the words that had followed. "And one of the strangest and saddest things in life is that some people cannot differentiate between the two."

They worked together, she topping and tailing beans and scrubbing Jersey Royals, he dressing a crab for starters. His hands worked deftly at the claws and she saw the muscles in his forearms flexing. Feeling her eyes on him, Will looked up. "Glass of wine?"

"Yes, please."

He ran his hands under the tap and dried them on a towel before heading to the aft cabin.

"Where are you going?" she asked.

"For the wine. I keep it in a locker below the water-line. It stays cool that way."

"No need. Have you forgotten?" She gestured towards the cool-bag sitting at one end of the worktop. He came back up, unzipped the top flap, plunged his hand in and withdrew the first of three bottles.

"Oh! What have you done?"

"I don't know what you mean." She began to scrub again at the potatoes.

"Bollinger!"

"I should hope so. This is a class boat – or so you tell me."

He kissed the back of her neck, and pulled three glasses out of a cupboard at one end of the galley.

"Shouldn't we break it over the bows or something? That's what the Queen does."

"Not on my boat she doesn't."

"Spoilsport."

"For a start it would ruin my paintwork, and as it's Bollinger it would be a criminal waste of champagne."

"Well, you'll have to give her a glassful, then." The voice came from outside. It was eight o'clock and Hovis had arrived punctually, which Will lost no time in pointing out to him.

"Not much traffic on the pontoon tonight. No hold ups at all. Normally get stuck among all those commuters on pontoon number two at bank holidays but those delights are a few weeks away yet."

"Don't remind me. How busy *does* it get here on bank holidays?"

"Oh, not terribly. Bit more bustle on the jetty, and the day-boaters turn up to dust off the cobwebs and hose off the gull-shit – oh, sorry, muck." He grinned apologetically at Amy, who laughed.

"You're just in time for a glass, Hovis." She greeted him with a kiss.

"Oh, I say. Things are looking up."

Will handed round tumblers that were more used to plain water than bubbly, popped the cork and let the golden liquid fizz into them. "Ladies and gentlemen," he said, struggling to keep any trace of emotion out of his voice, "I'd like you to drink a toast to two ladies."

"Hear, hear!" said Hovis, then, "Sorry. Jumping the gun." He looked sideways at Amy and raised his eyebrows. She giggled.

"Two ladies who mean a lot to me." Amy blushed. "One is sixty-eight years old, and the other–"

"Steady!" cautioned Amy.

"–isn't. But I wouldn't have survived the past few weeks without either of them." He looked pointedly at Amy and raised his glass. "Neither would I have managed without a certain gentleman, but we'll let his identity pass."

"Best thing," agreed Hovis.

Amy raised her glass. "Here's to *Boy Jack*. God bless her and all who sail in her."

The men repeated the toast and all three sipped their champagne, gasping with pleasure as the bubbles hit the back of their throats.

"Come on, then," urged Hovis. "Let's wet the old girl's bottom."

They climbed the wheelhouse steps to the deck, then stepped down over the beer crate on to the pontoon where Will hurled what remained in his glass over the bows of *Boy Jack*. He stepped back and looked at her, no longer an apologetic hulk but a graceful lady reclining on the rippling water that sent a mosaic of reflections dancing up her clean white hull. Graceful. He saw now that she had deserved her original name. He reached out his hand to grasp Amy's and squeezed. She returned his gesture with a flickering smile.

"God bless all who sail in her," he whispered, so that only she could hear.

The meal was as great a success as the one on Hovis's boat, and the conversation even more relaxed. They knew each other now, had been through things together. Appreciative noises were made over the crab; the duck with orange was cooked to perfection, but Hovis reckoned, with a wink in Amy's direction, that the vegetables were better than anything else.

Chablis followed the Bollinger, and Amy lay back against Will on the long bench seat. Over coffee the conversation became reflective. Nobody intended it to be sad, but Ernie's name could not be avoided. Will was determined not to be morose, and instead regaled them with stories of his early days at the lighthouse, and Ernie's generosity during that tough time so soon after Ellie's death. Then they returned to the present. To the fact that Evan Williams, Prince Albert Rock's second principal lighthouse keeper, had agreed to act as temporary custodian until a permanent replacement could be found. Hovis was reminded of young Applebee: he could not understand the boy's stupidity in being out in the storm.

Will explained what had happened at the police station.

Hovis was astounded. "You reckon Gryler's running a booze racket?"

"I don't know. The police told me not to mention it. Certainly not to Gryler."

"No. Certainly not. Oh, no!"

"I wonder if we'll ever find out any more," mused Amy.

"I don't know," said Will. "Maybe not. The police are on to it now, but I can't help being curious."

"Best to leave things alone," said Hovis sharply.

"That's what Ernie said," replied Will, ruefully.

"They've had Gryler in," added Hovis. "Questioned him all night, apparently."

"Let him go, though."

"Maybe they're watching him."

"Ooh! Makes you shudder," said Amy, nestling closer to Will.

"Anyway. Never mind all that. Who's for a spin around the Cove tomorrow?" offered Will brightly.

"What?" Amy pulled away a little.

"Tomorrow morning. Maiden voyage, I think. Weather looks fair. Tides are right. Engines are raring to go. Won't travel far. Just see how she feels in the water."

"But what about the studio?"

"Close it. We'll only be a couple of hours."

She looked at him squarely. "All right, then, I will. You're on. Hovis, what about you?"

"I think you two should do that on your own." Hovis eased out of his seat. "Make it special."

"Oh, come with us," pleaded Amy. "You've watched all the work being done."

"No. Not this time. This is your treat. I'll wave you off. I'll even dress overall if you want."

"What?" asked Amy.

"Dress overall. Put all me flags out. Look like a regatta."

"Don't you dare," said Will. "I want to slip out quietly, not with a fanfare of trumpets."

"If you insist. But I'll give you a push off and I'll be here to catch your line when you come back."

"That would be helpful."

"That's sorted, then. And now I must be off. I know I got here punctually, so I'll leave punctually. Stroke of eleven. Not bad. Oh, and that reminds me. Hang on a minute." He slid open the door and dived from view, returning half a minute later with a small wooden box. "For you. A boat-warming present. Bit of a cheek, really. It's broken but I thought you wouldn't mind, if you see what I mean."

Will took the brass-bound mahogany box, which was about six inches square. He knew precisely what it contained. "Hovis, I can't take this."

"Of course you can. I told you, it's broken, of no use to me. But I know you'll be able to fix it."

Will pressed the round brass button and lifted the lid to reveal the marine chronometer under its protective pane of glass. "I don't know what to say."

"Well, don't say anything. Just enjoy fixing it." And with a smile Hovis left.

Amy put her arms around Will's waist and looked with him at the clock face. "Charles Shepherd – Makers to the Royal Navy" was engraved in elaborate script across it. On the front of the box was a small ivory panel bearing the number 1205. "It's beautiful."

"Isn't it? What a man." He put the clock on the table and turned to her. "I wondered if you – would you . . ."

"Mmmm?"

"Would you stay the night? Here. On the boat."

She smiled. "I've no toothbrush."

"We carry a spare."

He pulled the wheelhouse hatch closed and picked up the brass oil lamp that had provided them with light to dine. He led her down to the aft cabin where the rosy glow of the mahogany panelling seemed warmer still by the lamplight. He slid the cabin door shut, put down the lamp on the bedside locker and turned to kiss her. She stepped back from him and began to peel off her clothes, looking at him all the while. He watched her entranced: the light caught the soft curves of her body and turned her hair to fire. Naked now she stood in front of him, her arms by her sides, quite still. Then she moved to the bed and slid under the quilt, never taking her eyes off him.

He watched her as she lay there, then undressed, gazing at her, until he, too, stood naked in the lamplight. He could hear the silence ringing in his ears and feel the passion rising deep inside.

"You're so beautiful," she whispered.

He walked to the bed, pulled back the quilt and looked at her for a moment before sliding in beside her and feeling the soft warmth of her body.

Spike was curled up inside the beer crate. Tonight he would sleep outdoors.

Chapter 21: Round Island

Amy woke first. She propped herself on one elbow and looked at him lying next to her in the bed. His dark curls shone in the early-morning sun that slanted through the port-hole. She listened to his slow, regular breathing. He was peaceful now, no creases on his brow, no troubled expression. Just a sleeping boy.

She realised how familiar she had become with his body. She knew each blemish, each mole, and the precise position of the darker flecks on the pale blue irises of his eyes.

His right arm rested on top of the quilt. She looked with the eye of an artist at the sculpted, lean biceps, the powerful forearms, the craftsman's hands – a combination of strength and sensitivity. She looked at his right hand; at the veins standing up beneath the weatherbeaten skin, the relaxed fingers. The callouses born of boat repairing could not disguise the delicate touch needed for mending a clock or making a model boat. There were scratches and grazes where the skin had been damaged, and paint ingrained where it had escaped the scrubbing brush and the soap. The short nails were chipped and battered, the cuticles irregular. How she loved his hands.

She reached out to touch his fingers and his eyes slowly opened. He looked at her, then reached up to cup her chin.

"Hallo."

"Hallo, you." She eased her body closer to him.

"I've been thinking," he said.

"No, you haven't, you've been sleeping."

"Yes, but when I was sleeping I was thinking."

She smiled at him. "Go on."

"You've only got a pair of white jeans. You're going to get a bit mucky crewing a boat in those."

"Is that the sort of thought that goes through your mind when you're lying naked next to me?"

"I'm only being considerate."

"I worry about you." She dug him in the ribs with her index finger and he jumped, then put his arms around her and squeezed her, nuzzling into her neck.

"What time is it?"

She looked at her watch on the bedside locker. "Half past seven."

He sat up and looked out of the port-hole. "And it's a lovely day. No wind. Sun on the water. Brilliant. Time we were up if we're to catch the tide."

She frowned at him. "Which tide?"

"We need to leave about an hour before high water if we want to avoid battling against heavy currents. That way we can get in and out without having to fight the tide."

"I see. I'm not sure I'll ever understand it. All those nautical terms and all those bits of rope – sheets and warps and shrouds and stuff."

"Don't worry about it." He bent over to kiss her nose. "The most important thing is still to feel the thrill of the water underneath you. Hang on to the enjoyment. Some sailors are so busy being technically correct in their terminology and their practices, and worrying about what might happen, that they forget to have a good time while they're doing it. Cowper said something like that."

"The poet?"

"No. The sailor. Frank Cowper. Wrote a series of books called *Sailing Tours* in the late nineteenth century. I lost them in the fire. He said, 'A boating book should be written by a man who has bumped ashore and afterwards has found the way to the proper channel. Such a man learns where the dangers lie.'"

"Sounds a bit irresponsible to me."

"He wasn't suggesting foolhardiness, just that

instead of taking notice of somebody else's wagging finger you rely on common sense and observation."

"Sums you up, really, doesn't it? Common sense and observation."

"Listen to me going on. Here I am stark naked next to a beautiful woman and talking about boats."

"Well, you could make it up to me."

"We'll miss the tide."

"Oh, bugger the tide. Let's just bump ashore."

"Have you opened the sea cocks?"

"Yes."

"Turned on the batteries?"

"Yes."

"Checked over the engines?"

"Yes."

"Go on, then, start her up." Hovis was standing on the pontoon. Will was at the helm inside the wheelhouse door. Amy crouched down on the foredeck, ready to catch the lines as instructed. She tightened the belt on an old pair of Will's jeans and pulled up the sleeves of the baggy fisherman's jersey beneath her lifejacket.

"Here goes, then." He turned the key of the port engine and the warning buzzer sounded. He pushed the port throttle forwards for about a third of its capacity and pressed the starter. The old Perkins engine turned over a few times then rumbled into life. He waited for the rev-counter to spring up to 500 revs, then repeated the process on the starboard engine. It refused to fire. He glanced at Hovis and tried again. Nothing.

"Once more. She's had a long rest," said Hovis encouragingly.

Will pressed the starter button a third time, giving just a little more throttle, and the engine growled into action, the rev-counter springing up to 700 revs.

Will looked at the dials in front of him. Water temperature low, as yet not warmed up. Oil pressure fine. Batteries fine. Rudder indicator amidships. He pulled the throttle levers to their lowest position, then stepped out of the wheelhouse and on to the deck.

"I think I'll just let her warm up for a minute or two."

"Good idea," said Hovis. "Everything else all right?"

"Seems to be. Have we got water coming out of the back?"

Hovis walked aft and confirmed that the engine-cooling system was working – regular squirts of water were slopping out of the exhaust pipes just above the water line. Will turned to Amy. "You OK?"

"Fine. Noisy, isn't it?"

"Should be better at sea."

"No, I like it. It's sort of comforting. Like a big cat purring."

"Talking of cats, where is he?"

Hovis pointed to a coil of rope on the foredeck of *Florence Nightingale*. Seated in the middle of it was Spike, ears up, eyes wide as he inspected the throbbing vessel that was his home.

"Oh dear. I think we might have upset him." The cat continued to watch their progress with detached interest from the comfort of the neighbouring vessel. Will walked around the deck of *Boy Jack* checking that the fenders were in position and that the mooring warps were secure.

"OK. This is it."

"Haven't you forgotten something?" asked Hovis.

Will frowned. "What?"

"Auntie Betty." Hovis pointed astern. "Bad form."

Will laughed, stepped into the wheelhouse, and returned with the red ensign wrapped around its newly varnished flagstaff. He unrolled it as he walked astern, and slotted it into the brass holder above the transom. Then he walked to the bows and picked up another, smaller flagstaff that had been lying on the deck. He slotted it into the jack-staff holder on the pulpit and unwound the smaller flag of St George, with its central shield – the emblem of the Association of Dunkirk Little Ships.

"Better?"

"Much better!"

"Daft bugger!"

"Well, there are standards to maintain. Mind you, your ensign will be better when it's faded a bit."

"Don't start!" He wagged an admonitory finger at Hovis. "Are we ready, then?"

"I can think of no further reason to detain you."

"OK. Cast off."

Hovis undid the two springs and threw them to Amy. She caught them both, then the head line, and finally the stern line.

"Can you coil them?" Will shouted at her.

"How?"

"Just tidy them up so you don't fall over them."

He moved the two throttles forward, relying on the paddle-wheel effect of the propellers to push him sideways from the pontoon, then eased them off to slow their forward progress to a minimum. Hovis leaned on the hull of *Boy Jack* to reinforce the movement. The boat swung slowly outwards, the bows creeping into the water slightly ahead of the stern.

"Lovely!" said Hovis, encouragingly.

Suddenly Will saw a flash of black and white. He looked up, wondering what had fallen from the mast.

Hovis pointed to the sharp end of the boat. There, seated in front of the Samson post, was Spike, like some feline figurehead.

"It looks as though he's coming, then!" cried Amy.

"I just hope he doesn't fall overboard. I haven't got a lifejacket for a cat."

Will eased the port engine into forward gear, keeping his helm amidships, and as they cleared the

245

pontoon to head towards the entrance of the boatyard he switched between the engines, using them, rather than the wheel, to steer the boat out into the cove.

"*Bon voyage!*" Hovis waved them off, and they cruised slowly past the other boats – Jerry McDermott's *Sokai*, gleaming like a newly scrubbed bathtub in the morning light, a couple of guano-spattered day-boats and Gryler's replacement for PZ 291, another redundant fishing boat.

The sea hove into view as they rounded the corner of the jetty, and they chugged out into the cove at a steady five knots. Now Will realized how it felt to have your own boat. He stood at the wheel, passing it slowly from hand to hand, remembering not to "take great fistfuls of it" as his instructor had taught him three years ago. The butterflies remained in his stomach, but he had a sense of freedom.

Small wavelets broke against the bows as *Boy Jack* slid through the water, and the sound of the engines was indeed, as Amy had suggested, comforting, now that they were clear of the harbour walls. He pointed his boat westwards, towards Bill's Island, the only thing in view on the calm, glittering sea.

"This weather is just unbelievable. It's as if it knew she was going out for the first time today. Sort of welcoming her back," Will said.

He stuck his head through the wheelhouse door and felt the gentle breeze of their forward motion. He pulled at the hatch in the coach-roof and slid it back to let in the fresh air. The boatyard receded into the distance behind them. He looked at the fluttering ensign and the foaming white wash that fanned out behind them. "Do you want a go?" he asked.

"Can I?"

"Just hold her steady and aim for the island." She took the wheel from him and he stepped away to stow the ropes. In the event he didn't have to.

"What have you done?"

"What do you mean?" She sounded troubled.

"With the ropes?"

"You said to coil them so I did."

"But I didn't expect this!" They were neatly wound into flat spirals. "She looks like the *Victory*."

"I should hope so. You forget, I'm a painter. I notice things."

He leaned through the door and pecked her on the cheek. "I'm just going to stow the fenders. Back in a minute."

"No. I'll do it. I'm the crew. Where do you put them?" She motioned him to take back the wheel.

"In the lazarette."

"Sounds like someone out of the Bible. Give me a clue."

"There are two hatches on the afterdeck. If you lift them up you'll find a stowage area under them. It's called the lazarette. The fenders can go in there."

"Aye-aye, sir." She mock-saluted him and went about her duties.

They had been out for about an hour, and Amy had observed how relaxed he was. She had been prepared for him to shout at her, as that was what most men in charge of boats did, but he had simply asked her to do things clearly and firmly.

Will felt a sense of release and vindication: release because of his new-found ability to escape the land, and vindication in that *Boy Jack* handled like a dream. He patted the wheel as if it were a well-behaved dog, and put his arm round Amy as she stood beside him.

"Better be getting back, I suppose."

"Suppose so. Not that *he* seems bothered at all."

Spike had hardly moved since the voyage had begun. He had eased forward a few times and looked over at the bow wave, but decided against leaping down and chasing it. He had ignored his two shipmates, which was not unusual, explained Will.

Will looked ahead as they began to round Bill's Island. It rose up out of the sea like a giant hump-backed whale, its rocks alive with chattering gannets and guillemots, its grassy slopes dotted with sea pinks and yellow vetch. They watched as the sea splashed on its shores, where sandpipers and oystercatchers paddled and prodded for food.

"Who was Bill?" asked Amy.

"He was Prince Albert Rock's lighthouse keeper in the nineteenth century. Did a bit of a Grace Darling. Rescued a family in a storm. Just like Ernie." His voice lowered. "Except that he survived." He felt the keen sense of loss again. How different the sea was today. Like another country. He was brought to earth by a sudden grinding sound. The boat juddered and slowed dramatically. Amy was thrown against the bulkhead and cried out as she bumped her head. Will braced himself against the wheel and pulled the gear levers into neutral.

"Are you OK?" he asked.

"Fine. What happened?"

"I don't know." Will leapt out of the wheelhouse door as the cat scampered in, frightened by the noise and the unexpected jolt.

The boat rocked gently from side to side as the engines continued to tick over. Will walked astern.

"What is it?"

"Something round one of the propellers, I think. Or both of them. I bet it's a bloody lobster pot. Damn. I should have been looking."

"Sorry." She felt guilty at having distracted him.

"Not your fault."

He leaned over the transom and looked down into the water. "Bugger." He could see it now: a lump of rope floating in the water with a dark grey plastic container at the end. The sort of cheap float fishermen used to mark their lobster pots.

"If they used proper fluorescent ones they'd be easier to pick out from a distance. Look at that. Bloody dark grey and half submerged. Nobody's going to spot that until they're on top of it. Shit!"

"Can you untangle it?"

"I'll have a try, but I bet it's bloody cold in there."

"Can't we just fish it out with a boathook?"

"No. It'll be wrapped round the propeller. I've got a diving mask. I'll jump over and hang on to the side and see if I can do it from there."

He stepped into the wheelhouse and turned off the engines. They were both aware of the silence, broken only by the gentle lapping of waves on the hull and the distant cries of seabirds on Bill's Island.

The sky was pale blue streaked with wisps of cloud. Amy suddenly felt the urge to reach for her paints. She watched him slip over the side clad in a pair of shorts and a face mask. He held on to a knotted rope secured to a stanchion and lowered himself over the transom. He came up several times, then at last raised his hand above the surface triumphantly with a coil of battered rope.

He scrambled aboard, tied the rope to a cleat and pulled off the mask, panting for breath. She looked at his body, running with rivulets of seawater and spattered with kelp. His chest heaved as he took in massive gulps of air.

"Not wound round too far – only one propeller . . . The other's OK." He bent double, his head between his knees, and she laid her hand on his back.

He raised his head, flinging water from his black curls, and smiled at her.

She gazed at him, her eyes speaking volumes.

He looked down at her in her oversized jeans, rolled up above her bare feet, at her body encased in the baggy sweater and the lifejacket, and at her hair tied back from her face. He wound his arms round her, dripping water over her clothes.

"I'm getting awfully wet," she said softly.

He eased away from her, grinning. "Shall we see if there's a lobster for our trouble?"

"Are we allowed to?"

"It's damn near taken off our propeller and it isn't properly marked. I think the least it owes us is a decent supper."

He untied the rope from its cleat and between them they hauled up the pot. But it did not contain a lobster. It contained a plastic food container, sealed in a polythene bag.

Chapter 22:
Trinitas In Unitate

"What is it?"

"I don't know. Pass me the knife."

Amy handed him the one that was kept in a sheath by the helm, and he cut away the polythene to expose the plastic food container, which was sealed with waterproof tape. He ran the knife round the seal and lifted the lid to discover several plastic bags filled with white powder.

Amy was the first to speak. "Oh, my God!"

Will looked up at her face, from which the colour had drained.

"Don't ask me how I know this," she said, "but it looks to me like heroin."

Will swore. Then he said, "The lowest drawer in

the chest to one side of the helm – there's some waterproof tape in it."

Amy disappeared into the wheelhouse and returned with it. Will resealed the plastic box, shivering as the breeze brought up goosebumps on his wet skin. Then he replaced the container in the lobster pot and lowered it back over the side, allowing the dark grey float to bob away from them on the water.

He stepped into the wheelhouse and returned with a nautical chart, then walked to the foredeck and motioned Amy to follow him He laid the chart on the deck, weighting it at each corner with their shoes, and looked about to get his bearings.

"If I had my GPS . . ."

"Your what?"

"My GPS – a navigation system that uses satellites to fix your position. If I had it I could get a precise bearing on where we are to within fifty metres or so."

"Impressive."

"Yes. But I haven't got one yet so we'll have to guess." He looked at the sun and at his watch, at the position of Bill's Island and at the mainland, then took a pencil and made a cross on the chart. "I reckon we're about here." He looked around him at the sea. "Can you make out any more lobster pots with dark grey floats?"

"They're difficult to see."

"I know. That must have been the idea."

"What do you mean?"

"Fishermen with lobster pots generally lay a string of them. They use individually coloured floats so that they can identify their own pots. That stops them pulling up pots belonging to other fishermen."

She looked at him and the significance of what he was saying became clear.

"So Christopher Applebee used dark grey floats?"

"Exactly."

"Which were difficult to see . . ."

"Unless you knew precisely where to look."

"And other fishermen would leave them alone?"

"That's right. He made them even more difficult to find by part-filling the floats so that they didn't stick out of the water too much."

Amy looked out across the water towards Bill's Island. "Is that one over there? Directly in line with that big rock."

"Probably." He screwed up his eyes and scanned the water. "Yes. And there's another one there – see? Just in line with the end of the island. All his pots are round this side, so nobody could see him from the mainland when he emptied them."

"Clever trick."

"Yes. But simple, really. It's surprising that the police haven't cottoned on to it. But, then, they were looking for booze, not lobsters."

"Or drugs. So what do we do now?" she asked.

"Head back. I'd better go into St Petroc and explain to my friendly sergeant what's happened."

"Are you sure you want to?"

"What do you mean?"

"Do you think he'll believe you? You said he was questioning you as though you might have been involved."

Will paused and looked at her. "Don't sow seeds like that in my head. What's the alternative? That I turn detective and stake out the lobster pots until someone comes and pulls up the booty? No, thanks. I think I'd rather face the music with a detective sergeant than with the West Country Mafia."

"I suppose so."

He felt the chill of the onshore breeze. "Earghhh! I need to get dry. Towel me down?"

"Towel yourself down!" She smiled at him. "We've got to get back. No time for pleasure. I have a studio to open and you have some explaining to do. Wait till Hovis hears about this. He'll wish he'd come along."

The sun rose slowly in the clear, pale sky, glinting on the soft peaks of the ripples that shimmied on the surface of the water. They said little as they motored back but stayed close, Amy with her arm on his shoulder as he steered for the Crooked Angel.

"I know this sounds stupid, bearing in mind what's just happened, but I'm desperate to paint," she said softly, as the jetty grew closer.

"Mmm?"

"I've been doing nothing but shop-keeping – I've been tied to that till for too long. And with the holiday coming I'll need more stock."

"But who'll mind the shop?"

"Primrose has a niece in St Petroc who helps her out sometimes. She said she doesn't need her at the moment, so I thought I'd ask her."

"What if the girl takes after her auntie? Gossip-wise, I mean?"

"Well, I'll have to decide that when I meet her. But I'm just desperate to paint."

He ruffled her hair, amazed that after their startling discovery she could still be thinking of painting. He didn't say anything, but felt a great surge of love for her, and a dawning realization that now he could remember Ellie without feeling guilty.

They rounded the corner of the jetty and the sound of powerful engines met their ears. Jerry MacDermott's boat was on the move and coming directly towards them. Will swung the helm of *Boy Jack* to starboard so that the boats would pass, according to the nautical rules of the road, port to port. But MacDermott was still clearly driving on the left and the two boats began to make a bee-line for each other. Deciding in a split second that a chance of salvation was better than the certainty of being crushed against the harbour wall, Will pushed both throttles forward and spun the wheel anti-clockwise, shooting *Boy Jack* across MacDermott's bows with inches to spare. His heart thumped in his chest as the great white iceberg of a boat rumbled past them, close enough to nudge their fenders, with the MacDermotts waving merrily from the top, unaware of the disaster that had nearly befallen their titanic Tupperware.

Amy looked at him with incredulity etched on her face. He looked back apologetically. "Close."

She gulped. "Very close."

They gently chugged round the boatyard to pontoon number three, to discover that Hovis was already there, waiting to catch their lines. He was shaking his head. "I don't reckon that man has a clue about boats."

"That's the understatement of the year. He's a bloody liability," confirmed Will. "Thank God he doesn't come here often."

"Yes, well, I think that's about to change," remarked Hovis. "How was she, by the way?"

"She was a dream, apart from a little local difficulty. But what do you mean 'that's all about to change'?"

Hovis tied off the four mooring warps of *Boy Jack* and then reached into his back pocket for a white envelope. "There's one of these for you inside *Florence Nightingale*." He waved the envelope aloft.

"What is it?" asked Will, shutting down the engines.

"An invitation." He read: "'Jerry and Trudie MacDermott will be at home on Sunday 24th May and request the pleasure of your company for lunchtime drinkies, 12 noon till 2 p.m. RSVP Benbecula, Bosullow Lane, Pencurnow Cove, Cornwall'."

"Lunchtime drinkies?"

"That's what it says."

"Lucky you," chirped Amy, mockingly.

"I think you'll probably have one, too," said Hovis.

"Oh, God!"

"Yes," said Will. "And you can't risk upsetting your customers, can you?" He grinned at her.

"I am not going on my own."

"Don't look at me." He raised his hands in front of him in self-defence.

"I don't really have to go, do I?" Amy moaned.

"Well, that all depends if you want to slight one of your patrons. Not really advisable, I'd have said, when you're new to the area. Not with a man who's spent as much as he has at your studio."

"Come with me?" She looked at him beseechingly.

"Can we talk about more urgent things? Like out there just now?" he teased.

"Yes, of course. Sorry." She perked up and looked in Hovis's direction. "We've had a very interesting voyage."

"Er . . . I think we ought to nip inside." Will motioned her and Hovis towards the wheelhouse of *Boy Jack*. "Cup of coffee, Hovis?"

"So what will you do?" asked Hovis, his face

displaying the sort of excitement more associated with the children in *Swallows and Amazons* than with grown men.

"Go to the police."

"Best thing, I suppose. Not right to keep that sort of thing to yourself. Be careful, though."

"What do you mean?"

"Don't breathe a word about it to anyone else. Best if it's kept between us three – and the police, of course."

"Well, I wasn't thinking of knocking on the door of Gryler's Portakabin and saying, 'Guess what I've just found.'"

"No. Of course not." He paused. "Clever idea, though. The smuggling thing. I mean, dreadful but clever." He took a gulp of his coffee. "Much safer to bring the stuff over from the continent and pass it on down here in sleepy Cornwall. It's quicker to nip it across the Channel at the shortest point, but that's also the busiest point, isn't it? Kent. Sussex. Coastguard always on the lookout. Customs hot on anything untoward. Makes more sense to get it over here in a little fishing boat, round the back of Bill's Island where a small boat could be relatively inconspicuous."

"Mmm," grunted Will, thoughtfully.

"Except to observant lighthouse keepers, of course," remarked Hovis, pointedly. "Shame about your diaries."

"I'm relieved they're gone, in a way."

"But not in another?" asked Amy, who until now had been listening quietly.

"No. I wish I could go through them and check. But then . . ." He thought of the past life he would have to wade through, and the emotional turmoil of reliving his recovery. "Perhaps it's for the best. Fate." He looked at Hovis. "Pointless worrying about the things I can't change."

Hovis drained his coffee cup. "I'd better get on." He rose and so did Amy. "Me, too."

"Good luck with Primrose," said Will. "I'll catch up with you later." He gave Amy a hug and kissed her, then watched as she walked towards the village. As usual he found it impossible to take his eyes off her until she was out of sight. Then he made sure that the boat was secure and set off to catch the bus for the police station at St Petroc.

"Do you mind if I hang on to this, sir?" The detective sergeant folded up the chart.

"No, not at all."

He blew his nose loudly on a large tartan handkerchief, then stuffed it back in his pocket. "It was just the one lobster pot you hauled up, was it?"

"Yes. The one that caught my propeller."

"Mmm. I see." He looked thoughtful, as though struggling with his conscience. "We carried out a search, you know."

"Sorry?"

"We searched the lad's room in the village. Young Applebee's room."

"I see."

"We found the usual sort of stuff – dirty magazines . . ."

Will found himself wondering if the sergeant meant *Loaded* and *FHM*.

". . . and we also found some bottles and some weedkiller."

For a split second Will mused on the unlikelihood of Christopher Applebee being interested in gardening, then realized what the policeman was getting at.

"According to Forensic, there's no doubt that he was responsible for the fire at the lighthouse."

"Oh." The pieces of the jigsaw fell into place, and the conclusion now seemed obvious.

"Whether or not Gryler knew anything about it we've been unable to discover. But I thought you ought to know. It clears things up. The fire, that is. At least we know who started it. What we don't know is if he was acting off his own bat. Maybe we never will."

"Yes." Will hardly knew what to say. The implications whirred in his mind.

It was Christopher Applebee who had set fire to the lighthouse. It was Christopher Applebee whom Ernie had been trying to save when he lost his life. Where was the justice in that? But Will knew better than to expect fate to mete out justice.

"I know how it must seem, sir," the sergeant spoke compassionately, "but I think it's best to just try to forget it."

"One of life's bitter ironies?" Will said.

"Something like that. The longer I do this job the less I try to understand the things that happen. Life's a funny old thing."

"Yes. Thank you for telling me."

"Oh, and again, sir. Under your hat if you would."

"Yes. Of course."

The sergeant smiled sympathetically as Will plunged his hands deep into his pockets and walked out into the bright, sunny day. If he had known how quickly he would have to return he would not have bothered leaving. He shopped for food in St Petroc then caught the bus home.

The police car intercepted him as he walked along the lane at Pencurnow from the bus stop. A uniformed constable was at the wheel and leaned over to wind down the window.

"Do you think you could get in, sir?"

Will opened the passenger door. "But I've just–"

"I'm afraid the sergeant needs to see you again."

"Why's that?"

"Didn't say, sir. Just asked if I'd pick you up and take you there."

On the way back to St Petroc, Will's mind worked

overtime, trying to understand what could be the reason for his return to the police station. It dawned on him as the sergeant walked into the interview room. "It wasn't there, was it?"

"No, sir. No sign. Just empty lobster pots. All six."

"You found six?"

"Yes, sir. All empty."

Will felt silly. "Well, it was there this morning, that's all I can say."

"Mmm. Did anyone see you around Bill's Island?"

"No. Not as far as I'm aware – no, I'm sure not."

"And you saw no boats in the vicinity?"

"Mine was the only one."

"Mmm. Bit of a bugger, that. Someone's been there between your visit and mine. But we don't know who."

Will sat at the Formica-topped table feeling like a schoolboy being interviewed by his headmaster. The sergeant did not question Will's honesty, but a hint of incredulity crept into his voice. He came at the problem from a number of angles and, finally realizing that he was not getting any further, agreed that Will could leave. He seemed annoyed, and Will hoped that the cause was the unresolved situation rather than his own involvement.

"Do you think I could have my chart back?" Will asked.

"Yes, of course you can." The policeman led the way from the interview room to the counter at the front of the station, and reached below it to retrieve the chart, now folded up and tucked neatly into a polythene bag. He dangled it in the air and looked at it. "Never understand these. Know where you are with a map, roads and that, but not one of these."

Will looked at him questioningly and the sergeant read his mind. "Oh, don't worry, sir. I wasn't on my own, I was with the coastguard. He can understand them. And so can the person who got to the stuff before we did," he added, under his breath. "Be in touch, sir." And with that he walked into the room behind the counter.

Chapter 23:
Beachy Head

"I just don't want to go. They're awful people." Amy snuggled up to him.

"Well, sometimes we all have to do things we don't want to do."

"Beast!" She dug him in the ribs with her elbow and he collapsed with a peal of laughter.

They were lying side by side in her bed at the studio. For the last week they had revelled in each other's company, Amy trying to put Will's voyage to the back of her mind, convincing herself that he might not go after all, and Will busying himself during the day with further work on the boat, and telling himself it would be a good while yet before she was ready.

It was early on a Sunday morning and the

MacDermotts' 'drinkies' party was just a few hours away. Will pulled her closer and she curled into him.

"What a way to ruin a Sunday."

Out of the skylight Will could see plump white clouds. "It'll probably rain on them. Anyway, it's only for a couple of hours. We can arrive late and leave early. Say you've got the studio to attend to."

"Which is true. Angela can only stay a couple of hours."

"How's she been?" He stroked her pale back.

"OK. She's very quiet. No danger of her providing Primrose with any useful information."

"I'm relieved to hear it."

"But at least I've managed to paint."

"How many?"

"Three."

"When can I see them?"

"Soon. I've got some finishing off to do and I don't want you to look until they're done."

"I suppose we could get out of going."

"It was you who said we ought to go, not me," Amy reproved him.

"I've changed my mind. I'd rather stay here with you. All day."

"No. You were right the first time. The MacDermotts spent a lot of money at the studio and I could do with more of their business."

"Oh, I see. Getting serious now, are we? Business-woman of the Year all of a sudden?"

She grinned. "Well, I suppose we don't have to get up just yet, do we?" She slid her hand down underneath the quilt and his stomach muscles contracted.

It was another hour before they emerged.

It was a quarter to one when they walked up the hill towards Benbecula, holding hands, Amy grumbling quietly and Will trying to suppress a smile, though he, too, was hardly looking forward to an hour or more of small-talk with the denizens of Pencurnow Cove. He was, he told himself, only there to provide moral support. He looked out across the deep turquoise sea and at the blue sky, gradually filling with cumulus clouds, then squeezed her hand reassuringly. It was a soft, delicate hand with long, fine-boned fingers, and he loved the feel of the tender skin in his own.

He darted a look at her face, shadowed by a wide-brimmed straw hat. The feeling of complete pleasure in her company grew daily. Often it was simply enough to be in the same room. He felt no need to say anything: he could draw strength and warmth from her presence alone. At other times he wanted to hold her so tightly that her body almost passed through his. And soon there would be his voyage. He put that thought to the back of his mind and held her hand tighter as they crested the brow of the hill and heard voices at the garden party.

Benbecula was a Victorian gentleman's residence

built of granite and planted squarely at the top of the lane where it commanded a fine view of the cove. Stone gateposts topped with pineapples supported ornate wrought-iron gates, which opened on to a gravel drive that led, in a sweeping curve, to the white-painted front door set in a generous porch equipped with a shiny brass ship's bell. There were two sets of mullioned bay windows at either side of the door on the ground floor, and four gabled dormer windows protruded from the blue slate roof. Virginia creeper, in its shiny late-May livery, caressed mullion and finial with its rampant tentacles, softening the harsh, chiselled lines of the architecture. It was a solid house, not elegant in the Regency sense but robust Victorian. William Ewart Gladstone rather than Beau Brummel.

The rear of the house overlooked the bay, and handwritten notices pinned to wooden stakes directed guests along the drive and round the side of the house towards the striped lawn. A sprinkling of tables decorated the turf alongside a newly created putting green speckled with scarlet flags. The terrace alongside the house boasted a tall white flagpole, and strings of bunting led from it to the surrounding trees of macrocarpa, bent by years of onshore breezes into crouched wizened shrouds of greenery.

"It looks like the vicarage fête," whispered Will.

"And here comes the vicar," murmured Amy, as Jerry MacDermott strode across the lawn in his pink sweater and white trousers, the ubiquitous cigar clenched between his teeth and a glass in his left hand.

"Glad you could make it," he boomed, patting Amy on the back. Will thought the wide-brimmed hat must have put MacDermott off giving Amy a kiss: the prospect of negotiating access with a glass in one hand and a cigar in the other might have been more than he could manage without one of them coming to grief.

"Squire," MacDermott acknowledged Will. "Come and meet everybody."

Will's heart sank as they were dragged across the lawn, where a Pimm's was thrust into their hands by a local girl dragooned into waitressing.

"Great place, eh? Bloody good views of the cove."

"Wonderful," Will admitted, truthfully. Benbecula might not have been the prettiest house in Pencurnow, but it was certainly the largest and boasted the best panorama of the bay. Beyond the house, the lawns sloped away towards the sea between banks of feathery tamarisk. Bill's Island rose up from the ocean, looking even more like a whale than it did from the shore of the cove, and Prince Albert Rock Lighthouse pointed immaculately skywards from its granite promontory.

"You should come and paint up here," suggested MacDermott – with the merest hint, thought Amy, that the location might improve her technique. She smiled noncommittally.

"Said to the missus when we bought it that it was the best house in the area. No point in settling for anything less, eh? Course, we had to do a fair bit of work on it. Decoration a bit on the dreary side. Still, the missus has a flair for that sort of thing. You're artistic, come and have a look."

Before either of them could demur, Will and Amy found themselves propelled towards the french windows at the back of the house to peer into a room that made the Sistine Chapel seem lacklustre. Gone was the country chintz favoured by the previous owners, and in had come silken curtains, fringed with gold and gathered in great folds and ruches on either side of every window by fat tie-backs that swept up yards of sumptuous fabric. The sofas and chairs were white and richly padded, coffee tables of gilt and onyx held glossy books devoted to racing cars and stylish interiors, and glass shelves on either side of the new marble fireplace displayed a quantity of Lladro and Capo di Monte that could have restocked Lower Regent Street.

The telephone was an ornate pseudo-Victorian confection in amber and gold, and Amy guessed that even the lavatory pan was probably equipped with swags and tails.

The two gazed on the profligate display of newly acquired wealth in silent bewilderment.

"Done well, hasn't she?" said their host, with pride. "Knows just what to put with what. No point asking me – I'm colour blind."

It was at this point that Amy noticed the two sculptures she had sold the MacDermotts. They were standing at either side of the double doors leading from the ornate sitting room into the hall, each placed centrally on a goatskin rug. Her heart sank when she thought that she had provided something that was to the MacDermotts' taste. But then she saw the funny side and wondered what Oliver would have said if he had known where his works of art had ended up. Poetic justice. She shivered, remembering his letter and his promise of a return visit, but her thoughts were interrupted by Jerry MacDermott's voice.

"Who do you know?" he asked, wheeling them away from his Aladdin's cave towards the scattered tables on the lawn.

Unless Will acted quickly they might be saddled with a detailed itinerary involving visits to most of the local population. He waved at a figure a couple of tables away. "Look, there's –" he stopped himself in the nick of time from mentioning Hovis's Christian name – "Aitch. We'll go and say hello."

Hovis hailed them. "Hallo, me dears. How are we?" He was sitting with a couple of old ladies from the village who ran the tea-shop. He rose, doffed his battered Panama and pecked Amy on the cheek. The two ladies beetled off in search of another gin.

Will glanced at the diverse groups of people seated

at tables and standing chatting. "A bit like an Agatha Christie whodunit, eh?" Hovis remarked.

"Mmm?" Will was preoccupied.

"All gathered in the garden for the inspector's revelations."

"What do you mean?"

"Well, the likelihood is that someone here knows about the . . . er . . . *catch* you made. All the usual suspects are present." He indicated the far end of the garden by the cliff, where Len Gryler, standing alone in a shirt of unusual whiteness, was swigging from a bottle of Newcastle Brown.

Hovis warmed to his subject. "Then there's the *nouveau-riche* set." Will looked towards the house, where Trudie MacDermott, her blonde hair whipped into an even more spectacular froth than usual, was giggling in the company of an elderly but distinguished man in a navy-blue blazer with gold buttons. She wore a short, tight white miniskirt and a pink T-shirt that left little to the imagination. Her red-faced companion was having trouble in lifting his eyes from her cleavage but she seemed to mind not at all.

"The Admiral's happy, then," observed Hovis.

"The Admiral?" asked Amy.

"Old Scalder. Very keen on the ladies. His wife's the one with the moustache leaning against the drinks table."

Amy sipped her Campari. "That's very wicked of you."

"Perhaps. But it's true."

She watched as the Admiral's bushy eyebrows twitched. He grinned lasciviously at Trudie, the ice-cubes rattling in his gin and tonic.

"Is he really an admiral?"

"No," chipped in Will. "Ernie used to say that he was a petty officer with delusions of grandeur. Sidney Calder, known to his shipmates as Scalder. Always getting into hot water with the ladies. Harmless enough, though."

"Unless you're a lady," added Hovis.

Will chuckled. "Unless you're not a lady!"

Amy looked around. "I didn't realize there were so many people in the cove I didn't know."

"They only come out in summer," said Hovis. "Spend most of the winter tucked away in their cottages making ships in bottles."

"Watch it," said Will, threateningly.

"Ah. Sorry about that. Bit near home, eh?" Hovis sipped his Scotch and water.

"How long do you think we'll have to stay?" asked Will.

"Well, we can't go yet," admonished Amy. "We've only just arrived."

"You don't look the most reluctant people here," remarked Hovis. "I'd say there were two others who will want to stay as short a time as possible." He nodded in the direction of a couple standing alone lower down on the lawn towards the sea.

Will shielded his eyes from the sun and looked in the direction of Hovis's gesture. "It's the Morgan-Gileses. I'm surprised they came."

"Very surprised," agreed Hovis. "It must be upsetting to be a guest at a house you once owned. Especially when the new incumbents are not exactly of the same water."

"Come on," said Amy, "let's go and have a word. They look really uncomfortable."

"But –" Will tried to stop her, but she was already crossing the lawn. He looked exasperatedly towards Hovis, who shrugged. Will sighed, then followed her.

The Morgan-Gileses brightened at Amy's approach. "How nice to see you." Hugo offered her his hand. His wife nodded and smiled distantly.

"We thought you looked a bit out of it," said Amy, as Will caught her up.

"Oh, well, you know . . ." Hugo's good manners prevented him from expressing his real feelings. "It's nice to be able to take in the view again, isn't it, Mouse?"

His wife lowered her eyes before turning them towards the terrace, where Trudie MacDermott was now walking with the Admiral, whose deep laugh echoed across the lawn. The four onlookers watched as she took the blazered old boy by the arm, clattering in her stilettos across the York stone flags that led to the old conservatory.

"Lovely vine, you know," remarked Hugo.

"Sorry?" asked Amy.

"In the conservatory. Wonderful grapes. 'Muscat of Alexandria'. Isobel was a dab hand at thinning, weren't you, dear?"

Mrs Morgan-Giles, her discomfort growing, finished the drop of sherry in the bottom of her glass, then looked at her watch. "I think we ought to be going now. The joint will be ready soon."

Hugo looked embarrassed at his wife's eagerness to leave. "Yes. Yes, I suppose we must. Would you excuse us? It's lamb and we do like it pink." He shook hands again with both of them and held out an arm to shepherd her towards the gate of the garden they had once tended together. Isobel Morgan-Giles barely acknowledged them as she hurried across the turf, her husband following her with his hands clasped behind his back. They looked, thought Will, just like the Queen and the Duke of Edinburgh, making a state visit to a country that had once been part of the Empire but which was now an independent territory. The Morgan-Gileses' Union Flag no longer flew from Benbecula's flagstaff: it had been supplanted by cheap bunting.

Chapter 24:
Royal Sovereign

They left each other at the entrance to the Crooked Angel, Amy to take over from Primrose's niece at the studio, and Will to visit May Hallybone in St Petroc. The sky looked angry: vast grey-bottomed clouds blotted out most of the blue, and a sharp breeze whipped at the waves in the cove. Will grabbed a jacket from *Boy Jack* and unfastened the padlock of his newly acquired bike. Tiring of frequent bus journeys into St Petroc, he had bought the old green Raleigh a few days previously from an advert in Primrose's window. He had chained it to the stanchions on the boat for safety. Already one or two new faces were appearing at the yard – like the surly youth with the day-boat who had turned up on pontoon number one. He looked shifty and seemed obsessed with his ropes. Will became more security-conscious and reminded himself to lock up whenever he left.

He wheeled the bike along the pontoon and on to the jetty, mounting as he approached the new shower block. Len Gryler walked out of his hut as Will cycled past, the white shirt now replaced by the familiar oily overalls and the Newcastle Brown with a pint pot of tea. He nodded silently, and watched as Will pedalled slowly up the lane, past Benbecula and on to the St Petroc road.

It was a steep climb for the first couple of miles, but he enjoyed the physical exertion after the hour of enforced politeness at the MacDermotts'. At the top of the lane the road flattened out. To the right were fields of sheep surrounded by hedgebanks, and to the left, rougher countryside of bracken and foxgloves, vetches and coarse grasses, running down to the sea-pink-studded turf that topped the cliffs.

He hopped off the bike and pushed it through the bracken towards a lump of granite that offered a good view of the cove. He perched there, looking out to sea through the swaying madder-pink spires of foxgloves and inhaling the fresh, crisp air. Shafts of sunlight beamed down between the clouds, high-lighting patches of sea with gleaming silver. The glittering water contrasted sharply with the blue-grey clouds, which threatened at any moment to shed their watery load. Perhaps the clouds would blow by today. Certainly, brighter sky seemed to be in the offing.

He looked at the patterns of light on the water, and again the crystal clear image of Ernie disappearing beneath the waves came into his mind. He rubbed his eyes as if to wipe it away, and turned his thoughts to his impending trip. For weeks now it had loomed ever larger in his mind. But so, too, had Amy. She had not brought up the subject since the day she first visited *Boy Jack*, and neither had he. Amy hoped it would go away, and Will wasn't quite sure what he hoped.

How long would it be before he was ready? Two weeks? Three? He could not put off his decision much longer. But was there a decision to make? He was about to sail around the coast of Britain. This is what he had planned all these years. It was why he had bought the boat, spent most of his savings doing it up and equipped himself technically, physically and emotionally for the journey of a lifetime, leaving behind the past and its tragedies – the loss of Ellie then Ernie – and making a new start.

But he had not accounted for Amy, or falling in love. He stared at the sea, hoping that it might yield up some sort of solution but, as ever, it was intent on its own business. It had its own agenda; if he wanted to be a part of it, all he had to do was put out in his boat. If he did not, he must remain as a spectator, watching from a distance, and wondering what it would be like to be involved. He sighed heavily. What had once seemed simple was now fraught with complications.

Below him a boat cut through the waves. A large white boat. A fast white boat, slapping against the crests and roaring on past Bill's Island. He recognized it. It was the MacDermotts'. Having said goodbye to their guests they had clearly decided to go out for a spin. He waited for the boat to come into view again at the other side of the island, but it did not. He looked at his watch. Half past two. It was five to three before the boat reappeared, travelling back in the direction whence it had come. It was returning to Pencurnow, as fast as it had left some twenty-five minutes ago.

Thoughtfully Will picked up the bike and cycled on towards St Petroc.

"Could just have stopped to admire the view." Hovis was sitting in the corner of the bench seat on *Boy Jack*.

"Did you see them go out?" asked Will.

"Yes. Usual fuss and bother with ropes, even though they had old Scalder with them. Mind you, he'd probably had too much gin to be of any help. But he looked the part, standing on the bridge in his blazer and peaked cap."

"What do you think I should do?"

"You've two choices, haven't you? Go to the police

to report something you think is suspicious, or keep it to yourself."

"Mmm." Will looked thoughtful. "It's not much to go on, is it?"

Hovis shook his head. "Not really. Odd, though, all the same. Especially as they were out of sight for less than half an hour. Not really long enough to drop the hook, put the kettle on and put your feet up, and too long to be simply turning round."

"Did you see them come back?"

"Yes. By then I think old Scalder was *persona non grata*. Probably tried to touch up MacDermott's missus." He winked.

"Did they have anything with them?"

"What sort of thing?"

"I don't know. Polythene bags or plastic boxes or something."

"Well, they had a couple of holdalls – you know, those things they use to keep bottles of wine chilled, cool-bags. But I expect that was just their picnic."

"Do you fancy a trip out there?"

"Where?"

"Bill's Island."

Hovis looked uneasy. "Oh, I don't think you should go there. Keep out of the way. Best thing."

"But if we go out there now and find that the lobster pots aren't empty any more then the chances are that the MacDermotts put the stuff in them."

"Don't you think the police will have thought of

that? They'll be keeping an eye. Bound to be. Don't get involved. And, anyway, the MacDermotts are presumably taking stuff out of the lobster pots rather than putting it in."

"Well, let's just go for a sail and see if anything's going on."

Hovis grew more agitated and made to leave.

"Just a quick trip. That's all. I'll show you how my new GPS works." Will felt driven to push the issue, even though to his own ears he sounded childish. Something inside him was goading him on.

"No. I'd rather not." Hovis walked towards the hatchway, intent on leaving.

Will blocked his way. "Why not? What have we got to lose? We might even see something that will help clear this lot up."

"I can't."

Hovis was panicking. He tried to push past Will. Will wondered what was the cause of this sudden fear. Surely Hovis couldn't be involved. His mind raced as he stood in front of the bearded figure.

"What is it you know that I don't?" asked Will, looking his friend straight in the eye.

Hovis avoided his gaze. "It's nothing."

"If it's nothing, why won't you come?"

"Because . . ."

"What?" Will snapped impatiently. "Because what?"

Hovis rubbed at his beard, then wiped his hand

over his forehead where beads of sweat were already forming.

"Because I get seasick." He slumped down on the bench seat, took a red and white spotted handkerchief from the pocket of his grubby corduroys and mopped his brow. He sat limply, the picture of despair. "Nobody knows. Not a soul. Truth is, I even get queasy in the boatyard when the wind blows up. I've tried to get over it, like Nelson. Thought it might subside with age, but it seems to have got worse."

"Dartmouth and Salcombe," Will whispered, half to himself.

"A dream, I'm afraid. I only ever go there by train. Old *Florence Nightingale's* destined to end her days here. Like me."

"But have you tried–"

"Everything. All the cures. Pills. Potions. Those little armbands with buttons on them. Nothing helps. Ten minutes on the flattest sea and I'm heaving over the side. Went to the doctor. He said it was something to do with my inner ear. Balance, that sort of thing." He looked up at Will with a feeble smile. "It's a bit of a bugger, isn't it? Always loved the sea, and all I can do is look at it."

"I won't tell anybody. Don't imagine that."

"Thanks."

"Just for a minute there I thought . . ."

"I know. I saw it in your eyes."

"Sorry."

"You weren't to know." Hovis exhaled loudly. "Would you mind not saying anything to Amy?"

"Of course not."

"Only I don't want . . ."

"I won't breathe a word."

Amy listened avidly to his story of the MacDermotts' boat and found herself agreeing with Hovis that this was something for the police, not Will.

"Should I tell them?"

"Supposing the MacDermotts had just broken down?"

"In a new boat?"

"It happens, doesn't it? New cars break down."

"Well, yes, but . . ."

"Just keep it to yourself for a while. You can always mention it later if you have to."

She was sitting on the sofa at the studio, her feet tucked beneath her blue and white striped cotton dress. She sipped at a glass of Chardonnay. In spite of the wide-brimmed hat the sun had caught her cheeks, and she seemed to glow. A shaft of sunlight darted in through the skylight, its beam turning the scrubbed wooden floor the colour of honey. The heavy clouds were all but gone and the evening was still. Will sat cross-legged on the floor, looking up at her.

"How was May?" she asked.

"I almost forgot." He took a gulp of the clear amber

wine. "She was a bit tearful. But pleased."

"Pleased?"

"They've awarded Ernie the George Medal." He felt his throat constrict.

Amy's face creased up with delight. "Oh! How lovely. I mean . . ."

"I know." He came and sat beside her, putting his arm around her and his head against hers. "At least his life hasn't gone unrecognized."

"She must be very proud."

"She showed me the letter. Somehow it seemed such a final thing." He put down his glass. "I went to his grave. Put some flowers on it. You know, butter-cups and foxgloves. He preferred those to garden flowers. It's a lovely spot. Looks right out over the sea."

They sat quietly for what seemed like an age, and then he said, "About my trip."

She sat perfectly still, her eyes fixed on the floor. She had put it all to the back of her mind; had tried hard not to think about it, imagining that if she were to distance herself from it sufficiently it would disappear. His words surprised her.

"I want you to come with me."

She swung round to look at him.

"I don't want to do it on my own. I want to do it with you." He watched her. Waiting for an answer. When, eventually, it came, he felt the pit of his stomach sink.

"I can't." She spoke gently and looked away.

He had half expected this, but still it came as a shock. "Why not?"

"Because." She found herself unable to meet his eye. "Because of all this. I've just got myself started up. I can't just leave it all."

He thought he must have heard wrongly. Perhaps that was not what she meant.

"But I thought . . . I thought you . . ."

"Wanted to come?"

"Yes."

She turned to face him. "Oh, I do. I really do. But I can't just throw it all in. Just like that."

He stared at her, shaking his head in disbelief. "I don't understand. I mean, do you want to be with me or not?"

"Yes. I do."

"Well, then, come with me." A note of exasperation crept into his voice.

"It's not as easy as that."

"It is. It's perfectly straightforward. I don't want to go without you. I don't want to be on my own any more; I want to be with you. You seemed to want to be with me so I thought you felt the same."

"I do feel the same, but I can't just up and come. I can't."

"But how can you say that?" He almost shouted the words. He was angry now. Angry at letting himself be lulled into what was clearly a false sense of security.

She had led him on. Made him think that he was important to her, got him to lower his guard to the point where he had offered her his life to share and she had rejected him. They had talked as he had not talked in a long time; shared their feelings so completely, made love in a way that he had never made love before; become soulmates, and here she was, turning him down simply because his voyage – which she knew about and had always known about – got in the way of her gallery, studio, shop or whatever she wanted to call it.

She interrupted his thundering confusion of thoughts.

"I thought you might have changed your mind about going."

He looked at her with real pain etched on his face. "But I've been planning it for so long. You know that. I've never made a secret of it. It's what I've always wanted to do."

"Until I got in the way?"

"Don't say that."

"But it's true isn't it? You had your life mapped out and then you bumped into me and I messed it all up."

"It's not like that."

"Oh I think it is." She tried to keep her voice steady and level. "You need this trip to clear your mind. Start you off on a new life. Leave the past behind. I know that. You've longed for it. Why should I imagine that you'd give it up?"

"Because I love you."

Amy looked at him hard, biting her lip to rein in her emotions. "But not quite enough." She looked away.

"Please. Don't say that. Don't think that I don't love you enough. I couldn't love you more."

"No. Well; there we are then."

He felt empty. Cold. Why had it all suddenly gone wrong? He wanted her to go with him, to make the trip of a lifetime and she had turned him down. They sat slightly apart on the sofa now, neither of them capable of taking the conversation any further.

Will got up. "I'd better go."

Amy said nothing.

He looked down at her, his feelings numbed. "I'm sorry."

She did not answer. Just carried on looking at the pictures on the wall. The pictures of white beaches and blue sea and clear skies.

The last thing she heard was the gentle closing of the door and the tapping of the 'Closed' sign against the glass.

Chapter 25: Nab

His jaw ached. For two weeks now he had been clenching his teeth, telling himself he was right to press on with his plans. He had offered to take her with him and she had declined. She knew it was his intention to go, always had been. He felt annoyed with himself for having given so much of himself away, betrayed, too, because she wouldn't go with him. How could she say that he didn't love her enough when he had offered to share his life and his dreams with her?

She continued to occupy his every waking hour. As he studied the charts he would need for his voyage her face kept smiling at him from harbours and creeks, compass roses and tide tables.

There were days when he felt low enough to call it all off, and others when his bloody-mindedness saw him ploughing ahead doggedly with his preparations.

From time to time he caught Spike looking at him questioningly with his head on one side. And Hovis had been quiet of late, allowing him to get on unhindered. He had told him of Amy's refusal to go with him, and been surprised at his reaction. Hovis had absorbed the information quietly, averting his eyes, as though the subject had nothing to do with him. Which, of course, reflected Will, it had not.

The late May bank holiday came and went. June had arrived and at weekends now the place would be alive with tourists. He would have liked to have been away by now, but there were still engine refinements to make, the anchor winch to be repaired, wind-screen wipers to fix — fiddly jobs that seemed to take up large chunks of his day. Two of the port-holes leaked during heavy rain and needed sealing; a small area of deck planking had sprung and needed recaulking, and a cleat had come away from its mounting. Old boats, like old houses, seemed forever in need of attention.

Half of him wanted to cast off, leave and sort out such problems along the way. What did it matter where he was berthed? He could make running repairs in any port. Yet the perfectionist in him wouldn't let him set off until everything was ship-shape. Only then would he have the satisfaction of knowing that his voyage was underway and the past left behind.

But where did the past end and the present begin?

He sat on the edge of the bed, weary of thinking. The brass clock on the bulkhead showed a quarter to eleven. He looked out of the port-hole and saw the moon glinting on the rippling water, heard the gentle slapping of the tide against the hull. It was a sound he loved: comforting, promising, exciting. The hairs on the back of his neck stood on end at the prospect of adventure, but a black cloud surrounded him as he slid under the quilt and waited for the soothing motion of the sea to rock him to sleep.

The tapping sound woke him slowly. At first he thought it was something in the water, knocking against the hull – a bottle or a can. He sat up. The tapping had stopped, but he could not settle. He heaved his weary body from the bed and walked up the cabin steps towards the door of the saloon. He pulled back the curtain and looked out. Nothing. Just a silent boatyard with vessels straining at their mooring warps. He turned to go back to bed, but a flash of white caught his eye. He looked down. A piece of paper lay on the cabin floor. He opened it and strained to read the words that were printed in capitals in handwriting he knew. The words were few but the message was clear: "0300 HOURS. OUTSIDE THE SALUTATION. TED.

He looked at the clock. It was half past two. He sat on the bench seat, rubbed his eyes and reread the note. It was like something out of a spy thriller, yet

Ted Whistler was not given to flights of fancy. He pulled on his clothes in the dark, slipped on a pair of deck-shoes, slid open the door and padded down the pontoon towards the jetty, his heart thumping in his chest. He must be mad. Ted must be mad. What was going on?

He eased open the hefty gate of the boatyard as silently as he could and squeezed through, closing it behind him before walking along the lane that led to the Salutation. The pub was dark now, its clientele having long departed to their beds. Alf Penrose had never been prosecuted for serving after hours – he was too partial to a good night's sleep.

Will looked around. Nothing. No one. Perhaps it was a joke. Perhaps he'd dreamt it. A hand touched his shoulder and he almost cleared the iron railings in one leap.

"What the – !"

"Ssh." The voice was familiar.

"Bloody hell! What's going on?"

"Sorry," Ted whispered. "Come over here." He led Will to a stretch of railings overshadowed by buildings, where the moonlight failed to provide illumination.

"What's wrong?"

Ted pointed out to sea in the direction of Bill's Island. "Just wait."

The two men had little in common other than a shared background of lighthouse-keeping, but each knew from experience that once the eyes were fully accustomed to the dark they could see almost as well as in daylight – especially on a moonlit night when the shadows were as contrasting as any provided by the sun.

Will's eyes were used to the darkness, but he could see nothing other than the hump of Bill's Island rising out of the water, the glint of the moon on the rippling tide and the wavelets breaking on the island's shoals. The regular flash of the lighthouse added its own intermittent brilliance.

For fully twenty minutes they stood there, and just as Will was about to suggest there were better ways of spending the early hours, his eyes focused on a small inflatable dinghy making its way back from Bill's Island.

"Night fishing?"

"In one of those?"

There was only one alternative. "Smuggling?"

Ted nodded.

"How do you know?" He kept his voice low.

"Been watching regular."

"How long?"

"Three weeks."

"Why?"

"Dunno. Had a feeling, that's all. Pissed off about Ernie."

"You've been out here every night?"

"Mostly."

The two men watched as the dinghy made its way towards the shingle bank – not to the boatyard or the adjacent hard. Ted spoke again softly. "Seems to happen on Thursday nights, about this time. Not always, but twice before. The other night there was too much wind. Sea was too rough."

"Fancy going out in a boat that small. Any kind of sea and it would be over. Must be mad."

"Desperate, more like."

"Why haven't you been to the police? Come to think of it, why haven't the police spotted it?"

Ted ignored the second question and answered the first. "Didn't want to get involved. Anyway, there never seems to be anything in the boat. No fish. Nothing. But they must be up to something."

"Why have you got me out here?"

Ted shrugged.

"What happens now?"

"Watch and you'll see."

As the boat approached the bank of pebbles the rower shipped the oars and stepped out before pulling it clear of the tide. He bent to pick something from the bottom of the dinghy. Will could not make out what it was.

"That's a first," said Ted, a note of surprise in his voice. The oarsman deflated the tiny vessel, folded it and stuffed it into a large holdall. The night was calm and silent, apart from the sucking of the tide on the shingle, but all the while the figure looked about nervously, clearly waiting for something or someone.

Ted nudged Will's arm and nodded in the direction of the cliff path. Will screwed up his eyes and could just make out another figure descending towards the beach. The first figure had also seen the newcomer, but made no move to depart. The newcomer walked down the shingle bank and picked up the object that had been removed from the boat, put it into a bag, then took the handle at one side of the holdall that now contained the dinghy. The figures then set off with their two pieces of baggage towards the cliff path.

For a moment, Will and Ted looked at one another, unsure of their next move. Then Will cocked an eyebrow, Ted nodded, and they walked silently across the narrow lane to climb a small, steep path that would join the one that ran along the top of the cliff. In the space of two minutes they would be able to intercept the oarsman, his companion and their cargo.

The suddenness of it all took them both by surprise. As they breasted the grassy knoll before them, two large figures blocked their path.

Both Will and Ted stopped in their tracks, straining hard to make out the features on the faces that confronted them. With the moonlight behind them it was difficult, but Will thought he recognized one of the men as the policeman who had driven him back to the station in St Petroc. The other looked vaguely familiar but Will could not place him.

"Stop there, please," commanded the second figure, quietly but firmly. Will and Ted did as they were told. His companion, the young policeman, looked back over his shoulder towards the path where the oarsman and his companion must have been climbing. Will could see nothing over the knoll.

The four stood silently for what seemed like an age, until the young policeman said, "That's it. They're in the bag," in his voice a mixture of relief and triumph.

"Right," said his companion. "Down there, please." He pointed to the path they had just climbed, signalling them both to make their way down. Silently they descended, looking neither right nor left, until they reached the lane. A police car purred silently into view and Ted and Will were motioned into the back seat by the second policeman, who then climbed into the front. No siren sounded, and no words were spoken during the short, speedy journey to St Petroc at half past three on a Friday morning.

Will knew what would happen when they arrived at the station. He could hear the voice of the detective sergeant now, could see the expression on his face.

Who could blame him for the conclusions he would draw?

On arrival at the police station they were split up and shown into separate interview rooms. Will sat alone for twenty minutes before the sergeant arrived with the young constable in tow, switched on a machine, gave time and date details and uttered the words that previously Will had heard only on television: "You do not have to say anything, but it may harm your defence if you do not mention, when questioned, something which you later rely on in court. Anything you do say may be given in evidence."

Will felt a cold sweat break out on his brow.

"I think you need to explain a few things to me, don't you?"

Will recounted the events of the night – Ted's message, how he had accompanied him to the coast road and watched the boat bringing back its cargo.

The detective sergeant looked grim. He listened attentively, asking questions that showed clearly he had already talked to Ted. For the best part of an hour the interrogation was relentless, the sergeant's manner intimidating. Then he sighed and got up. "You're lucky, aren't you?"

"Sorry?"

"Lucky I believe you. And at least your stories tie up."

Will could think of nothing to say.

"I know you were drawn into this by a series of events, sir, but you'd have helped more if you'd just stood back and left us to get on with it."

"I thought I had."

"Until tonight."

"Yes. I'm sorry."

Will was unsure where the conversation was leading, but relieved that the sergeant was not treating him as a suspect. His curiosity got the better of him.

"Did you get them? The two on the cliff path?"

"Yes, sir. We did. No thanks to you. A couple of minutes more and you'd have blown it. Do you know how long we've been watching them?"

Will shook his head apologetically.

"Four weeks. Every night for four weeks. Along with your friend next door. Well, actually, we've been at it eight days longer than him."

Will looked at the sergeant enquiringly. "Ted?"

"He didn't do anything, only watched, so we thought we'd leave him alone. Just keep an eye, you know."

"He wasn't . . . ?"

"No. He wasn't. From the start we were fairly sure he wasn't, but we didn't want him to do anything that might prejudice the outcome, so we decided to leave him be, provided he didn't overstep the mark. Only this was the first night they actually came away with anything. You can't arrest people for rowing around in a rubber dinghy late at night. You might want to arrest them for stupidity but we chose not to. Waited until we had something a bit more serious to go on."

"Did they pick it up, then?"

"I can't really say any more, sir."

"No, of course not."

"I'd be grateful if you'd keep tonight's events to yourself. It will be public knowledge soon enough, but I'd like to be in charge of the timings myself, if that's all right with you?"

Will was conscious of the sergeant's sarcasm.

The policeman moved towards the door. "Wait here for a few minutes and I'll arrange for someone to drive you back." He left the room, along with the young constable, and Will stared unseeingly at a poster advising against drink-driving. It was then that he remembered where he had seen the other police constable before, not the one who had just left the room but the one who had stood beside him on the cliff path. He was the surly youth who had arrived on pontoon number one in the battered day-boat. He must have been watching Will, Gryler and the boatyard ever since. Will shuddered, remembering how close he had come to revisiting the lobster pots.

The door reopened and the boating police constable gestured to Will to follow him, his face expressionless. Ted was waiting outside, looking as though he had only just survived an attack by a

Rottweiler. As they walked down the corridor together they passed another interview room. The door was in the process of being closed, but as they walked past, Will saw the two figures sitting at a table.

The door slammed shut but the vision of Hugo and Isobel Morgan-Giles remained imprinted in his mind.

The sergeant was careful never to let his personal life spill over into his work. He had endeavoured, over the last few years particularly, to keep the two separate. Whenever they looked as though they might conflict, he made sure that someone else took the reins. His colleagues knew this, and knew, too, that he never let his own experiences colour his judgement.

He questioned Hugo Morgan-Giles calmly and thoroughly, with little display of emotion. "You do know what was in the packages?"

Hugo considered. "I'm not sure."

"Do you know what they were worth?"

"No."

"Around fifty thousand pounds each, street value. That's a quarter of a million pounds."

Isobel Morgan-Giles shot at her husband a glance laden with reproach.

Hugo's head jerked up. "I'd no idea!"

"How much were you getting?"

He hesitated. "Five thousand."

"Each?"

Hugo looked crestfallen. He shook his head.

"Where from?"

Hugo turned to his wife, who stared at him with disgust. He realized he was now on his own. "A few years ago, when we were still living at Benbecula, we encountered financial difficulties." He looked almost embarrassed to admit to it. "We lost a lot of money. Lloyds. I was a Name. We found ourselves heavily in debt. We struggled to keep the big house going for a long time but in the end we only just managed to hang on to what we used to call the Dower House – the Moorings – and we moved in there and sold Benbecula to . . . other people." He said it politely, without any hint of recrimination. His wife let out a suppressed but scornful snort.

"I tried to find a couple of consultancies in the City, but I failed, and I realized that very shortly I would have to declare myself bankrupt, which would mean losing everything, even the Moorings. I was desperate to find a way of just hanging on in there, I think you'd call it. The children are both at private schools and that was the one thing I was determined they should continue to have – at any cost. Benbecula had been in the family for three generations. I'd already let them down enough.

"I tried everything I could think of. Went to see old friends, almost begged for work, but nothing was forthcoming. You're not equipped for much when you've been retired from the Army for ten years. Except for being chairman of the village-hall committee. I just didn't know where to look. People were very sympathetic but . . . nothing." He spoke calmly, almost relieved to get it all off his chest.

"So you found an easier way to make money?"

"I'd never done anything illegal in my life. I haven't even had a parking ticket. It wasn't easy. I didn't do it without a lot of soul-searching. But in the end I couldn't afford self-respect. Too much pride for that, I suppose. Too much family pride. If you see what I mean." He didn't wait for an opinion, but continued, "Just over a year ago I caught the two boys up in the attic smoking pot."

The sergeant raised his head. "The two boys? I thought you only had one son."

"He had a friend. A lad from the village. Used to muck around together. I gave them a hell of a tongue-lashing, bawled them out. Told them if I found them at it again I'd give them what for. Tim – my boy – went back to school and I thought that was that. It was about a week later when the lad came to see me at the house. I wanted nothing to do with him. Told him not to come back, and not to see Tim again either. He left, shouting something abusive about money. About how I was wasting an opportunity."

"Who was the lad?" asked the sergeant.

Hugo spoke very quietly. "Christopher Applebee."

"Go on."

"I never thought much about it. Then this man turned up at the house the following week. Said he was from the Inland Revenue. I invited him in, thinking that this would be the end of things, that we'd lose what little we'd managed to save. I took him into my study. He said that I owed more money than their calculations had at first shown, and what was I going to do about it? I thought I'd reached rock bottom. Then he smiled. Said he wasn't really from the tax office but now I knew how I'd feel when they really did come.

"I didn't understand what was going on. I asked him what he was doing, who he was, why he thought he could come into my house and talk to me like this. I asked him to leave. Then he said he was a friend of the lad's and that he'd heard I needed money. I told him I wasn't interested, that I wouldn't do anything underhand or illegal. He said what he was suggesting was quite safe. He explained that I could earn money by joining his import-export business."

The sergeant rested his chin in his hands and sighed.

"Yes. Deep down I knew what was going on, but it was the first offer anyone had made to me."

"And you took it?"

"Not at first. He was very persuasive. Said that he had plenty of people who could collect things for him. What he needed was someone reliable – senior management sort of thing – who could make sure that goods were delivered to a prearranged address at weekly or monthly intervals. That was all. There was no need for me to know what was in the packages. All I had to do was make sure they were delivered. That was all."

"So you said yes." The sergeant's voice was devoid of emotion.

"Eventually," Hugo agreed wearily. "You've probably never been there, but it's amazing what you can make yourself do when there's nowhere else to go. When you've explored every conceivable avenue and found no way out. I even managed to convince myself that the packages contained nothing illegal. Stupid, isn't it?"

Still no reaction.

"And so it started. Christopher would collect the parcels from the lobster pots and bring them to me."

"Always on a Thursday?"

"Yes."

"But not every Thursday?"

"No. We weren't told when they were coming. The man said that's the way it would be."

"Were there always five parcels?"

"No. Sometimes fewer."

"And did you meet the man again?"

"He said there would be no need."

"So where did you take the parcels?"

"To a waste skip behind a hotel near Green Park,

in London."

"And where did you get your money?"

"By post. In a padded envelope."

"And Applebee?"

"I don't know."

"And you always got five thousand pounds?"

"Always."

"Not a lot, considering the value of what you were delivering."

"But I didn't know that." Hugo realized as he said it that his claim of ignorance would count for little.

The sergeant persisted with his questioning until he was satisfied that there was little more to be gained by continuing at this hour of the morning.

As the sergeant stood up to go, Hugo said, "I do just want to say one thing. My wife has had nothing to do with this. It was entirely my doing."

The sergeant looked balefully at his interviewee. "Until Christopher Applebee was drowned trying to pick up the packages and you had to start collecting the stuff yourself. Then, of course, you needed someone to help you carry the dinghy up to the house."

Hugo gazed at the floor.

"The firebomb at the lighthouse?" The sergeant asked the question as though he were asking the time of day. "Your idea or Applebee's?"

Hugo answered, without hesitation, "Mine. Applebee knew that the lighthouse keeper's diaries were there. Heard about them in the pub. Said we ought to steal them. I thought a firebomb would be quicker. Neater."

"And who threw it?"

"I did."

"Noble of you to admit it," the sergeant said flatly, "but the stuff we found in Christopher Applebee's flat tells us otherwise."

The Morgan-Gileses were detained for further questioning. The sergeant returned briefly to his desk before going home to snatch some sleep. He picked up his car keys from the desk drawer, then looked at the framed photo that stood next to an overflowing in-tray. It was a picture of his daughter. She had been only fifteen when the picture was taken. She had died four years ago now, after taking a single Ecstasy tablet at a disco in Penzance.

Chapter 26: Nash

Amy rose early. She had become accustomed to lying awake from around six o'clock and had decided after several days of moping until eight that the only way ahead was to work. The bank holiday weekend had gone well, and she needed more stock. She contacted the jewellery maker, the patchwork stitcher and the rest of her suppliers to make sure she had enough for what she hoped would be a good season ahead.

Her three new paintings were finished, but she was not sure she liked them. They were bright enough, but lacked sparkle. She hung them where they would catch the eye of a prospective purchaser as soon as the studio door opened. She took a shower and sat down to orange juice, bran flakes and slices of banana.

Just occasionally it was impossible not to think of

him. Just occasionally, several times a minute. She pushed back her chair and crossed to the sink with the glass, the bowl and the spoon, slamming them into the washing-up bowl with unwise ferocity. The glass broke. "Shit!" She clutched at the rim of the sink and closed her eyes to prevent the tears spilling over. "Oh, shit!" A wave of sorrow engulfed her and her body contracted in wild sobs.

She reached for the kitchen roll, tore off a couple of squares and blew her nose loudly, cursing herself. "Stupid woman! Pull yourself together and get on with it. He's not worth it. They never are."

She mopped up her tears, sniffing all the while, and wiped away the smudges of mascara before they descended from her lower eyelids on to the freckled cheeks.

"Oh, God! What a state! What have you done? Why did you turn him down? So bloody anxious to prove you can go it alone. So keen to be bloody independent. Well, now you are, and where has it got you? On your own again. Huh!"

She sniffed again and binned the kitchen roll, heading for the bathroom to sort out her face before opening the studio. It was, after all, what she had always wanted.

Will sat on a canvas chair at the bows of *Boy Jack* looking out across the cove to the lighthouse. It seemed ages since he had been there, but there was little reason to return now. May Hallybone was staying in St Petroc with her sister. She'd decided to make a home nearer her friends. That's what she'd said when he'd called in the week before. Will had been worried about her, but May had allayed his fears. "Got to get on with life. No use moping about," she'd said. "I just remember all the good times, forget the bad. You can't brood on what might have been."

"Will you stay with your sister?" he'd asked.

"Good Lord, no! We're all right for a while but we'll drive one another mad if we have to spend the rest of our lives together. I'll find a little place on my own. I'll be happy – always comfortable in my own company. And with the animals." Will smiled at the thought of her living out her days with her pigs and chickens, a woman contented with her lot, accepting what life had given her – and taken away.

The sound of a hatch opening came from the boat next door, and the sandy-whiskered head popped out. "Good morning! Looks as though it's going to be a nice day. Suit all those trippers."

"Hallo." Will grinned reluctantly.

Hovis looked at him, sitting in his faded director's chair, surrounded by coils of rope. "Your boat's beginning to look like mine."

Will looked down at his feet where the snaking mooring warps and sundry strings were sprawled like some gigantic cat's cradle, defying his efforts at measuring them and getting them into any order.

"Just trying to make sure that I've got enough of them."

"I should think the answer to that question is almost certainly yes," Hovis remarked.

"Do you want some coffee?" asked Will.

"Not just now. Going shopping."

"I think you might want to put it off for a while when I tell you the news." Will remembered the sergeant's request to keep things to himself, but he considered Hovis to be pretty near to family.

"What do you mean?" Hovis's eyebrows were raised. They rose even higher when Will explained the events of the previous night.

"Well, bless me! Who'd have believed it? Have you told anybody else?"

"No. The sergeant asked me to keep it to myself."

"It'll be out in the open soon enough, though. You can't keep that sort of thing quiet round here. Not with Primrose on the lookout." The prospect of her reaction made Hovis chuckle. "She'll have a field day with this one." But then the sadness struck him. "Poor buggers. I wonder what made them get involved."

"It's not too difficult to see, I suppose," offered Will. "Lost all their money in the Lloyds business – house, everything. Still have two kids at expensive schools. Needed to keep them there. Found a way of doing it."

"Yes, but drugs. I wouldn't have thought that was

312

the Morgan-Gileses' way of getting out of a hole." He shrugged. "Still, that's modern society for you. In the old days it was rum, now it's heroin and cocaine."

He looked reflective. "Just a minute, though. What about the MacDermotts? I thought we had them lined up for it, with their flash boat and their half-hour wait behind Bill's Island."

Will gestured to the other side of the boatyard where Len Gryler's legs stuck out of the engine-room hatch of the MacDermotts' bathtub.

"Engine trouble. Gryler's been up to his elbows in grease and diesel since first thing this morning."

Hovis perched on the side of his boat. "You know, I will have that coffee." He looked up at the sky where just a few wisps of white cloud floated in the increasingly rich blue. "It does make you count your blessings, doesn't it?"

"I suppose so."

For the next half-hour, while they chomped their way through digestive biscuits dipped in coffee Hovis endeavoured to piece together the jigsaw, quizzing Will after the fashion of Dr Watson with Sherlock Holmes. The only difference was that Will was less sure of the answers.

"Christopher Applebee. Presumably he was doing it for the Morgan-Gileses?"

"I guess so."

"But you'd have thought that they'd have called a halt to it after the accident, wouldn't you?"

"Depends how desperate they were for the money. And they didn't know that the drugs had been found, only that Christopher Applebee and Ernie had been drowned. As far as they were concerned, everybody still thought Applebee was catching lobsters."

"Do you think that they were the brains behind it all?"

"Don't know. Either that or just couriers. The stuff would be put in the lobster pots by some foreign fishing boat and the Morgan-Gileses would pick it up and pass it on, getting a cut for their trouble."

Hovis looked back towards Pencurnow. "Just a sleepy little Cornish fishing village and it's caught up in all this. Well, well, well."

Will looked out towards the lighthouse. "I think I'll take a walk. Haven't been over there for ages."

Hovis risked a question. "When do you think you'll set off?"

Will threw the dregs from his coffee cup over the side and they landed with a plop in the water. "Next week, I hope. Get a few more jobs done and then be on my way."

"Which direction will you go?"

"West. Thought I'd go to Scilly first. Put in at New Grimsby on Tresco. Sheltered harbour. Good seafood. Stay there a while. No rush."

Hovis slapped at the bows of *Boy Jack*. "We'll miss you, you know."

Will looked at him, temporarily wrong-footed.

Spike padded from the bows and wrapped himself around his master's leg, tail held high. Will looked down then back at Hovis. "We'll miss you, too."

There was a pause, neither knowing how to proceed with the conversation. Hovis broke the silence. "Still going on your own?"

"Yes," replied Will softly. The cat rubbed against his leg again. "Well, not entirely. If he stays." Spike looked up at him, inscrutable as ever, then hopped off the boat and down the pontoon in search of amusement.

"I'm sorry," Hovis said.

"Yes. Me too." Will took the proffered mug from Hovis and put it with his in the saloon before he locked up and headed for Prince Albert Rock. In all probability, it would be the last time he saw it for a long while.

He walked slowly along the coastal path, aware that as the weeks passed, it would become more populated. The smell of the vegetation filled his nostrils – a rich mixture of herb robert and foxglove, bladder campion and kidney vetch. It seemed as colourful as a herbaceous border. Below, the sea glinted and glimmered, fresh white waves breaking on the Cornish granite and catching the sun in rainbows of spray. It was all tantalizingly beautiful.

He stood and watched as a kittiwake keeled through the air, shrieking its name to anyone who would listen. The granite-sand path beneath his feet crunched as he trod, and he wished now that he'd put on a pair of shorts. The day was turning into a scorcher. He walked faster now, forcing positive thoughts into his head. He would go it alone. No problem. He'd done it before, could do it again. He kicked a shard of granite, which bounced down the cliff to be swallowed up silently by the waves.

The beach beyond sported half a dozen deck-chairs – the early arrivals had landed – but there was no sign of the woman with the Labrador. It struck him in an instant that she must have been Isobel Morgan-Giles. He stopped and wondered if her walks with the dog had been part of the set-up. The same dog that had been towing Hugo when Hovis and he had bumped into him on the cliff. The day that Christopher Applebee went out in his boat for the last time.

He walked on, gradually descending towards the lighthouse as the cliff path curled around Prince Albert Rock. It was hard not to feel a pang of fear, coupled with sorrow at his leaving. The white-painted granite tower had been the place where he had sheltered from life – and death. The physical rock to which he had turned when he most needed comfort. He had found it there, in the company of Ernie and May and, to a lesser extent, Ted Whistler, whose dourness now seemed less forbidding. But that was yesterday. It was time to move on. Impatience bit into him, but not so much that he could not stop to think.

He perched on a rock that was almost on a level with the lantern, and watched the sunlight glinting on its lattice panes. Through the mantle of forced optimism came the echoes of Ernie's voice: "Prince Albert Rock Lighthouse was constructed in its present form by William Tregarthen Douglass, the same engineer responsible for the construction of Bishop Rock Lighthouse." Soon he would see Bishop Rock for himself, when he sailed off in the direction of Scilly. On his own.

He missed her. He who had learned to prefer his own company. What had happened to the loner?

He cursed himself for having let down his guard then cursed himself for losing her because of his single-minded desire to sail away. Here he was, on the verge of his lifetime's ambition, so why didn't he feel more elated? He knew why. He just chose not to admit it to himself.

He looked at the sturdy white tower and forced his emotions to one side. Built all those years ago, when there were no elaborate pieces of lifting gear, no JCBs and no electricity. How many ships had it kept away from the rugged Cornish rocks below? How many had perished there before it was built? And since? The bitter pain stabbed at him. He breathed in deeply and continued down the final stretch of path.

If Evan Williams was in a good mood there might

be a bottle of beer for him. After all, they were neither of them on watch any more. All Evan Williams had to do now was take care of the fabric of the place and show around the tourists. A bottle of beer seemed a safe bet.

Recently Amy had managed to keep Oliver Gallico out of her mind. If she had considered the odds she would probably have laid money on his returning when emotionally she was at her lowest ebb. It would have been a safe bet.

The studio was busy. The early tourists, enjoying a lunchtime stroll after their long journey down the A30, were looking at pictures, fondling ethnic jewellery and scrutinizing pieces of sculpture. Amy and Angela – who had fortunately agreed to help out for the rest of the summer – wrapped gifts, popped postcards in envelopes and hoped constantly for a sizeable sale. Angela was getting better at the job. She was more chatty with the customers now, and her course in bookkeeping at the local tech was coming in handy. Primrose had taught her about stock-taking, too, and she did her best, during quieter moments, to explain to Amy what it was all about. Amy did her best not to glaze over.

There was little time for such conversations at lunchtime, though, and that was when Oliver chose to make his entrance.

Angela mistook him for a customer and was not

surprised by his arrogance: they saw all types down here. It was only when he said he was a friend of Amy's that she went across the studio to interrupt her employer, who was explaining the firing process of a salt-glazed pot to a couple who had driven all the way from Chalfont St Giles.

Oliver watched her reaction. It was not what he expected. Instead of looking hunted, her normal response, she glanced in his direction then continued dealing with the couple before she even raised her eyes to his. He felt uneasy.

She walked towards him and flashed him a polite but steely smile. "Hi!"

"Are you OK?" Oliver asked, with genuine concern for the first time.

"Fine. And you?"

He didn't like this approach. What was the matter with her? "You seem strange. You sure you're all right?"

"I told you, I'm fine. What are you doing down here again? Looking for talent?"

Oliver found it hard, in such circumstances, to bring his customary conceit to bear. There was nothing to push against. Nothing to respond to. "I've come for you."

Amy raised her eyes heavenward. "Oh, not that old chestnut again, please. I'm busy. I've an army of customers and only one assistant. Today is not the day for all that. It's all done with, Oliver. Go and find a young thing from the English National to go to Nice with you. I've had it." And with that she turned on her heel and went to sell the salt-glazed jar to the couple from Chalfont St Giles.

Oliver looked after her with blank disbelief, then searched for his sculptures. They had vanished, like the Amy he had once known. Even his hopes for a dramatic exit were dashed when a family with buckets and spades, windbreak and cool-bag almost fell over him as he tried to sweep out of the studio.

Amy closed the till and cast a surreptitious eye in his direction as he lurched down the stone steps. She was surprised to find she wasn't shaking. Surprised but somehow saddened.

Will was walking along the other side of the lane when he saw Oliver Gallico leaving the gallery. He looked different from the last time they had met. He was no longer swaggering. Will wondered what had brought about the change in his demeanour. And then he thought he knew. Clearly Amy had a good reason for not leaving the studio and sailing away with him. He watched as Gallico rounded the corner and was lost from view. Yes. It was definitely time he got on with his life.

Chapter 27:
Crow Point

All weekend Will stayed on *Boy Jack*, concentrating on his charts and keeping out of the way of the seething mass of humanity. Pencurnow was not in any way Newquay or Padstow, but the influx of even a modest population of tourists turned it from the quiet village where most of the locals knew one another into something approaching a coastal resort between the months of June and September.

Things quietened a little after the half-term week, but he still felt safer on board than in town. He looked from the deck towards the Roundhouse from time to time, allowing himself to wonder what she might be doing, if she were missing him as much as he was missing her.

Spike, like most domestic animals, could sense something new in the offing. Instead of spending the better part of every day looking for free fish, he relied on Will's offerings of tinned catfood and watched the preparations for the voyage with intense curiosity.

Will found himself talking more to Spike, sharing his thoughts, until he realized that he did not even want to share them with himself. He sat up late into the night, poring over pilotage books, making notes and plotting courses, checking tide tables and working out passage plans.

It irritated him that the raw thrill of the voyage had been replaced with a more methodical approach, that the technical, navigational and mechanical aspects had come more to the fore than the romance and escapism. Perhaps that would return once he had finished the basic planning. He hoped so.

By Wednesday he was ready to take the boat out for the day to brush up on his solo handling. He didn't want to involve Hovis in the exercise, which he felt he ought to be able to carry out alone, so he waited until he was out shopping and slipped a note under the cabin door of *Florence Nightingale* explaining that he would be back in the early evening. There were two high tides and he could enjoy a day away from it all, still confident of being able to return with enough water beneath him.

The moment of slipping his moorings made him apprehensive. But the engines pounded reassuringly beneath his feet and he let go first of the springs, then the head and stern lines before using a little throttle to nudge the boat away from the pontoon. Slowly he motored through the boatyard, past the jetty and out into the open sea. Len Gryler watched him go from the doorway of his cabin, raising a hand aloft as he chugged by. It was eight thirty in the morning, bright but overcast, force three, maybe four.

Amy was walking down the hill from Primrose's with her shopping when she saw the boat leaving. She stood quite still, leaning on the sea wall, watching *Boy Jack* butting gently through the low waves. She knew it was him, not just from the shape of the boat but because she could see a black and white cat sitting like a figurehead on the prow. Her heart sank, and she could not remember ever feeling so empty.

The boat sailed well. It pleased him that after a while he did not hear the engines. In the days when he had been convinced he wanted a sailing boat it was the sound of wind on canvas and hull cutting through the water that had given him pleasure. Now it was the foaming white wash that appeared in his wake, the reliability of forward motion that could never be guaranteed under sail, and the feel of the sturdy boat beneath his feet as he took the helm.

Spike had surprised him by finding the whole exercise an adventure. There was no timidity about him when it came to the water. He sat, mesmerized, looking over the side at the bow wave, as if waiting for a fish to leap into his clutches.

Will tried out the autopilot. It maintained the set course and he allowed himself the satisfaction of knowing that his calculations of tidal streams had been correct. He checked his position on the chart with the pocket GPS and discovered that they seemed to agree. None of the gauges – water temperature, oil pressure or battery level – showed anything untoward. It would, hopefully, be an uneventful shake-down trip.

He dropped anchor further along the coast at a smaller, unpopulated cove, and a weak sun glinted though the thinning clouds. He tipped cat biscuits into a saucer for Spike, whose appetite had been sharpened as much as his own by the short voyage, then tucked into a Cornish pasty and an apple.

They bobbed gently on the water, the hook holding well, and Will watched as the head of a grey seal emerged above the water ahead. It blinked, then dived. Spike sat wide-eyed. It was the largest fish he had ever seen.

After an hour at anchor, Will switched on the winch and hauled up the hook before motoring down the coast. They hugged the shoreline pretty well and a germ of what it would be like to sail away from it all finally began to grow inside him. For three hours they cruised on autopilot, before Will changed course, came about and set off back in the direction of Pencurnow. The sky was still grey, but the wind had risen a little and the sea now had a distinct swell. He felt uneasy, unsure how the boat would cope with such conditions, and how Spike would take to the more violent motion.

Both questions were answered quickly. The boat turned not a hair, simply put its head down and pressed on, neatly parting the waves and snaking its way through the swell with a comfortable, predictable motion. Will rode the waves as though standing on the back of a bucking bronco, bending his knees to counter the rolling, and Spike made for the saloon, where he spent the rest of the voyage curled up on a cushion.

It was seven o'clock in the evening by the time they returned to the calmer waters of the cove, and Hovis was waiting for them, beaming from the pontoon as they came alongside. He caught the lines as Will threw them, and tied them to the rusty cleats on the pontoon before hailing the crew and asking how it had all gone.

Will had hosed down the boat to remove all traces of salt, scrubbed the decks, checked the warps, eaten his supper and fed the cat. *Boy Jack* was ready. There was no apparent reason for him to stay here any longer. All he needed now were provisions for the first leg of the journey. He would go to Primrose's in the morning and stock up. The tides would be right for a mid-morning departure. There was no sense in delaying. He might as well be off.

He picked up *The Shell Channel Pilot*. He put it down. He went up on deck. Dusk was falling. There was no sign of Hovis. Spike lay curled up in a coil of rope as if waiting for further instructions.

Will looked up towards the Roundhouse. The lights of the village glinted. A gentle breeze stirred the halyards in the boatyard. He would go for a walk.

He ambled down the pontoon, hands in pockets, feeling the walkway bob under his feet. He strolled out along the jetty and up the lane.

Through the windows of the Salutation he could see the orange glow of lights on glass fishing floats and brass binnacles, and hear the conversation and ribald laughter of tourists through the open door. He walked on, staying on the other side of the lane to the Roundhouse, from which a different sound emerged.

He paused, strained to catch a little more, then crossed the empty lane. Hesitantly he mounted the steps to the studio and heard more clearly what he thought he had caught from a distance. It was the sound of a cello playing Elgar. He felt his heartbeat quicken and found it difficult to swallow. The sound of voices in the Salutation died away and all he could hear now was the music.

Calmly he turned to face the sea, leaning back against the wall of the old building. In the pine and the granite he could feel the notes as they vibrated through timber and stone.

It began to rain, softly at first, then more heavily. He pushed himself away from the wall, walked silently down the studio steps and along the lane towards the beach. He approached the water's edge and paddled through the waves, finally sitting down on the wet sand just beyond their reach. He could feel the damp rising through his clothing, and the sea against his skin. He could still hear the cello.

His breathing was slow and deep, and the rain eased off to a steady soaking drizzle as he sat on the sand and looked out to sea. His head felt clear. A calm acceptance took the place of the self-pity that had gone before, and for a long time he sat motionless in the cool, wet evening, gazing out towards the horizon in the direction of the rest of his life.

Chapter 28:
Bishop Rock

The popping of webbing carried from the back room of Pencurnow Post Office and General Stores as it had every morning since heaven knows when. Will waited patiently for the proprietress to appear and finally, after much snipping of plastic and muffled cursing, Primrose Hankey bustled in with the piles of newspapers to dump them on the counter in front of her. Will waited for her to start asking questions, but she did not refer to his domestic life, his travel arrangements, or even to the news that shrieked in banner headline from the front of the local paper: PENCURNOW COUPLE HELD IN DRUGS SWOOP. She spoke quietly and simply: "We'll be sorry to see you go, Mr Elliott. What can I get for you?"

This was not at all what Will had expected. Surely

Primrose had never had a better time for gossip, what with the Morgan-Gileses' arrest and his own departure. There was enough material for conjecture here to keep Primrose in inquisition mode for the better part of a year. But she seemed reserved, pre-occupied.

Angela came out of the back room, pulling on a jacket and munching a slice of toast. She tossed a cheery goodbye in the direction of her aunt and opened the door with its customary ping. For the first time, Will noticed that it sounded slightly flat.

"I've got a list." Will pushed the sheet of A4 paper across the counter.

"Mmm. Shipping order." And then, realizing her unintended pun, "Oh. Sorry."

He watched as Primrose mumbled to herself as she worked her way through the list, slowly piling his goods upon the counter.

"You setting off straight away?" she enquired.

"As soon as I've said goodbye to Mrs Hallybone."

"I see." Primrose ferried packets of cornflakes, cans of pilchards, bottled water and tins of five-minute rice towards the ever-increasing mountain of groceries.

"You'll never carry all this. I'll ask the postman to drop it off on his way down, if you like. He'll be here in half an hour."

"That's very kind. Thanks."

"Funny to think of the two of you leaving at the

same time."

"Sorry?"

"You and Amy Finn. You arrived in the village within a week of one another and now you're leaving in the same week. Strange, really, how things work out."

Will was numbed by the news, even though he had suspected what was about to happen. She had decided to leave the studio after all. She was going away with Oliver Gallico.

"Why has she . . .?"

"Angela's going to look after the gallery for three weeks. They had a good bank holiday weekend, sold quite a lot of stuff, by all accounts. Nice, after all this time, to have a success story in the village. I think Amy just wants a break."

He was half relieved, half disappointed. Relieved that it did not appear she had gone back to Gallico. Disappointed that she seemed to be sorting out her life without him.

As Primrose systematically piled up his provisions, the truth of the situation hit him with the force of a fifty-ton juggernaut. With a clarity of mind that he had not experienced for a long time, he saw clearly what he must do. He could only hope he had not left it too late.

He excused himself and walked smartly out of the door, sprinted down the lane and slowed up only when the Roundhouse came into view. He paused at the foot of the old stone steps, hesitated, then climbed up and pushed open the door.

The studio was empty, apart from the two figures standing on either side of the counter. He stood just inside the door, suddenly self-conscious. Amy looked across at him, paused, then said to Angela, "Could you go and get some milk? And a packet of biscuits or something?"

Angela took in the situation quickly, grabbed her coat from the hook behind the counter and walked out as fast as she could, without breaking into a run. She closed the door quietly behind her. Will and Amy stared at each other.

It was she who spoke first. "I thought you'd gone. I saw you setting off yesterday and I thought you'd gone."

"No. Just seeing how she sailed, that's all."

"I see. When do you go?"

"This morning. I was going to go this morning."

"Going to go?"

"Yes."

"But . . . not any more?"

He sighed and turned towards the door. She thought he was about to leave. Perhaps the tides were wrong or something and she ought to have realized. But he turned the key in the lock, flipped the Open sign to Closed and pulled down the blind.

"I saw Oliver leaving the gallery."

"Yes. I finally got rid of him."

"But I thought . . ."

She looked at him, disappointed.

"And I just wanted to go. To run away from my past and start again. That's what I was doing before you . . ."

She nodded resignedly and looked down. "I know."

"But I got it wrong. It isn't the past any more. It's now. The past has sailed away on its own, without me having to sail away from it. There I was, heading off in my own direction, expecting you to fall in with my plans and thinking that if I offered to take you with me you'd give up everything and come. I thought you must, if you loved me as much as I loved you."

She looked up.

"I'd been so wrapped up in this voyage. It had become so important – all my life was pointing towards it – so the need to do it became . . . a mission, if you like."

"I know."

"But when it came down to it, when I really thought about it, there was no reason to go. Just one big reason why I should stay."

She looked at him, hoping that what she had heard was what he really meant. "But what will you do if you don't go?"

He answered without hesitation. "I'll look after the lighthouse and live with you."

It took her breath away. She gulped. "But you

can't. It will drive you mad. You'll hate all those people."

"Not half as much as I'll hate being on my own without you. Evan Williams doesn't want the job full time and they'll be happy to let me do it if I want to."

She stared hard at him, half afraid to let go, then ran into his arms. "You can do the last bit but you don't have to do the first. I can't have you being in charge of a tourist attraction. It's just not you. Build model boats. I've sold out. You'll earn far more doing that. Here."

She opened the drawer of the till and took out an envelope on which was written 'Will – £500'. "They walked out of the studio. Couldn't price them high enough. You'll just have to work faster." She stuffed the envelope into his shirt pocket and grinned at him through her tears.

He wiped them away with his fingers as she looked up at him and said, "You know why I wouldn't come, don't you?"

"I do now. I didn't see it then."

"I'd had my fill of being at the beck and call of men. However much I loved them. I needed to know that someone loved me enough to give up what they had just for me. Until now I've always been the one to give it up, and then it's always seemed to go wrong."

"I know." He threw his arms around her and held her tightly. "I know, I know."

334

"I'd have given up anything for you – painting, dancing, studio, anything – but I had to be sure you would do the same for me, and it didn't seem as though you would."

"Well, I have, and I'm here, and I will."

"Don't sail away without me," she sobbed.

"I won't, my love, I won't." He stroked the back of her head and the deep love that had eluded him since their parting came flooding back. He was home now.

They stood for a while, until Amy broke the silence. "What about *Boy Jack?*"

He smiled, but sadly. "I'll sell her."

She shook her head. "No, you can't. *Boy Jack* was meant for you, I've always known that." She eased away from him. "Wait a minute." She turned and ran up the spiral staircase, returning with a package wrapped in brown paper.

She held it out to him with both hands. "Here. I didn't have time to wrap them up. I got them a couple of days ago from one of my artists, then when you sailed yesterday I thought it was too late, so they're still in the paper from the shop."

He looked at the package and felt its weight. He knew instantly what it was.

"Hey! Open it!" She watched him with sparkling eyes as the brown paper fell away to reveal the five gilt-decorated volumes of Frank Cowper's *Sailing Tours*. "Only now, Mr Lighthouse Keeper, there is no way you're going on your own."

He gazed at her through his own brimming tears.

"We're not going to do it all in one go, but over the next three weeks you can take me exactly where you want."

"Any preferences?" he asked, his eyes gleaming.

She smiled. "Well, I've asked a friend of mine who owns a Cornish yawl, and he tells me that of all the places around Britain there is one particularly sheltered and secluded harbour in the Isles of Scilly called New Grimsby. Now, it doesn't sound much like the Bahamas, but I expect it will be quite pleasant when we bump ashore."

If you liked *The Last Lighthouse Keeper*
don't miss

Animal Instincts

by
Alan Titchmarsh

Chapter 1: Angels

(Geranium robertianum)

"Could you fold your table away, sir?"

He was miles away. Half a world away.

"Sir?"

"Mmm? Sorry."

"Can I take your cup?"

"Oh, yes. Sorry." He managed a weak smile

She was quite pretty, her hair tied back in a smooth, shiny dark brown bun, her lipstick the same bright red as the pattern on her uniform. The sort of lipstick his mother used to wear. Strangely old-fashioned now. He folded up the table and secured it with the clip, then leaned sideways to look out of the window.

The landscape was gradually rising up to meet him. It should have been grey – he had been convinced it would be grey, to match his mood and the image of the country he had left behind ten years ago. But it was soft green and dusky purple, pale russet and dark brown. There was no hint of battleship grey anywhere, except on the roads that snaked though the countryside. He sighed, and looked down at the newspaper folded open on the seat next to him in row fourteen. It should have been row thirteen, but they had left out that number, skipping straight from twelve to fourteen. On this occasion the thoughtful adjustment by British Airways seemed futile.

The *Daily Telegraph* was less tactful. On page 13 he read, again, his father's obituary:

Rupert Lavery, who has died aged sixty-two, was best known for his work at the West Yarmouth Nature Reserve in Devon where, over the space of thirty years, he built up a reputation as a conservationist of unusual stance and individual reasoning.

The writer had clearly known his father well.

Not for Lavery the left-wing activist approach. He concentrated, instead, on influence by example. He steadfastly refused to allow hunting on his land, but remained on good terms with the Lynchampton Hunt, whose territory surrounded him. He made sure his own land was farmed organically, but took a broad view of genetically modified crops, refusing to join in with those who condemned them as 'Frankenstein foods'. On one occasion, when interviewed, he suggested that the widespread invasion of ragwort was currently the greatest threat to the British countryside and was being overlooked by both farmers and government alike.

Here, at least, was something upon which they agreed. Ragwort was deadly to horses.

Lavery endeavoured to reintroduce the red squirrel to Devon, with little success, alas, but is credited with contributing to the saving from extinction in Britain of the large blue butterfly.

He looked up, blinking back the tear that had came to his eye. Dear old Dad. A failure with the red squirrel but a winner with the butterfly. What a legacy.

Those who perceived Rupert Lavery as a crank missed the point. A tall man, with a gentle but deter-mined nature, Lavery regarded himself as a respon-sible custodian of 300 acres of Devonshire. Though never an evangelical animal rights campaigner, he maintained steadfastly that the link between badgers and bovine tuberculosis was largely unproven, and won a following for his dedication to local natural history in South Devon. But for his tragically early death due to a fall, there is no doubt that he would have continued to be one of the country's most influential conservationists.

Rupert Christopher Lavery was born at West Yarmouth, Devon, on 2 May 1937, and educated at Radley and Trinity College, Cambridge. He attended the Royal Agricultural College, Cirencester, before beginning a career in estate management, finally taking over the family farm from his father in 1970.

He was a Fellow of the Linnaean Society and a member of the Royal Corinthian Yacht Club, but was seldom seen on the water.

Rupert Lavery married, in 1965, Rosalind Bennett, who predeceased him. He is survived by a son.

Kit folded the paper so that he could no longer see the obituary. An insistent *ping* accompanied the illuminated 'Fasten Seat Belts' sign, and the 747 tilted slowly to reveal, through the small oval window, the sprawl of London. Now it *was* grey, with only the muddy ribbon of the Thames to guide the aircraft towards Heathrow.

He would stay just long enough to sort things out. A few weeks. Maybe a month. Perhaps two.

Had he known what lay ahead of him, he would have transferred his baggage to a Qantas flight and headed straight back to Balnunga Valley.

— *Animal Instincts* —

He had completely underestimated the ladies. But, then, he hadn't met any of them yet.

POCKET
BOOKS

MR MacGREGOR

Alan Titchmarsh

When Rob MacGregor is picked as the new
presenter of a struggling gardening programme,
he quickly becomes a favourite with everyone.
And that's half his trouble . . .

Having a gardener who's also a sex symbol might
be a godsend for the TV bosses, but there are
plenty of others who are not so happy: Bertie
Lightfoot for one, the expert Rob replaced; Guy
D'Arcy, another TV rival and insatiable woman-
iser; and most importantly Rob's fiery girlfriend,
Katherine – an investigative journalist on the local
paper. As Rob becomes more and more wrapped
up in his career, and she is involved in a big story
for the paper, the relationship comes under strain.
Especially when a misunderstanding causes
sparks to fly and things get really complicated . . .

PRICE £6.99

ISBN 0-7434-7847-9

POCKET
BOOKS

ANIMAL INSTINCTS

Alan Titchmarsh

When Kit Lavery's father dies, he is forced to return
home after a ten year stint in Australia to sort out
his affairs. A well-known conservationist and
champion of wildlife, Rupert Lavery has left behind
a nature reserve in Devon, staffed by two very
determined women; Elizabeth Punch and Jess
Wetherby, both of whom are committed to keeping
his work alive.

As if these two women weren't anough, Kit falls
under the spell of the beautiful Jinty O'Hare, niece of
the local Master of Foxhounds.

When a buyer is found for the estate, Kit is torn. Will
he stay or will he go? Perhaps Wilson the Gloucester
Old Spot pig has the answers. In moments of stress
and high anxiety, she seems to be the only one who
will listen to the outpourings of a bewildered Kit
Lavery . . .

PRICE £6.99

ISBN 0-7434-7848-7

POCKET
BOOKS

ONLY DAD

Alan Titchmarsh

According to their friends, Tom and Pippa
Drummond have the perfect existence – an
enviable lifestyle, a happy marriage, and a great
kid in Tally.

A rare summer holiday is planned – an idylic
retreat in the Italian hills. Tom takes time off from
running his restaurant, Pippa leaves her herb
garden in the charge of a dotty neighbour and
Tally takes a break from the two men in her life.

Tuscany is everything they hoped it would be –
cicadas in the trees, the scent of sage and citrus
and suppers under the stars. But their joy is short-
lived. Overnight their lives, their circumstances,
their very identities are altered, and life will never
be the same again.

PRICE £6.99

ISBN 0-7434-7846-0

**POCKET
BOOKS**

Read the new bestseller from
Alan Titchmarsh . . .

ROSIE

'It's your grandmother.'
'Yes?'
'She's been arrested.'

Nick Robertson thought he had become used to his
grandmother Rosie's dotty behaviour. At 87,
a widow now, she is determined that before life
passes her by, she will live a little.
Or, preferably, a lot.

There is no time like the present, Rosie insists.
Life is to be enjoyed to the full and to hell with the
consequences. She will help Nick find the soul mate
he clearly lacks, and he can help her find out about
her past. It seems a simple task, but it turns out to
involve far more skullduggery than Nick had
anticipated . . .

PRICE £6.99

ISBN 0-7434-3010-7

POCKET
BOOKS

This book and other Alan Titchmarsh **Pocket Books** titles
are available from your local bookshop or can be ordered
direct from the publisher.

0-7434-7845-2	The Last Lighthouse Keeper	£6.99
0-7434-7847-9	Mr MacGregor	£6.99
0-7434-7848-7	Animal Instincts	£6.99
0-7434-7846-0	Only Dad	£6.99
0-7434-3010-7	Rosie	£6.99
0-7432-0771-8	Love and Dr Devon	£17.99

Please send cheque or postal order for the value of the book,
free postage and packing within the UK, to
SIMON & SCHUSTER CASH SALES
PO Box 29, Douglas Isle of Man, IM99 1BQ
Tel: 01624 677237, Fax: 01624 670923
Email: bookshop@enterprise.net
www.bookpost.co.uk

Please allow 14 days for delivery. Prices and availability
subject to change without notice